W9-BYA-358

Also by J. C. Eaton

The Sophie Kimball Mysteries
Broadcast 4 Murder
Dressed Up 4 Murder
Molded 4 Murder
Botched 4 Murder
Staged 4 Murder
Ditched 4 Murder
Booked 4 Murder

The Wine Trail Mysteries
From Port to Rigor Morte
Death, Dismay and Rosé
Divide and Concord
Sauvigone for Good
Pinot Red or Dead?
Chardonnayed to Rest
A Riesling to Die

Railroaded
4 Murder

J.C. Eaton

KENSINGTON
PUBLISHING CORP.

www.kensingtonbooks.com

KENSINGTON BOOKS are published by

Kensington Publishing Corp.
119 West 40th Street
New York, NY 10018

All Kensington titles, imprints, and distributed lines are available at
special quantity discounts for bulk purchases for sales promotion,
premiums, fund-raising, educational, or institutional use.

Special book excerpts or customized printings can also be created to fit
specific needs. For details, write or phone the office of the Kensington
Sales Manager: Attn.: Sales Department. Kensington Publishing Corp.,
119 West 40th Street, New York, NY 10018. Phone: 1-800-221-2647.

First Printing: September 2021
ISBN: 978-1-4967-2457-1

ISBN: 978-1-4967-2460-1 (ebook)

10 9 8 7 6 5 4 3 2 1

Printed in the United States of America

Dedication and Acknowledgments

This book is dedicated to the Sun City West Model Railroad Club and the Rhythm Tappers

Keep chugging and tapping!

We'd like to give special thanks to the members of the Sun City West Model Railroad Club for taking the time to explain all the fascinating things about running model trains. We are in awe! And a very special shout-out to President Bob Rose and Choo-Choo Chick extraordinaire, Bev Rose.

We are extremely grateful to our incredible support team of readers and tech wizards. We could not do this without you. Susan Morrow, Gale Leach, Larry Finkelstein (U.S.), Susan Schwartz (Australia), you are phenomenal!

Without our amazing agent, Dawn Dowdle, from Blue Ridge Literary Agency, none of this would be possible. If only we had half your energy!

Indeed, we are genuinely appreciative of Elizabeth May, our editor at Kensington Publishing, and Rebecca Cremonese, our production editor. Thanks, Elizabeth and Rebecca, for your dedication and commitment to our novels.

Our publicist, Larissa Ackerman, works tirelessly to ensure we have readers. Boy, are we ever in your debt!

And to the staff at Kensington, a tremendous thanks. From the editors to the art department, you dazzle us every step of the way.

Finally, we thank you, our readers, for bringing our quirky, looney characters into your lives!

Cast of Characters:

Protagonist:

Sophie (Phee) Kimball, forty-something bookkeeper/accountant from Mankato, Minnesota, turned amateur sleuth.

The Sun City West, Arizona, Book Club Ladies:

Harriet Plunkett, seventy-something, Phee's mother and book club organizer. Owner of a neurotic Chiweenie named Streetman.

Shirley Johnson, seventy-something, retired milliner and teddy bear maker.

Cecilia Flanagan, seventy-something, devout church-goer and more modest than most nuns. Sneaks off holy water when needed.

Lucinda Espinoza, seventy-something, attends Cecilia's church and translates Telemundo soap operas for the club.

Myrna Mittleson, seventy-something former New Yorker and aspiring bocce player with a penchant for self-defense weapons.

Louise Munson, seventy-something avid bird lover and owner of precocious African gray parrot.

Ina Melinsky, Harriet's sister and Phee's aunt. Married to saxophone player and gambler, **Louis Melinsky**. More eccentric than Lady Gaga and Andy Warhol combined. Seventy-something, but don't tell her that.

The Sun City West, Arizona, Pinochle Crew:

Herb Garrett, Harriet's neighbor and pinochle crew organizer, seventy-something.
Bill Sanders, seventy-something bocce player.
Wayne, seventy-something, carpenter, jack of all trades.
Kevin, seventy-something.
Kenny, seventy-something, married.

Williams Investigations in Glendale, Arizona:

Nate Williams, sixties, owner, retired detective from the Mankato, Minnesota, Police Department.
Marshall Gregory, forties, partner and retired detective from the Mankato, Minnesota, Police Department, Phee's fiancé.
Augusta Hatch, secretary and Wisconsin transplant from a tool and die company, sixty-something. As quick with a canasta hand as she is with her Smith & Wesson.

Maricopa County Sheriff's Office:

Deputy Bowman, fiftyish, grizzly in looks and personality.
Deputy Ranston, fiftyish, somewhat toadish in looks and personality.

Sun City West Residents:

Cindy Dolton, sixty- or seventy-something, local community gossip and dog park aficionado.

Gloria Wong, sixties or seventies, Harriet's former neighbor.

Paul Schmidt, seventies, avid fisherman and radio show host.

Friends and Family:

Kalese Kimball, twenties, Phee's daughter from her first marriage. Teacher in St. Cloud, Minnesota.

Lyndy Ellsworth, forties, Phee's friend. Works for a medical billing company in the area.

CHAPTER 1

Office of Sophie Kimball, Williams
Investigations, Glendale, Arizona

Ugh. Another phone call from my mother during my break time.

"Of course you can get him into the Glendale City Hall," she said. "He's a service dog."

It was a good thing I swallowed my last bite of a donut before hearing my mother's comment or I would have choked to death. "A service dog? Have you gone bonkers? Streetman is anything but!"

"Well, he'll be performing a service, won't he? He'll be carrying your wedding rings in a pretty little gauze bag and bringing them down the aisle or whatever setup they have for a civil ceremony."

Not if Marshall and I have anything to say about it. "Look, Mom, I've got to get back to work. My break is almost over. And the wedding isn't until June. The end of June, to be precise. That's three months from now. We wanted to make sure Kalese will be done teaching so she can fly in from St. Cloud."

"My granddaughter would want Streetman at the ceremony. She adores that dog."

"Look, I know you have your heart set on having him take part in the wedding, but maybe we can bring him back a doggy bag or something from the reception. Besides, you know how that neurotic little Chiweenie gets around people. He'll either duck under the seats, grab someone's sweater and refuse to let go, or, worse yet, lift his leg on the podium."

"He's making progress, Phee. He now stands on his rear legs and does this adorable little doggy dance to get treats. Or when he hears music on the radio or TV. He's improving every day. He just needs some time."

And a refill of his doggy Xanax . . . "I'll keep that in mind. Talk to you later."

No sooner had I hung up the phone when Augusta, our secretary, leaned against the doorjamb to my office. "I wasn't eavesdropping. Honest. But you did get a bit loud. Especially the bonkers part. Don't tell me. Your mother wants the dog to be in the wedding party?"

I groaned. "It's not a wedding party. It's a simple civil ceremony for family and friends, followed by a nice luncheon at the Renaissance Hotel in Glendale. And yes. She does. She wants the dog to participate. And worse yet, if I relent and say yes, she'll get her friend Shirley to design an outfit for him that would put Lady Gaga's designers to shame."

"Maybe you and Marshall could elope or something. Vegas is nice that time of year."

"Trust me. We thought of that, but she'd only follow us, along with that book club of hers. Anyway, I need to get back to these spreadsheets. The accounts aren't going to reconcile themselves."

Augusta chuckled and walked back to the outer office. She and I comprised half of the four-person team at Williams Investigations, about twenty miles northwest of Phoenix and a stone's throw from my mother's community of Sun City West, Arizona.

My boss, Nate Williams, was a retired detective from the Mankato, Minnesota, Police Department, where I had worked in accounts receivable. A few years ago, I'd gotten a good taste of Sun City West when my mother and the book club ladies became convinced they were reading a cursed book responsible for a series of unexplained deaths. Tired of listening to her histrionics, I flew out west to see what was going on and, within minutes, found myself embroiled in murder and mayhem. Not to mention gossip, exaggeration, and downright wackiness. But that wasn't the worst of it—Streetman, my mother's dog, was.

When one of her friends went into assisted living, she rehomed the litter guttersnipe and proceeded to spoil him like nobody's business. The dog came with a litany of behavioral issues, but none of that mattered to Harriet Plunkett. As far as she was concerned, Streetman was her little prince. Go figure.

Then there was my mother's Booked 4 Murder book club, where the gossip and innuendo traveled faster than the speed of light. I vowed not to return anytime soon, but Nate made me the proverbial "offer I couldn't refuse" to relocate to Arizona and handle his bookkeeping and accounting. Using the old what-have-you-got-to-lose? ploy, he convinced me it would be a good move. Go figure.

I was a mid-forty-something divorcee and a licensed bookkeeper and accountant. Now I'm engaged to be married. Sometimes I look at the ring on my finger and have to touch it to be sure I'm not imaging things. My fiancé, Marshall Gregory, is the third employee at Williams Investigations. Like Nate, he's a retired Mankato Police Department detective, albeit fifteen or so years younger. My age, to be precise.

I'd had a schoolgirl crush on Marshall for years while I was employed in Mankato. Little did I realize, he felt the same way. So, when he moved out here to join Williams Investigations, we both "came clean," and our relationship took off.

We share a rented home in Vistancia, a multigenerational neighborhood not far from the office, and unless our wedding ceremony gets mucked up because my mother decides to sneak that little dog of hers into the Civics Building, the next ring on my finger will be a wedding band.

Thirty seconds later, my cell phone rang, and like a Pavlovian dog, I answered it immediately. It couldn't be my mother again because she always used the office line. Something about needing "a real connection."

"Hey, Phee! It's me, Lyndy. I figured you'd be on break. Just checking to make sure we're still on for Mexican at Abuelos after work."

"Absolutely. I can taste their guacamole already. Marshall won't be back from Yuma until tomorrow afternoon and I dreaded the thought of a frozen dinner, or worse."

"He must get tired of testifying on some of those cases."

"The long drives are a pain, but I don't think he minds the rest of it. Anyway, I can't wait to tell you about my mother's idea for a ring bearer. It's a doozy."

"Does it have four legs?"

"Aargh. You know her too well. See you after work."

I ended the call and smiled. It was good to have a friend my age who understood about wacky families. Lyndy Ellsworth moved out west following her husband's death and found herself dealing with an eccentric aunt who, like my mother, also lived in Sun City West.

It was a little past six when I spied Lyndy at Abuelos. Because it was a weekday evening and some of the snowbirds had already headed home, the place wasn't as packed as usual. Our table was adjacent to the indoor courtyard fountain and flanked by two giant ficus plants. Lyndy waved me over and proceeded to tell me about her day.

"I swear, they deliberately change the health plans just to frustrate me. Do you know, I can recite the nuances between the old Medicare Supplemental F and now the new plans in my sleep?"

"Ugh. Glad I just work with numbers, not health plans like you do."

A twenty-something waiter with wavy, brown hair took our drink orders as we perused the menus. Enchiladas with carnitas for Lyndy and a giant bowl of shrimp and jalapeño chowder for me.

No sooner had I put down the menu when I glanced across the room. "Oh no. Oh no, no, *no*!"

"What?" Lyndy asked. "What's wrong?"

"Don't make any sudden moves that will call attention to us. If we move quickly, maybe we can leave some cash on the table and sneak out of here."

"Why? What's going on?"

"Whatever you do, do not turn around. That's my mother across the room from us with two of her book club friends, Shirley Johnson and Lucinda Espinoza. They must not have noticed us when they came in. Thank God for these giant ficus plants."

"Are you sure it's them?"

"Of course I'm sure. I can recognize my own mother. Even if she changes her hair color every time the wind blows. And there's no mistaking Shirley and Lucinda. One tall, elegant black woman accompanied by a frumpy woman with blondish-gray hair. Yes, it's them. We'd better make a move. Now! Good grief. What are they doing here? They never leave the compound. Unless—"

"HomeGoods is less than a quarter mile from here. They must be having their March sundown sale," Lyndy said. "Maybe we can just keep our heads down. I'm starving."

Just then, the waiter returned with our drinks and asked for our orders. I was doomed. It was only a matter of minutes. Minutes? Who was I kidding? Seconds. I detected a slight movement from across the room, and all of a sudden, my mother was standing shoulder to shoulder with the waiter.

"Phee! I thought you'd be heading right home from work." Then she nodded to Lyndy. "Nice to see you again." Then back to me. "I'm with Shirley and Lucinda. HomeGoods is having a late-day sale. We thought we'd eat first."

Lyndy kicked my ankle under the table and I tried not to laugh. "Uh, sounds like fun."

"You're welcome to join us, you know. Dinner and shopping. We can move the place settings in no time."

I threw my hands over my bread plate as if protecting a government document.

Meantime, the waiter stepped back. "We're more than happy to accommodate you."

"No," I all but shouted. "I mean, that's not necessary. Um, you've got our orders, so we'll stay where we are."

He nodded and took off before my mother could call him back or, worse yet, grab him by the sleeve of his jacket.

"Thanks for asking, Mom. How about we stop by your table for a few minutes after we eat. Coffee maybe?"

"All right. I'll tell the girls. And think about Home-Goods. There must be something you need. Especially because we had to return all those stolen goods from that garage sale a few months ago."

"You don't have to remind me. Anyway, Marshall and I are all set. Enjoy your meal."

"Good seeing you again, Mrs. Plunkett," Lyndy said.

"Same here." My mother traipsed back to her table, and I waved to Shirley and Lucinda. "Whew! That was a close one. Usually she nags until she gets her way. Of course, we're not off the hook yet. I had to open my big mouth and tell her we'd join them for coffee."

"That's okay. Your mom's friends are really quite entertaining."

"That's a nice way of saying 'loony.' I'll give you that much."

And while my meal with Lyndy was slow-paced and relaxed, our desserts with my mother and her friends made up for it.

"I'm telling you, Harriet," Lucinda said, "one of these days Roxanne Maines is going to wind up murdering her husband. It's just a matter of time."

Lyndy dropped her spoon and it clanked on the small dish under her coffee cup.

"You'll get used to this," I whispered. "Just play along. It'll make sense eventually."

"Are they talking about a soap opera?" she whispered back.

"No. It's not one of the Telemundo names I'm familiar with, and believe me, I get a weekly earful from them. Lucinda translates the Spanish, if you were wondering."

"I wasn't."

Shirley wiped the sides of her lips with a napkin and sighed. "Lordy, Roxanne must have the patience of a saint. I could never put up with that man's nonsense."

"The pack rat business is one thing," my mother said, "the philandering is another. I would have given that geezer the boot decades ago. What did he do now?"

Lucinda leaned into the table, forcing the rest of us to follow suit. "He was seen locking lips with some floozy from the Sun City West Model Railroad Club. One of the Choo-Choo Chicks."

Lyndy and I looked at each other and I shrugged.

"I give up," I said. "What's a Choo-Choo Chick?"

"A female member of the club," my mother answered. "But if Roxanne gets her way, that woman may find herself face down on the railroad tracks."

My mother's comments weren't usually prophetic, but in this case, she came awfully close.

CHAPTER 2

I was used to the conversations the book club ladies had. It was like dealing with Swiss cheese. One slice per speaker. Holes and all. But if you put another slice behind the first, some of the holes would get filled in. A few slices later, you might know what was going on.

In our case, it took Lyndy and me two cups of coffee and I lost count of the Swiss cheese slices.

"You remember Roxanne from my Bunco group, don't you, Phee?" my mother asked.

"I, uh, um . . ."

"Of course you do. She's in the Rhythm Tappers and the Jazzy Pom Tappers, too. You and I went to one of their shows at the Stardust Theater a few years ago. Tall, blond woman, shapely legs. She was a former Radio City Rockette. Of course, I'm not sure if she's still blond. I haven't seen her in a few weeks."

Lyndy took a spoonful of her flan and stifled a laugh.

"I'm sure I'd recognize her if I saw her," I lied. I'd never met the woman up close and personal, but what the heck.

Lucinda stabbed one of the caramelized bananas from her dessert bowl and held it still for a moment. "Her husband is Wilbur Maines. He's the president of the Sun City West Model Railroad Club. Been president since the discovery of dirt, from what I've been told."

"Wilbur Maines. Why does that name sound familiar? Is he one of Herb Garrett's friends?"

Herb was my mother's neighbor and for some reason seemed to be involved in everything—theater productions, the broadcast club, and, of course, his own pinochle crew.

"Nope, not one of Herb's cronies." Lucinda faced my mother. "He isn't, is he, Harriet? I mean, you haven't seen him going over to Herb's place, have you?"

My mother shook her head. "No. Only the usual gang. Every Thursday night. Kevin, Kenny, Bill, and Wayne. Of course, it's not like I'm keeping tabs on his house, but I have to take Streetman outside after the news at seven."

Shirley, who had been relatively quiet up until that point, clasped her hands together and took a breath. "Phee probably recognized the name because there was an article about the railroad club in the *Sun City Independent*. Something about a ruckus over which size train track to use for the new display across from the little pavilions at Beardsley."

"Train-track size?" Lyndy asked. "We're talking model trains, right? Not a full-size one, like the Santa Fe Railroad exhibit in Wickenburg?"

"Oh, it's model trains all right," Shirley continued. "Those model railroads come in two sizes. At least I think that's what the article said. Wilbur Maines was adamant the Beardsley display use a G track. Or was it an H track? Wait. I think it was H. I think G is my new health insurance supplement. Of course, G track sounds familiar. Hold on, maybe it was an—"

"Eight track?" The words slipped out of my mouth, and Lyndy nearly spat out the sip of coffee she'd just taken.

"Sorry, Shirley," I said. "I couldn't resist."

"That's okay. I have to admit, it was funny. Anyway, there's a lot of grousing going on at that club over the train-track size. Good thing the project is a year off."

My mother pushed back her chair from the table and sighed. "Well, if we don't take off, we'll miss that sale. Sure you girls don't want to join us?"

"We've got work tomorrow, Mom," I said. "Maybe another time." *Or decade.*

Lyndy grabbed me by the arm after we exited the restaurant and walked toward our cars. "My God! It was like trying to follow a stream-of-consciousness dialogue, but without the printed version."

"No kidding. And trust me when I tell you, tonight's dinner conversation was pretty clear-cut. Usually it takes me days to unravel it. And we were lucky it was only my mom and two of her friends. You can't possibly imagine what it's like when the entire Booked 4 Murder book club gets together. Maybe they'll put today's gossip to rest."

"I hate to tell you this, Phee, but I don't think you've heard the last of the Roxanne-and-Wilbur saga. And those train tracks? What difference does it make?"

"Beats me, but I'm sure I'll find out. Whether I want to or not."

* * *

I hadn't given Roxanne Maines or model railroads another thought until I walked into the office the following morning.

Augusta was already at her desk and the Keurig was ready to go. "Nice dinner out last night?"

"It was. Until my friend Lyndy and I ran into my mother at the restaurant. She was eating with Shirley and Lucinda."

"You went to dinner in Sun City West?"

"Oh heavens no. I know better than to take a risk running into one of the book club ladies. Nope. We went to Arrowhead in Peoria. Thought we'd be safe. Ha! My dumb luck my mother and her friends were on their way to a sale at HomeGoods and decided to eat at the same restaurant we did."

"Oh brother. Don't tell me you wound up at the same table."

"Only for dessert. And that was bad enough. Got an earful about some woman and her philandering husband. Oh. And model trains, too."

"Must be the morning for women with philandering husbands. Nate's meeting with one of them right now. Lady by the name of Roxanne Maines."

"Roxanne Maines?" *It can't be.*

"Uh-huh. Do you know her?"

"Tall? Blond? Maybe in her sixties or seventies?"

"As a matter of fact, yes. Don't tell me she's in your mother's book club?"

"No, only their gossip. I mean, *if* it's the same lady. The one my mother was yammering about was a former Radio City Music Hall Rockette."

Augusta shrugged. "Wouldn't know. Want me to buzz

you on the phone when she walks out of Nate's office? You can see for yourself if you think it might be her."

"Geez, that's so unprofessional. But yes, buzz me. I'll be discreet. I'll bring my coffee cup out here and act nonchalant."

"I'll say one thing. The apple doesn't fall far from the tree."

"That's not funny, Augusta. I may have professional reasons to find out if it's her."

"Really? Professional reasons? You plan on offering your accounting services?"

"One can never tell."

"Harrumph. I'll be sure to let you know when it's time for your entrance."

Both of us laughed, and I walked into my office, but instead of closing the door, I left it slightly ajar. For the next forty minutes or so, I immersed myself in invoices. The phone rang once, but it turned out to be one of our vendors, who had a question for me. Another ten minutes went by and, sure enough, there was a buzz from the outer office. I reached for my coffee cup, got out of my chair, and threw open the door.

A tall, blond woman wearing dark slacks and a clingy cowl-necked sweater walked to the front door accompanied by my boss. I pretended to select a coffee pod while eyeballing both of them. It was hard to say, but the woman certainly fit my mother's description.

Suddenly, she turned and was face-to-face with Nate. She latched on to his wrist and, in a voice that owned the room, said, "So help me, if I find out he's having an affair with one of those train-chugging, Choo-Choo chickens, the next thing his lips kiss will be the stone-cold pavement."

Yep, it was *the* Roxanne Maines all right. Not a single doubt in my mind. I tapped the floor, waiting for the K-cup to quit brewing, and locked gazes with Augusta.

Satisfied? she mouthed.

I nodded back and smiled.

By now, Roxanne had left the office and Nate walked toward us. "The two of you will have to do better than that if you ever plan to do surveillance work. Why the sudden interest in our new client?"

"Not my interest," Augusta said. "Phee's the one staking a claim to this case."

"I'm not staking a claim. It's just that—well, if you must know, Roxanne Maines was the subject of a long conversation my mother and her friends had last night at the restaurant. My friend Lyndy and I happened to be there, and before we knew it, we got swooped up and deposited at my mother's table for dessert."

Nate burst out laughing and shook his head. "Like fish in a pelican's mouth, huh?"

"In a manner of speaking. And yes, Lyndy and I were privy to some idle chitchat about Roxanne, but nothing that Roxanne probably hasn't already told you."

My God! I've become the gossip-mongering washerwoman in all those fairy tales.

Nate moved closer to Augusta's desk, where I was now standing. "And what exactly did you ascertain from your enlightening conversation? And dare I ask which of your mother's friends were passing along their intel?"

I gulped. "Shirley and Lucinda."

With that, Nate leaned over and belly laughed so hard, I thought he'd lose his breath. "Shirley and Lucinda? I'm afraid to ask, so I won't."

Nate had gotten to know my mother's friends in the

past two years as a result of a few murders that took place in Sun City West. Had it not been for the exaggeration, gossip, and innuendo the ladies were famous for, Williams Investigations, along with the Maricopa County Sheriff's Office, would have solved those cases a whole lot sooner.

"We've got the gist of it," Augusta said. "Rotten, cheating husband. And no innuendo there. We heard it straight from the horse's mouth, so to speak. I thought the part about the lips kissing the pavement was a bit overdone, but what do I know?"

"About the same as I do at this point," Nate replied. "And I'm going by the book on this case. A little digging around and some undercover surveillance. Shouldn't be all that hard to find out if the husband is stepping out on her. From what I understand, the guy spends most of his time at the Model Railroad Club on R H Johnson Boulevard when he's not working on the train exhibit at the Beardsley Rec Center. Won't take a herculean effort to see if he leaves either of those places with anyone."

"I might as well really make myself a cup of coffee," I said, "as long as I'm standing here. I don't even know Roxanne, but I feel sorry for her if what she says is true. I hate the idea of infidelity."

Nate gave me a tap on the shoulder. "I hate the idea of it, too, but let's face it, this office profits from it. In the past month alone, Marshall and I investigated at least five similar cases. It's a miserable thing, but it pays the bills."

"That's what my uncle Orson used to say about running his chicken farm. At least you won't get stuck with manure, Mr. Williams," Augusta said.

"No, but if things don't go right, I might wind up stepping in it."

* * *

As a matter of fact, Nate wasn't the one stepping in anything unsavory. I was. And it happened early the next morning, before I was fully awake and my coffee had a chance to kick in. It was Saturday morning and Marshall leaned over the bed and gave me a gentle nudge.

"Last night went by *way* too fast," he said. "At least I don't have any out-of-town cases this week unless something comes up. I'll get those steaks on the grill the minute I get home this afternoon. Lucky you, it's your Saturday off."

"Yay. And I plan to snooze for another half hour at least. Then I'll tackle a few home projects I've been putting off."

"Forget the projects. Try to have a fun day. See you later, hon."

I closed my eyes, but I was too awake to sleep yet not awake enough to function. I threw a sweatshirt on over my nightshirt and walked into the kitchen to make myself a cup of coffee. I had barely taken the first few sips when the phone rang.

My mother's voice made my hair stand on edge, like static electricity. "Phee! You're up. Good. How soon can you get to the Beardsley Rec Center?"

"Please tell me this is a general reference question and not something else. It's a quarter to eight."

"Cecilia thinks she might have discovered a dead body in the train exhibit next to the horseshoe tossing area."

"Then have her call the posse. And what was Cecilia doing by the horseshoe area at this ungodly hour?"

"She goes for her morning walk around Beardsley's perimeter every day."

"Like I said, have her call the Sun City West posse."

"It's not as easy as you think. Cecilia has, well . . . a reputation with them, so she called me instead. Streetman and I are going over there right now."

Terrific. A possible dead body and a neurotic Chiweenie. There's a recipe for disaster. "What did you mean by a 'reputation with them'?"

"Long story. Last year, during one of Cecilia's walks, she was positive she saw a dead body by the small berm between the Ramada picnic area and the main building. She was convinced it was a woman with a large, round face and long, brown hair that was somewhat unkempt."

"And?"

"It turned out to be a large river rock with one of those palm fronds wrapped around it. Those fronds fall off the trees any time there's a breeze."

"Oh brother. Was that it?"

"Not exactly. A few months ago, when she was leaving church in the evening, she glanced into the car parked next to her and was adamant there was a dead woman in the back seat. Even went as far as describing the woman's deep-set wrinkles and scraggly hair."

"I take it there was no dead body."

"Nope. It was someone's scarecrow they bought earlier in the day at one of the local nurseries."

"Um, it sounds like this is going to be a wasted trip for you and Streetman. Still, if Cecilia is that concerned, she needs to call the posse."

"Oh, she's concerned all right. Says she saw an outstretched arm."

"An outstretched arm? That could be anything! A large tree branch, a pipe, one of those decorative wooden borders—"

"Maybe the third time's the charm. Maybe Cecilia really did find a body."

"My God! This isn't a game show."

"For heaven's sake, Phee. Are you going to come or not?"

"Fine. It's better than listening to you nag for the next ten minutes."

Chapter 3

I couldn't believe I had just done that. I got so exasperated with my mother that I agreed to drive over to the model railroad display at Beardsley. By now, my coffee was lukewarm, so I chugged it, washed up quickly, and got in the car. Twenty-five minutes later, with an old-fashioned Dunkin' Donut in my hand that I bought along the way, I pulled into the Rec Center's parking lot.

Sure enough, I spied my mother standing next to Cecilia. It was impossible not to miss them. With my mother's flaming red hair—her latest color choice following the mulled wine fiasco—and Streetman sporting the green-and-tan-plaid doggy sweater he won at the Irish leprechaun contest on St. Patrick's Day, they were a stark contrast to the woman dressed entirely in black: Cecilia. And by entirely, I mean entirely—black pants, a long, black coat, and a black cloche. Oh, and a black scarf, too, in case the ensemble needed more color.

True, it was the end of March and the days were considerably warmer, but the mornings were downright frigid. My mother's car was the only one parked at the far end of the lot. Both women stood facing the small train tracks that circled around an idyllic village complete with tiny houses, stores, a school, and a church.

With her hands hugging her hips and Streetman's leash wrapped around one of them, my mother looked as if she was surveying the aftermath of a hurricane. Cecilia, on the other hand, stood perfectly still, her hands in the pockets of her coat. As soon as they heard my car pull up, they turned.

"Okay, I'm here!" I shouted to be heard above the slamming of the car door. "Where's this supposedly dead body?"

The minute he heard my voice, Streetman positioned himself between my mother's legs. She waved me over to the edge of the display and pointed. "Well, doesn't that look like an arm to you?"

"Where? All I see are train tracks and little houses."

"Take a closer look under those benches at the far side of the tracks. On the right. Looks like an arm is protruding."

I squinted and stared. Just past the benches was a drop-off that morphed into some sort of a garden area with lantanas, boxwoods, and Mexican bird of paradise plants. "Like I said on the phone, Mom, it could be anything. Did either of you try to get a closer look?"

"With Streetman, I couldn't," my mother said. "He'd pee all over the expensive trains and next thing you know, the Rec Center would be sending me a bill for damages."

Cecilia, who was still standing upright with her hands in her pockets, shook her head. "I was afraid I'd trip over the train tracks, and to get to the benches from the other side, I'd have to climb that steep incline. Who puts benches where seniors can't even get to them?"

I shrugged. "Fine. I'll venture across the tracks and take a look. I don't feel like walking all around to the other side."

"You should be fine," Cecilia said. "The trains don't start running until nine forty-five."

"Seriously? These trains run?"

"Of course they do," she said. "The electricity is hooked up to the same lighting as those pole lamps. And the only reason I know is because last year the lighting went out, and the Rec Center people took their own sweet time fixing it. It was only when the Railroad Club pitched a fit about the trains not being able to run that they fixed the electrical circuit. Or whatever it was."

"Great. Good to know. Give me a second."

I climbed over a small bed of granite rocks and side-stepped across the first set of train tracks. "Did you mention this to anyone else who walked here this morning?"

"I didn't see anyone else. Everyone's walking at the new setup on Meeker Boulevard. They installed some cushy material and posted flashing lights so you can tell how fast you're moving."

"Why do people need to know how fast they're walking?"

Cecilia and my mother both shrugged.

Then my mother spoke. "I have no idea. Another way

to spend money around here. Look around, Phee, do you see anything yet?"

"How can I? I'm still in the middle of the setup. Give me a minute."

The ground wasn't meant for walking or, in this case, trespassing across a costly model train exhibit. I took my time, making sure my feet were steady as I maneuvered around small rocks, assorted pebbles, and an abundance of gravel. Finally, I was in full view of the bench with the questionable object beneath it.

I bent down, leaned forward, and caught my breath, not realizing I'd been holding it. For a moment, I thought I detected the scent of cinnamon rolls, but it dissipated quickly. Maybe I was hungrier than I thought.

"What?" my mother shouted. "What do you see?"

It was an arm all right. There was no mistaking it. As for the rest of the torso, it was draped precariously over the berm a few feet from the bench. No wonder Cecilia and my mother couldn't see it. It was almost as if the poor victim had tried to climb up, having succumbed to whatever demise did him in. Definitely a him and not a her. Not many women had dark hair on their arms and hands. Or chrome domes with feathery wisps of hair at the base. But it was the heavy burgundy sweatshirt with the words, "Railroad Dude # 1" on the back that was the dead giveaway. No pun intended.

"Um, I think Cecilia may have hit pay dirt this time." Then I was immediately sorry for being so insensitive and callous. "I mean, she spotted some unfortunate individual who probably suffered a heart attack or stroke. Better call the posse."

"Get a good look, Phee. In case it turns out to be someone we know."

And so much for sensitivity in our family. "It isn't. I mean, I don't think it's anyone I recognize. Not one of Herb's buddies or any of the men who were in that play with you."

"So, it was a man?"

"Yes. A man."

Cecilia crossed herself at least three times while my mother pulled out her antiquated cell phone and placed the call. I was about to work my way back to where they were standing when something caught my eye. I knew from firsthand experience, and the myriad of crime shows I watched on TV, evidence should never be tampered with, so I did the next best thing. I pulled out my iPhone and snapped a few photos.

"You're not going to post those pictures on that Facebook thing, are you?" My mother's voice was amplified by the still air, and I was positive half the county would hear her.

"No. Of course not."

"Then what are you doing?"

"It might be nothing, but maybe this person was hit over the head with the bottom of a shoe. I'm taking a picture of a shoe."

"A shoe isn't going to kill anyone. And it might have come off one of those homeless people who meander by here."

"I don't think this came from a homeless person. I'll tell you why later."

A few inches from the man's head was a woman's tap shoe, facing up. If I wasn't mistaken, it looked like there was blood on the tap plate near the toe. Then again, it could've been the reddish dirt that was everywhere around here. As far as I could tell, the plate on the heel was clean.

Stepping gingerly so I didn't upset a possible crime scene, I made my way back to where Cecilia and my mother were standing. Streetman had ventured out from between my mother's legs and sauntered over to me.

"Look," she said. "He's ecstatic to see you."

"I wouldn't exactly call it ecstatic."

The dog sniffed my feet and looked up. I bent down, petted him, and told him what a good boy he was. While I petted the dog, I heard my mother on the phone.

"That's right, Shirley. A dead body. The railroad exhibit at Beardsley. Let Lucinda know, will you?"

"Good grief, Mom! Don't tell me you and Cecilia called the book club ladies while I was checking out the body? They'll race over here and interfere with a possible investigation."

"Only Myrna, Louise, and Shirley," Cecilia muttered, then turned to my mother. "Still want me to get ahold of Herb?"

I shuddered. "Not Herb! Whatever the two of you do, do not call Herb. He's like an old maid in pants. He'll call all his buddies and probably announce it on that radio show he's got. *Pinochle something-or-other*. Somewhere between explaining what meld is, he'll work this discovery into the conversation."

"Oh my gosh," my mother said. "That reminds me. Myrna and I will be on the air next week with our murder mystery show. Darn that Herb, he'll beat us to the punch."

I shot her a look. "Don't even think about it."

"Thankfully," she said, "Paul Schmidt won't be joining us. He's going up to Lake Powell on a fishing trip."

Paul Schmidt, along with my mother and Myrna, as well as Herb, had radio talk shows on KSCW 103.1 FM. It was a local radio station with a commanding reach in the West Valley of Phoenix. A few months ago, in what could best be described as an "on-air debacle," my mother's murder mystery show and Paul's fishing show were scheduled for the same air time. Neither one would relinquish the spot and the end result was a hodgepodge of both shows at the same time. Audiences loved it, and from that time on, they wound up doing some shows together.

"Do you hear that?" I asked. "It's a siren. The posse is on its way."

"Not as fast as Myrna," my mother replied. "That's her car pulling into the lot. And if I'm not mistaken, isn't that Shirley's maroon Buick turning into the driveway?"

"How did they get here so fast?" I was all but screeching.

"Shirley was on her way to the Creative Stitchers when I called. I'm not sure about Myrna."

Within seconds, Myrna Mittleson parked her car next to mine, got out, and marched toward us. I swear, the woman looked even taller than she did the last time I saw her. Maybe it was the beehive hairdo and all that spray. "Where's the body, Harriet? Quick! Point it out before the posse arrives."

My mother and Cecilia stretched out their arms as Shirley approached.

She took a breath and let it out in a huff. "Lordy! What a tragic way to start a morning. Was it a heart attack?"

Myrna walked to the train exhibit and stood on the balls of her feet. "Where is it? I don't see anything."

"Under the bench," I said.

"Looks like a tree branch, if you ask me. Are you sure?"

I did a mental eye roll. "Yeah, I'm sure, Myrna."

She surveyed the scene and folded her arms across her chest. "Posse's taking its time." Then she looked at Cecilia. "Were you the one who called them? No wonder they're taking their time."

Before Cecilia or any of us could respond, the unmistakable sight of blue and red flashers on a Sun City West Sheriff's posse vehicle came into view.

"Satisfied?" Cecilia asked Myrna.

"I suppose."

Streetman plastered himself against my mother's leg and she bent down to pet him. "The trauma must be getting to him."

I tried not to groan. "What trauma? He doesn't even know what's going on. He's not close enough to get a good whiff of the body. Not like the last time."

"Shh! The deputy's walking over here."

"Okay. While you and Cecilia tell him what you discovered, I'm going to walk back to my car and call the office. Nate and Marshall should both be there."

Shirley latched onto my wrist. "Oh Lordy, Phee! You don't think it's a heart attack at all. It's murder, isn't it? A full-blown murder right in the middle of the railroad exhibit."

CHAPTER 4

Nate and Marshall were tied up with clients, so I told Augusta what was going on. "Tell whoever gets freed up first to call me."

"What did the body look like? Could you tell if it was foul play?"

"Geez, Augusta, you're sounding like the book club ladies. And no, I couldn't tell. I couldn't even see the face. Just the back of the guy's head and one arm. But I did see a tap shoe, complete with those metal cleats on the bottom, a few feet from the head."

"I've heard of dancing on a grave, but not before they got there. Think it was the murder weapon?"

"I'm not sure, but—wait a sec. I'll email you the photos I took. Just in case."

"In case of what? It's not our investigation."

"No, but if it turns out to be a suspicious death, it

might wind up on our plate. The county deputies can barely keep up with the city homicides, the recent rash of hit-and-runs, and, lest I forget, the drug-related crimes. Done! I sent you the email. Forward it to Nate and Marshall."

"Will do. And while I'm at it, want me to get a new placard for your office that reads 'Sophie Kimball, Detective-in-Training'?"

"Very funny. See you Monday, Augusta. And thanks."

I slipped my iPhone into my pocket and walked straight ahead to where my mother and her friends were standing. The deputy was making his way across the model train tracks.

"To the right," my mother yelled. "Over more. About three more feet."

Then Myrna, Shirley, and Cecilia added their commentary.

"Watch out you don't knock over the church steeple! Step back. You need to step back."

"Now you're going the wrong way!"

"No! To the right. The right!"

The last time I heard directions like that, I was in the third grade and playing a game of "Hot and Cold" with my classmates.

"He's not mapping out the Louisiana Purchase!" I announced. "Let him be. He knows where to look."

Finally, after what seemed like an inordinate amount of time, the deputy waved to our group and shouted, "I'm calling this in."

"What does that mean?" Cecilia asked.

I spoke slowly and enunciated every word. "That we can expect more cars."

Sure enough, another Maricopa County Sheriff's car

arrived, only this time it wasn't a posse car. It was one of their official vehicles, and it was followed by a county coroner's car. No sirens, but enough flashing lights to ensure anyone coming out of a club room at Beardsley was certain to investigate.

Within minutes, a substantial crowd had engulfed the entire area. But that wasn't the worst part of it. The official deputy car was driven by Deputy Bowman, the one who'd investigated the other unfortunate deaths in Sun City West and had had more than one unpleasant encounter with my mother's dog.

"That's not Streetman, is it?" He walked toward us. "That dog better be leashed and muzzled."

As soon he said the word "muzzled," my mother scooped up the dog and pressed him to her chest. "I'll have you know, my little man is working on socialization, something you might want to consider for yourself."

"Nice seeing you again, Mrs. Plunkett. Dare I ask what brought you to a possible crime scene? Oh, never mind. I don't have an hour to sift through everything. I'll find out from the posse volunteer. Whoever notified the posse needs to stay here so we can get a statement."

With that, he headed to the posse car, where the volunteer was now standing, and my mother gave me a nudge. "Did you hear what he said? 'An hour to sift through everything'? Is he implying something?"

"He doesn't have to imply it. It's pretty obvious. You and your friends take forever to get to the point. My gosh, the last time Cecilia was questioned by the posse, she stopped and gave the deputy a recipe for brisket."

By now, the coroner had parked his van directly in front of the model train exhibit and walked to where the posse volunteer and Deputy Bowman were standing. I couldn't tell what was going on because the men blocked my view of the body. Next thing I knew, the coroner walked back to the van, got in, and exited the parking lot.

"Do they intend to leave the body right there?" Myrna asked.

I watched as the van turned left on Beardsley Road. "No. Looks like the coroner's going to remove the body from the other side of the exhibit. Just below the incline. It's steeper, but they won't have to sidestep over the train tracks and model village."

Myrna put her hand under her chin and shook her head. "Darn it. I can't see anything from here."

"Not much to see," I said. "The coroner's getting out of the van and his assistant, who must have been in the passenger seat, just opened a side door and is unloading a gurney."

Suddenly, another posse car pulled into the lot and a second posse volunteer approached the scene. This time, a woman. With a medium build, gray hair pulled into a bun, and round, black glasses. Within seconds, the two posse volunteers, along with Deputy Bowman, had cordoned off the area with yellow crime scene tape.

"Lordy!" Shirley exclaimed. "That man must have been shot. Or stabbed. Or—"

I took a few steps to where she was standing and shook my head. "It's just a precaution. Until they finish their investigation. Most likely it was natural causes." *Except for maybe those heavy-duty cleats on that shoe, but I'll be darned if I open that Pandora's box in front of my mother's friends.*

I was so fixated on the process involved to move a dead body from its resting place into a van, I hadn't noticed Deputy Bowman had left the two posse volunteers and skirted around the crowd until he spoke from directly behind me.

"I said, Miss Kimball, may I please have a word with you?"

"Huh? What? Sorry. I was kind of engrossed."

My mother and her friends were a few feet from me and had inched closer as soon as he spoke.

"Uh, maybe we should have this conversation in my car. If you don't mind," Bowman said.

"Sure. No problem."

I gave my mother a look and shrugged. "I'll be right back."

As we got closer to Deputy Bowman's car, he spoke. "This is probably a freak accident, or maybe even a medical thing, but there may be some evidence pointing to the contrary. I didn't want to get into it with your mother and, dear God help me, that group of women that seems to be attached to the hip around here, but can you possibly fill me in on the circumstances surrounding the original call to the posse?"

"I will, if you answer my question. Is that tap shoe near the victim's head the evidence you were referring to?"

"That old shoe? No. It probably got tossed onto the berm by one of those homeless people we get notified about. I'm referring to—Hmm, you know what I'm about to tell you must remain confidential, don't you?"

"I'm engaged to one of your consulting detectives. Of course I know."

"All right. Looked to me as if someone tampered with the electrical box used for the train's circuitry. It was adjacent to where the man's arm was, and if I'm not mistaken, those were chemical burns on the guy's hands. The man could have been electrocuted."

Or hit in the temple with a tap shoe . . . "What makes you think the box was tampered with? Maybe the guy was making a routine repair. Those Model Railroad clubbers seem to know what they're doing."

"Uh-huh. And they have keys to those boxes. This one was pried open. Scratch marks everywhere. Still, until we get the official verdict from the coroner, it's all speculation."

"Um, yeah. Speculation. I still think that shoe—"

"Yes, yes. I left word with the posse for the forensics team to bag and tag it. The crew should be arriving any minute, and they'll scour the place for anything noteworthy. So, now it's your turn. Suppose you tell me what brought you here and how the body was discovered in the first place."

For the next three or four minutes, I gave Deputy Bowman the rundown on the entire situation, beginning with my mother's phone call following Cecilia's discovery.

"Okay, then. I'll get their names and phone numbers and that's it for now. If we need to speak further with any of them, we'll let them know."

"Lots of luck getting out of here unscathed. They'll want to know everything."

"Good point. I'll direct the posse volunteers to handle that task. From my phone. No sense taking a chance and walking over there. And now, if you don't mind, I'll be on my way to the coroner's office."

"By the way, the dog really *is* getting better," I said.

"Than what? A snapping turtle? Next time your mother decides on a pet, suggest a goldfish."

With that, he started the engine, and I walked back to where my mother and the book club ladies were standing.

"What was that all about?" my mother demanded. "Does he know who the victim is, and why did he just leave?"

"He left because his part of the investigation is over for now. A forensics crew is on its way, and they'll be busy evaluating the scene. And for your information, he spoke with me because he knows you and your friends. And he doesn't have an hour or so to waste while they go off on tangents."

My mother let out a groan.

"You, Cecilia, Myrna, and Shirley need to leave your contact information with one of those posse volunteers. In fact, the woman volunteer is walking toward us right now. Then you're free to go."

"Does the Sheriff's Office plan on calling us to let us know what they found out?"

"I seriously doubt it. Look, for all we know, that man could have suffered a stroke or something. The only reason the place is cordoned off is because it's a public area and the Sheriff's Office needs to rule out anything out of the ordinary. Just give the posse volunteers your name and address."

"Fine. And the next time you find yourself inches from a dead body, sift through the pockets and look for identification. Now we have to wait until one of the news stations spells it out for us."

CHAPTER 5

My mother invited me to join her and her friends at Bagels 'N More, or maybe even the Homey Hut, once she dropped Streetman off at home. I had to practically restrain myself from shouting, "Oh heavens no," and instead explained I had lots of housework to do.

Then she bent down and petted the dog. "It's too cold for us to eat on those patios. And I didn't bring Streetman's outdoor bed for him. The ground is way too hard." She paused and gave me one of those looks that could only mean one thing–I was in trouble.

"If you're not joining us, Phee, you could drop Streetman off at my house. You've got a key. Just be sure to give him a handful of his kibble and two or three of those mini biscuits I keep in the glass jar on the counter. That way I can go straight to the restaurant with the girls. And if you can find the time, I've got a recording on a cassette tape of a pizzicato dance. He loves to get up on his hind feet and move to the music."

"No dance. No music, but if it means getting right out of here, I'll drive him home. And for goodness' sake, please don't pester the posse volunteers for the victim's name. They have no way of knowing."

"But you might. If Deputy Bowman contacts your office."

"He'll only do that *if* it's a suspicious death, and *if*, for some reason, they want to bring Williams Investigations into the case. My money's on the nightly news. DVR it or something if you're not going to be home. Catch you later."

She handed me Streetman's leash, and the little Chiweenie pranced over to my car without incident. Then something dawned on me. The car! Where was the victim's car? When I pulled up, only my mother's car was parked in the far end of the lot. That meant the victim either walked to the model railroad exhibit or got dropped off by someone else. The likelihood of him parking by the main building made absolutely no sense. I mulled that thought over and wondered if I should share it with Deputy Bowman. Then I thought otherwise. *He's the detective. Let him figure it out.*

Back at my mom's house, Streetman swallowed one of his mini biscuits without even tasting it right before Marshall phoned.

"Is everything okay? Augusta said you called. Something about finding a body by the railroad exhibit in your mother's community."

"Oh yeah. Not the greatest way to start off my day. Cecilia spotted it when she took her early morning walk. Actually, she spied an arm and called my mother. Long story. Apparently, Cecilia and the posse have a history regarding her emergency calls. Anyway, the posse arrived and called it in, and Deputy Bowman showed up."

"Without Ranston?"

"Uh-huh. I consider that the high point of my morning. Maybe he got the day off. I didn't ask."

Marshall chuckled. "What's your take? Heart attack or other?"

"Other. And Bowman thought so, too, only his take on the situation differed from mine. I spotted a tap shoe with those heavy cleats on it. A good thrust on the temple and it would knock someone out. Or worse."

"And Bowman?"

"He said it looked as if the man might have been electrocuted while he was working on the train's junction box."

"So, an accident, then?"

"Um, no. The box was pried open. Tampered with. Bowman thought the man might belong to the Model Railroad Club and, if so, those guys have keys to the junction boxes. I guess the forensics team will figure all that out. Meanwhile, my mother and her friends are beside themselves wondering who the victim was."

"They should know the drill by now. Next of kin gets notified and then the TV stations will air the information."

"Oh, they know all right. They just don't want to wait. It slows down the gossip."

Just then, Streetman let out a yelp.

"You've got the dog with you?"

"More like the other way around. I'm at my mother's house. I dropped Streetman off so she could hurry over for coffee with the ladies. That's when you called. I'm heading home now. I've got corned beef and cabbage in the Crock-Pot, so we should be all set for dinner."

"Great. I should be home before five. If for some reason I happen to find out more about your mystery victim, I'll let you know."

"Happen?"

Then the dog yelped again. "Hold on, I think someone's at the door."

I walked to the window and, sure enough, my mother's neighbor, Herb Garrett, was a few yards from the front door.

"Herb's coming up the walkway. I'd better see what he wants. Try not to get into too much trouble today."

"Nah, you already took care of that for us."

I laughed and ended the call as Herb knocked on the door.

He sucked in his stomach and smiled. "Hey, cutie, is your mother available?"

"Only if you feel like chasing her down at Bagels 'N More or the Homey Hut. Is it something important? I was on my way out."

"I wanted to give her the heads-up on some news I heard from Wayne. You remember Wayne from my pinochle crew?"

"Uh-huh." *And Bill. And Kevin. And Kenny. And their nonstop grumbling about everything.*

"Tell your mother Wayne was driving by on Beardsley Road and it looked to him like someone took a header off that incline by the model railroad tracks. Wayne saw everything."

"Driving by?"

"Oh hell no. He pulled over across the street. Got out of his car and took a good look. Saw the coroner's guys loading the stiff into their van."

"So Wayne saw the aftermath, not the actual incident." *Or my mother standing there with her friends.*

"Duh. He said there was a crowd of people, but they were too far away for him to see if he recognized anyone."

I figured my mother would eventually tell Herb she was part of that crowd Wayne had spotted, so I filled him in. Somehow, he didn't seem all that surprised.

"Does Harriet have any idea who bit the dust? Was it foul play? All Wayne could tell me was there were a few sheriff's cars, but what the heck, they send out a militia for the tiniest fender bender."

"Um, I don't think so. Like I said, you could always stop by Bagels 'N More or the—"

"That's okay. I'll catch her later. Nice running into you, cutie." Then he paused for a minute and coughed. "Damn allergies. I never know what's pollinating around here."

I tried not to groan as I shut the door. Then I gave the dog a small handful of kibble, retrieved my bag from the counter, and left, making sure I locked up. It was unbelievable. This place was a veritable rumor mill and now, with the latest incident, I could practically guarantee the phone lines would get plenty of use before the day was out. What I didn't realize at the time was that it would be my phone, with me fielding all the calls.

It began the moment I set foot in the house. The red light on the landline was blinking, so I pushed the button and played the message.

"Phee! It's your aunt Ina." *Like I wouldn't recognize*

that voice. "Your mother left me a message about a dead body and some railroad tracks. I wasn't sure if it was a book she wanted us to read for the book club or if she happened upon a corpse while she was walking that dog of hers. The message wasn't that clear. I called her back, but she's not home, and the voice mailbox on her cell phone is full. Tell her she needs to erase old messages. Call me if you know anything."

I contemplated returning the call right away so I could get it over with, but before I had the chance, the phone rang again. I looked at the caller ID and I saw it was Lyndy. I was safe.

Lyndy sounded as chipper as always when I answered. "Hi, Phee! You're not going to believe this, but my aunt called. You know, the busybody who lives in your mom's community. Anyway, she wanted to let me know she saw the coroner's van by Beardsley. Said they were loading up a body from that steep slope by the railroad exhibit. She was driving and pulled over. Couldn't get a good look, though, because some guy was in front of her and had the better vantage point. Can you believe it?"

"Not only can I believe it, I was there."

For the next five minutes, I filled Lyndy in on all the details, beginning with my mother's phone call and ending with Herb's impromptu visit to her house.

"Holy cow! I guess the deceased must have had a heart attack or stroke, huh?"

"I don't think so."

Then I expounded on my original rendition of events. This time with my full-blown theory about the tap shoe and Deputy Bowman's observation about the junction box.

It took Lyndy all of three seconds to come up with her

own theory. "I'll bet the victim got shocked from messing around with all those wires in the circuit box and was knocked out for a second. Then someone took advantage of it and whooped him over the head with the tap shoe. Hard enough to kill him. You said it was a woman's tap shoe, right?"

"Uh-huh."

"Well, maybe the victim was having an affair with her and things went south. Oh my gosh. You don't suppose it was the guy with the lip-locking floozy, do you?"

"Oh my gosh, Lyndy. You're getting as bad as my mother."

"Yeesh. Well, if it turns out to be something more than a medical reason or natural causes, I'm sure you'll find out soon enough. Let me know, huh? I live vicariously through your escapades."

"I doubt this will be much of an escapade, but sure, I'll let you know. Catch you later."

Finally, I was able to make myself a cup of coffee and a sandwich before tackling some of the smaller house projects I'd been putting off, like organizing my closet. True, it wasn't exactly a "house project" in the real sense of the term, but it *was* a project for me, and technically, it had to be done in the house.

When we first moved in here, we were happy to get as many boxes as we could unpacked and, in a rush to free up floor space, I'd hung and stacked my clothing wherever it would fit, regardless of season. I had bathing suits hung next to heavy jeans and long sweaters draped over tank tops. The whole mess gave me the willies. But not as creepy as the message I got from Augusta about a half hour after Lyndy and I finished talking. I was in the closet working and didn't feel like charging over to the phone.

The hair nearly stood up on my neck when I played the message back.

"Phee, it's Augusta. Mr. Williams and Mr. Gregory blew out of here as if someone lit their pants on fire. They wanted me to tell you Deputy Bowman called. He got an ID on that body, and when he went to deliver the unfortunate news to the maybe-not-so-grieving widow, he found out she was one of Mr. Williams's clients. The one from yesterday. The Choo-Choo Chick affair? Call me when you get a minute. I'm going to be here for another hour."

Of all the coincidences in the world, Lyndy had managed to hammer down the entire situation with a darned good guess. The hairy arm Cecilia saw under the bench by the model railroad tracks belonged to Roxanne's husband. What was his name? Willis? Winton? Oh crap . . . Wilbur. It was Wilbur.

I stared at the phone, not knowing who to call first. Lyndy? And tell her it was time to consider a new career as a psychic? My aunt Ina? What was I? Crazy? Without giving it any further thought, I dialed the office and waited for Augusta to pick up.

CHAPTER 6

"She's not a suspect, is she?" I blurted out the minute Augusta answered the phone. "Is that where Nate and Marshall went? To Roxanne's house? Or did Deputy Bowman arrest her?"

"Hold your horses. You're starting to sound like your mother. And no, Mr. Williams's client wasn't arrested. Yet. And I say *yet* because the way things go around here, it wouldn't surprise me. Anyhow, the men went to have a chat with Deputy Bowman. Something about a tampered circuit box for that model railroad. If you ask me, Bowman must think his office is going to be up to its elbows with that investigation, so he figured he'd get ahead of the game and clue Mr. Williams and Mr. Gregory in. Besides, the wife is already one of our clients."

"Knowing how things work, the county lab won't get definitive results on that box for days. And as far as the body is concerned, other than any obvious wounds, toxicology results can take weeks."

"Yep. Got that right. Even if a body was mauled to death by a pack of hungry javelina, they'll still want to know what the victim ate and ingested prior to that."

Yeesh. That's a vision I can do without. "So, Wilbur Maines, huh? I wonder if he had any enemies."

"If he was flitting around with one of those chickadees in the Railroad Club, could be that woman's husband wanted to put a stop to it."

"Geez, Augusta. This guy's death is going to play out like a never-ending soap opera for my mother's book club ladies. I suppose all the news channels will release his name later today."

"My money's on the four p.m. slot on channel three. After that, anything's fair game."

"So you think Nate and Marshall will get called into this?"

"If it turns out to be murder, I do. Like I said, Bowman's getting ahead of the game for once. The Sheriff's Office is understaffed as it is. More cost efficient to hire consultants."

"Yeah, I suppose you're right. Thanks for keeping me posted. Have a good weekend. See you Monday morning."

"With bells on."

I decided not to make any other phone calls or I'd be mired in them for the rest of the afternoon. No doubt my mother would call me as soon as she watched the evening news. Lyndy, too, I imagined. Taking advantage of the remaining few hours in the day, I rearranged my closet, organized our kitchen drawers so the cutlery would be adjacent to the microwave, and threw in a load of wash.

By the time Marshall walked in the door, our Crock-Pot dinner was ready and I was itching to know what he'd found out. Thankfully, he was just as eager to spill the beans.

He planted a quick kiss on my lips. "I know Augusta told you about Bowman, but whoa! I think everyone's going to be stepping into a landmine."

"What do you mean?"

"It doesn't take a rocket scientist to figure out Wilbur Maines didn't die of natural causes or an accident. Even if it does take days for the forensics team to issue an official report. And don't get me started on the autopsy. Roxanne was adamant her husband's body remain unscathed. Went berserk at the mention of the word 'autopsy.' According to Bowman, she put up such a scene, it made him suspicious she had something to do with the guy's death."

"Did you and Nate speak with her?"

"Nate went over to her house while I had the pleasure of continuing the conversation with Bowman *and* Ranston back at the posse office in Sun City West."

"And?"

"Among the items taken in as evidence from the scene was that tap shoe you mentioned, a Phillips head screwdriver, which could have belonged to the victim, and get this—a few of the granite rocks near the circuit box that were covered with blobs of what appeared to be superglue or something similar."

"Superglue?"

"Uh-huh. Maybe Wilbur was using it for something in that circuit box, but there was no glue jar in sight, or on the body for that matter. The forensics team dusted everything for prints, but you know how that goes. Unless someone's in the system or willing to offer up their prints, it won't tell us a thing."

"Was Nate able to get any information from Roxanne?"

"More like finger pointing. I met up with him for a quick cup of coffee at a Starbucks, and he relayed his conversation with the wife. Nothing she hadn't already told him the day before."

"A possible affair?"

"Yeah. And all the messiness that goes with it. Too bad she couldn't offer up more than that. Then again, if she could, she wouldn't have needed our services, I suppose."

"Bowman didn't tell her about the evidence they found, did he?"

"Not a word. Trust me, if any of that evidence links back to Roxanne, she'll need a lawyer, not a detective."

And she'll have to hide the other tap shoe if it was her. "If it does turn out to be murder, and you and Nate get called into the case, wouldn't it be a conflict of interest?"

"Roxanne hired our office to find out if her husband was cheating on her. The contract was nullified by both parties once Deputy Bowman informed her of her husband's demise. That's why Nate went over there in the first place. He'll let Augusta know on Monday. Between you and me, he's fairly certain this is a suspicious death and we'll be working this case as well."

"What makes him so sure?"

"Intuition, I suppose. *That* and another bit of evidence Bowman uncovered. Wilbur had two restraining orders issued for former members of the Model Railroad Club. Both were filed in the past month. If that's not suspicious,

I don't know what is. And before you ask, Roxanne didn't know a thing about them."

"Guess we'll have to sit tight till Monday and see what happens. Meanwhile, there's a hot corned beef and cabbage meal waiting for us to devour it."

We let the subject of Wilbur drop as we chowed down on one of my favorite comfort foods. Unfortunately, that hot topic emerged with a new vengeance as soon as the evening news came on.

"Do you want to get that phone call or should I?" Marshall asked. "It's probably—"

"I know. I'll get it."

Expecting the call to be from my mother, I wasted no time getting right down to it. "Yes, yes, we caught the news, too. Wilbur Maines. Roxanne's husband. Er . . . late husband."

"I don't know any Roxannes. Or Wilburs. Is this about the corpse on the railroad tracks? I caught the last part of the news and missed the story. Is that what your mother's message was about? Another dead body in Sun City West and not a novel I need to order online? She's still not answering her phone, by the way."

"Aunt Ina?"

"Of course Aunt Ina. Who did you think it was?"

"Actually, I thought it was my mother. She must have gone out to dinner with one of her friends. It's Saturday night. Cheeseburger night at Putters Paradise, if I'm not mistaken."

"Well, as long as you seem to know what's going on, you can tell me."

I turned to Marshall, rolled my eyes, and mouthed, *Aunt Ina.*

Have fun, he mouthed back and picked up the remote.

I tried to be short and succinct as I gave my aunt the salient details, leaving out anything that could remotely compromise a murder investigation. *If*, indeed, that was about to happen. Unfortunately, my aunt preferred the long version and not the CliffsNotes.

CHAPTER 7

"Wouldn't be the first time a woman did her husband in for cheating. Do you think that's what happened? And why pick a public spot? Hmm, now that I think of it, I guess it's better than having the body in the house."

"It may turn out to be an unfortunate accident, Aunt Ina."

"An unfortunate accident is when you overcook a casserole. Hold on a minute, I want to see if Louis recognizes the name. He's in the other room, practicing his saxophone. He didn't watch the news."

Before I could say a word, I heard her yell, "Louis! Do you know anyone by the name of Wilbur Maines? Louis! Can you hear me?"

"That's okay, Aunt Ina," I said. "It really doesn't—"

"Give me thirty seconds and I'll call you right back."

The line was dead in an instant.

"What was that all about?" Marshall asked.

"Aunt Ina. She's checking with my uncle to see if he knows the deceased."

Sure enough, the phone rang as promised. "Your uncle Louis doesn't know Wilbur Maines, but he knows Montrose Lamont."

"Huh?"

"Montrose Lamont is a clarinet player. Widowed. Lives in Sun City West. He and your uncle have worked the same gigs in the area."

"What does that have to do with Wilbur?"

"I'm getting to that, Phee. You're as impatient as your mother. Montrose was in that Railroad Club with Wilbur until the two of them got into some big row over a proposed railroad track expansion. According to Louis, Wilbur was a real jackass and used his authority as the club's president to boot Montrose out. Then Montrose threatened to get even, so Wilbur had a restraining order placed on the guy."

"You got all of that in thirty seconds?"

"Your uncle doesn't waste time getting to the point. Anyway, if your mother calls, tell her to call me. I want to know what to bring for the potluck book club meeting this month."

"Um, sure."

Marshall leaned over on the couch and gave my shoulder a squeeze. "So, what tidbits of wisdom did your aunt have to share?"

"Half the equation on those restraining orders. My God! Louis Melinsky knows everyone."

I gave Marshall the quick rundown and we both uttered the same word at once: motive.

"Seems that way," I said. "If he was murdered, the wife had motive, and so did this Montrose guy. Although I really can't fathom how a little spat over a railroad design could result in a homicide. By gosh, I'm not even sure whether he was murdered, but I've got a list of suspects, beginning with the unknown, jealous husband of a woman who might have been having an affair with him and two legitimate people who may have had their own reasons."

"I'm sure Bowman and Ranston will be going over those restraining orders with a fine-tooth comb. They've got the same information your uncle Louis has, plus the other name."

I widened my eyes and waited for him to continue. Nothing. "Did Bowman give you the other name?"

"Nope. But if the lab comes back with a definitive homicide verdict, I'm sure Nate and I will get all the information we need. Face it, Wilbur was president of the Model Railroad Club. Got to be a zillion members in that one. Think of all those interviews Bowman and Ranston don't want to conduct."

"Yikes."

The rest of our weekend, oddly enough, was a normal one. Except for a few pestering phone calls from my mother. Apparently, Cecilia was so distraught over finding a real dead body and not river rocks covered with pond fronds, she all but sequestered herself in church on Sunday, attending every Mass they had. In fact, according to my mother, Cecilia asked Father Mulroney if the church would consider adding an additional four-hour Mass.

Monday at work went by without incident and Tuesday started off the same way. Until eleven fifteen. That was when Deputy Bowman called our office to deliver the news. The autopsy confirmed Wilbur Maines suffered a serious blow to the right temple from a blunt, flat object. That hit on the head turned out to be the cause of death. The coroner also confirmed Wilbur suffered a minor electrical shock prior to receiving that fatal strike. Bravo, Lyndy!

Up until now, I had put the thought of that tap shoe on hold because it could have belonged to any one of the women in those tap-dancing clubs, or maybe even someone who wasn't associated with Sun City West. But once the victim's name was revealed, I seriously wondered if it wasn't his wife who did him in.

"Kind of hard to pull fingerprints off a shoe that's been on the ground for who-knows-how-long," Marshall said when I mentioned it that afternoon. "And why leave it there to be discovered? Unless, of course, something spooked the culprit."

"You know what this means, don't you?" I tried not to laugh.

"Oh, I know all right. We'll be called in to assist with interviews. First that Railroad Club, then those tap-dancing, pom-pom women, or whatever you call them."

"I think my mother said they were the Jazzy Poms and the Rhythm Tappers, but I could be wrong."

"It doesn't matter. If the shoe fits, Nate and I will be wearing it."

Six hours later, the early evening news came on, followed by the Booked 4 Murder Club's own gossip hotline. By ten, the women were convinced poor Roxanne was going to be arrested for murdering her husband. Somehow, the news anchors got wind of the tap shoe and offered their own speculation about the case. So much for the journalism of Edward R. Murrow and Walter Cronkite. My mother had called at ten twenty-five, insisting, "Nate and Marshall, do something before an innocent woman is placed behind bars."

"First of all," I tried to restrain myself, "they haven't been called to consult on the case. And second, need I remind you they're private investigators, not defense attorneys?"

"Hogwash. If they're decent investigators, Roxanne won't need an attorney."

As things turned out, Roxanne *did* need an attorney. She became a person of interest almost immediately, but, thankfully, an arrest hadn't yet been made. As for my boss and my fiancé—well, they got the official word the next morning.

No sooner had Augusta turned on the Keurig than the phone rang and it was Deputy Bowman. Sure enough, the Sheriff's Office needed our office to assist with the investigation now that the ruling on Wilbur's death was declared a homicide.

"It's those interviews. That's why they're calling us in." Nate stared at the coffee maker and tapped his foot. "Enough to turn a twenty-year-old's hair gray. And the family photos. Now everyone has a damn smartphone. Why is it these people insist on showing us photos of their grandchildren playing soccer or eating in a restaurant? Bowman and Ranston had the right idea –stick to the gangs and the drug dealers."

"You're eating it up and you know it," I said. "Besides, wasn't it you who told me there's nothing quite like solving an old-fashioned homicide?"

Nate watched as the K-cup he'd put in the machine started to brew. "I probably muttered that during a weak moment. Anyway, I'll head over to the posse station and speak with one of those deputies as soon as I'm done with my morning appointment. It should be a quick one. What does Marshall have today, Augusta?"

"He should be done with that early appointment he had at eight with a woman who wanted him to track down a missing necklace. Then he's got a guy from Buckeye who's trying to locate a birth parent."

"If he's still with a client when I drive over to Sun City West, I'll fill him in later. If not, he can join me."

Nate had picked up his coffee cup and started for his office when he spun around and let out a sigh. "You might as well tell your mother we're on the case, Phee. No doubt she'll be nagging us one way or the other, wanting to know if there's a serial killer loose. One ray of light, though: Wilbur was killed with a blunt object and not an ax. Can you imagine what Harriet Plunkett and those book club women would be like if the murder weapon was an ax? Between their imaginations and those books they read, they give new meaning to the term 'going off the deep end.'"

"If you don't mind, I'll wait until lunchtime. No sense getting my nerves in a tizzy so early in the day."

I made myself a cup of McCafé's medium roast and marched directly to my office, where I remained glued to spreadsheets for the next two hours. It was only when Augusta rapped on my door that I looked up from the screen.

She took a step forward. "Want me to get you a donut or anything? I can't enjoy my midmorning break without a munchie, and we're all out. So, if you'll man the phone, I'll get us reinforcements from Dunkin'."

"Deal. Vanilla or maple-frosted. Leave my office door wide open, okay?"

Augusta took off and I went back to my spreadsheets. Then, for some inexplicable reason, I pulled out a piece of scrap paper and wrote, "tap shoe, Phillips head screwdriver, glue." It was an odd combination of objects found at a crime scene, but, then again, this wasn't a game of Clue. I reasoned the Phillips head screwdriver might have belonged to Wilbur because he most likely needed one for his work on that circuit box. That left the tap shoe and glue on those rocks.

I folded the scrap paper and tucked it in the top of my right-hand drawer. *Let the crime lab mull over those things. At least they'll be able to get a shoe size, and maybe even a brand name for the glue. Then what?* I reached for the mouse and clicked on one of the spreadsheet columns. At least the numbers didn't pose any mysteries for me.

CHAPTER 8

"Hallelujah!" my mother exclaimed when I called her at a little before noon to tell her that Nate and Marshall would be assisting with the investigation into Wilbur's death. "The news anchors on channel five thought the killer might have used a tap shoe. Why didn't you tell me it was a tap shoe when you saw it? All you said was 'shoe.' You said you saw a shoe. That's like saying you saw a fly when it was a dragonfly."

"Honestly, Mom, it wouldn't have made a difference. Forget the news anchors. I think they get paid to banter."

"I need to let the ladies know Williams Investigations is looking into the murder. I *can* say 'murder' now, can't I? Everyone else is saying *murder*."

"Yes, yes. You can say 'murder,' 'homicide,' 'foul play,' or whatever you'd like."

"Good. By the way, the potluck book club meeting is

going to be at Shirley's tomorrow at six thirty. You're welcome to attend, you know. We're discussing a Harlan Coben novel. Then we move on to culinary mysteries with Linda Reilly's *Fillet of Murder*."

"Sounds very appetizing, but I've got a full schedule and most likely will be working late."

"Fine. Let me know if you hear anything. Cecilia is a basket case. If that murderer isn't caught soon, I don't know what she'll do. At least I have Streetman for protection."

And a family-size bottle of Resolve *for the carpets.* "Um, sure. Have a nice time."

If I thought I was getting off the hook easy, I was wrong. Dead wrong. I should have known my mother would come up with some harebrained scheme to plunge a professional investigation into a free-for-all so everyone—including Herb, who was practically bald—would be pulling the hair out of their head.

It was two days later, on Friday, when my mother called during my break and gave me indigestion. She wanted me to know she and the ladies had devised an ironclad plan to "ferret out" the murderer and clear Roxanne's name.

"Clear Roxanne's name? She hasn't been arrested. She's still a person of interest, that's all."

"For heaven's sake, Phee, one minute someone is a person of interest and then they're behind bars right before the commercial break."

I rubbed my right temple and took a deep breath. "On TV. Depending upon the screenplay."

"It's that tap shoe you found. Face it, Roxanne is a tap dancer. And the spouse. If we don't act quickly, she'll be carted off to the Fourth Avenue Jail in downtown Phoenix. We can't sit around and wait like we always do when one of these heinous things happens in our backyard. This time we're being proactive. Myrna used that word. It was on some committee report for the bocce club. Anyway, do you want to hear about this plan or don't you?"

I shifted the receiver to my other hand and rubbed my left temple. "Sure."

"We call the plan 'Operation Agatha.'"

"As in Agatha Christie?"

"Naturally. Louise Munson wanted us to call it 'Operation Rawhide,' because that was Ronald Reagan's secret service code word, but we're not reading any westerns, so we thought we'd stick to a name more reflective of our book club rather than Louise's obsession with the late president."

For a moment, I was speechless. All I could envision was a twenty-minute, heated dinner discussion about which secret code word to use.

"Phee? Are you still listening?"

"Uh, um, yes. I'm still listening."

"Good. Because here's the plan. We're going to infiltrate the Model Railroad Club and the Rhythm Tappers. Go undercover, so to speak, and find out who had a reason to kill Wilbur."

"What? You and your friends plan to join those two clubs? Yikes. I think you have to know something about building model railroads before you join that club, and as far as the Tappers are concerned, you have to know how to tap dance! And where are you going to find the time? Shirley's in all those sewing clubs, Myrna plays bocce—or makes a stab at it anyway—Cecilia and Louise are busy with their church functions, and you have a broadcasting program. And don't get me started on Aunt Ina.

She and Louis are way too busy with all the gallivanting around they do."

"Are you finished? Because we figured all this out."

I closed my eyes for a moment and inhaled deeply. "How?"

"We divvy up the surveillance. Cecilia used to take tap-dancing lessons when she was in parochial school. She even performed with her fourth-grade class. She'll sign up for the Tappers next week. Shirley already designs some of their costumes, so she'll join Cecilia and attend their meetings, or practices, or whatever they do. Lucinda will also sign up."

"Lucinda? Pardon me, but the woman was born with two left feet! Worse than Myrna."

"Cecilia will coach her."

If there was any possible way I could have rubbed both temples at once, I would have, but I needed one hand to hold the phone.

"And what about the Model Railroad Club?"

"Louise, Myrna, and I will join."

"Do Louise or Myrna know anything about model trains?"

"Just that they go around in circles."

"Dear Lord. This is going to be a disaster. Let the Sheriff's Office deal with Wilbur's death. Nate and Marshall, too, for that matter. I think you may be going way over your heads."

"Oh, I forgot to mention it. Herb will be joining the Model Railroad Club as well. He got wind of the potluck dinner and wound up at Shirley's. I've always said the man's worse than a homing pigeon when it comes to food. Anyway, he used to have a model train set when he was a kid. Said he still remembers some of the stuff."

"I'm at a loss for words, Mom."

"Well, you should be congratulating us for our fast thinking. Operation Agatha is now underway. I'll talk to you later."

I stared at my computer monitor as if all sense of reality had escaped me. I swear, it took me a solid minute to regain my senses and step into the outer office.

Augusta was flabbergasted when I told her about Operation Agatha. "Look at the bright side. At least it doesn't involve anything outrageous like their plans usually do."

"You mean like dumpster diving or going into someone's house under a false pretense?"

"For starters, yes. Although . . . hmm, now that I think of it, those plans started out innocuously enough."

"Aargh. This whole thing has disaster written all over it and trust me, somehow I'll get dragged into it."

"You can always tap your way out of it."

"Very funny."

I didn't get caught up with Nate or Marshall until late in the day, when we were almost ready to close. The minute I heard their voices, I walked to the front office. The two of them looked as if they had just sat through a screening of *War and Peace*.

"Any news?" I asked.

Nate gave Marshall a look and then turned to me. "If you can call revisiting the timeline with Bowman and Ranston news, then sure."

"So they were able to narrow down something?"

My boss scratched the back of his head and walked to the Keurig. "Good. There's still water in the cylinder. Oh, the timeline. Seems Roxanne drove her husband to the railroad exhibit at sunrise. Said she dropped him off on her way to her early-riser-yoga-stretching class at Palm

Ridge. That's about a mile or so away from Beardsley. Normally, the guy walks over to the exhibit because they live only a block or two away, but because she was heading out at the same time, she did him a favor."

"Harrumph," Augusta muttered. "Could do without favors like that. And what was the man doing at those train tracks at the crack of dawn?"

By now, Nate had popped in a K-cup and was waiting for it to fill. "According to the wife, Wilbur got a late-night call from someone in the club telling him the train didn't make its last run. Thought something went wrong with the circuit box."

"Did she say who called?"

"Nope. No idea. Wilbur took the call, so she doesn't know if it was a man or a woman."

Marshall took a step toward me and gave my shoulder a squeeze. "Bowman plans to get a search warrant for their house. He's determined to find out if that tap shoe belonged to Roxanne."

"And how's a search warrant going to do that?"

"If the mate to the shoe is found, it's pretty clear-cut."

A flat, blunt object all right. That rules out the Phillips head screwdriver and the jagged granite rocks. "If she did kill him, and used that tap shoe, she wouldn't be stupid enough to leave its mate in the house where it could incriminate her. And she wouldn't have left the shoe there in the first place. This whole thing reeks of a setup."

"Bowman doesn't agree," Marshall said. "He thinks Roxanne panicked and left the shoe."

I bit my lower lip. "This is looking worse by the minute."

Then Augusta chimed in, "Not as bad as Operation Agatha."

"What?" Nate and Marshall asked, almost as if on cue.

"I'm sure Phee will be happy to explain."

I shot Augusta a look and groaned. By the time I finished detailing my mother's latest fiasco in the making, my boss and my fiancé were roaring with laughter.

"Well," Nate regained his voice, "I can't really see any harm in that. I mean, those women are in to everything. Remind me to buy tickets for the next tap-dancing show. *This* I've got to see."

"Oh, they won't be around for a show. Trust me. All they want is gossip so they can concoct their own theory and plague us to death."

Marshall smiled at me. "Been there before, hon. I wouldn't worry about it."

Maybe he wasn't worried, but he should have been. Operation Agatha was a plan that needed to be feared.

CHAPTER 9

True to form, the Sheriff's Office supplied ours with a complete list of everyone in Sun City West who belonged to the Model Railroad Club and the Rhythm Tappers. By Monday morning, Augusta was fast at work scheduling interviews with them. I had just returned from a quick run to the deli for breakfast sandwiches, because all of us were hungry.

The lists were formidable, especially because it was March and the snowbirds were still in town. Nate opted for the Railroad Club, while Marshall wound up with the Tappers.

"Not that it really matters," Nate said, "but some of those women go on and on. Do you have any idea how many photos of cats I had to look at the last time we interviewed a club?"

Marshall, who was a few feet away at a file cabinet, looked up. "From what I hear, I need to be on the lookout for those Choo-Choo Chicks."

"I think you can hold your own." I laughed.

Between interviewing club members and handling their other investigative work, Nate and Marshall went nonstop for the next few days. But they weren't the only ones. My mother made sure Operation Agatha was up and running.

It was a little past three when she called me on Thursday.

Augusta took the call and then transferred it to my office, announcing, "Trouble in paradise."

My mother's voice was louder than usual. "The most dreadful thing happened at the Rhythm Tappers practice session today. Poor Cecilia!"

I saved the file I was working on. "What? Did she fall? Break a leg? Break someone else's leg?"

"Roxanne was arrested. For murder. Right in front of everyone. Those two barbarians from the Sheriff's Office slapped handcuffs on her and marched her out of the social hall as if she'd committed a crime."

"Um, I think *they* think she committed a crime or she wouldn't have been arrested. Did they read her the Miranda rights?"

"You mean that whole spiel about 'You have the right to remain silent'?"

"Yes. That."

"Yes. I can't begin to tell you how distraught Cecilia is over this."

"Cecilia? What about Roxanne? How did she appear?"

"For a woman who just lost her husband a week or so ago and who's trying to get on with a normal life, she appeared fine. Until those deputies marched in. Oh, I forgot to tell you. Roxanne planned a celebration of Wilbur's life to be held at the Railroad Club room next week. Catered. Of course, I'm not so sure that will happen if she's rotting behind bars."

"Okay. I'll let Nate and Marshall know, although I'm sure Bowman will have sent them a text or something. I'll call you tonight. Tell Cecilia to pull herself together."

When the men arrived back at the office an hour later, I learned Bowman had gotten in touch with them regarding the arrest. The term "waiting for the other shoe to drop" now had a whole new meaning for me. It seemed the mate to the tap shoe I found at the crime scene was resting comfortably in Roxanne's spare closet, along with at least three other pairs. Talk about incriminating evidence. So much for Bowman's circuit-box theory.

"It's way too easy," I told Augusta. "Only a dunderhead would be so careless."

"Yep. Got to agree with you on that one. If you ask me, the woman's being railroaded. Railroaded for murder."

"Do you think Nate and Marshall will still be needed for those interviews?"

"Hell yes. One shoe might not hold up in court, so the Sheriff's Office will need more evidence. Those interviews are bound to lead to something."

I had to admit Roxanne did have a motive if she thought her husband was cheating on her, but knocking him over the head with her tap shoe in a public place? Unless she was going for the dramatic, it made no sense whatsoever. I tried to picture a heated argument during which someone grabbed the nearest object and hurled it at their target, but again, how do you preplan having a tap shoe in your hand?

And if it was preplanned, why a tap shoe when another blunt object, such as a small hammer, would make more sense? Then again, those metal taps, depending on the size, can be formidable. One good bang to the right spot on someone's head and it's all over. I cringed. Two years ago, my mind never would have come up with gruesome scenarios for murder. Now I was one step away from opening shop in the noir section of the library.

"You okay, Phee? You have a strange look on your face."

"Uh, sorry, Augusta. Just thinking. I'd better get back to work."

And while Augusta and I locked the office and left at a little past five, Nate and Marshall remained to get caught up.

"Want me to pick up dinner on the way home?" Marshall asked. "Or better yet, meet me at Texas Roadhouse. I've been dying for a decent steak. We can turn off our cell phones and commiserate in private."

"Deal. Sevenish?"

"Sounds good."

Texas Roadhouse was one of those casual places where peanut shells on the floor weren't uncommon and western music gave the place a down-home feel.

Marshall tossed his fork around the bowl of Caesar salad he'd ordered and then let it drop. "Nate plans to visit Roxanne tomorrow at the jail. He's got some names of decent defense attorneys."

"Bowman and Ranston think they have a strong-enough case?"

"They hit the big three: motive, means, and opportunity. Good grief. The woman even admitted to driving her husband to the location."

"But it's too easy. You know that as well as I do."

"Too bad the deputies don't. This whole thing smacks of a setup. The good news is that while Bowman and Ranston have us interviewing club members to gain more solid evidence, we'll be trying to figure out who set her up in the first place."

"That's a relief. Meanwhile, Operation Agatha didn't get off to such a great start."

"Think your mother will let it go?"

"Let it go? Not on your life. She'll be more determined than ever to find the real killer."

We tried to focus on other topics of conversation during dinner but kept coming back to Wilbur's murder. At one point, Marshall jabbed his steak with a fork and then paused. "Who uses a bloody tap shoe when there's enough cutlery around to take out an army?"

I thought about it for a moment and bit my lower lip. "Maybe it wasn't the tap shoe at all. Maybe the tap shoe was a distracter . . . a ruse . . . you know, something that would lead people to assume one thing when it was something else altogether."

"Well, you can forget those rocks. They're all jagged and sharp. Wilbur's face would have scratches and gouges. The coroner was pretty clear about cause of death from a flat, heavy instrument, and those cleats are pretty substantial."

"I suppose." I bit into one of the mushrooms from my skewered steak and sighed. "Listen, I know we've both got a full slate tomorrow, but what does your weekend look like?"

"Ugh," Marshall said. "I'll be working on my smaller cases and picking up with interviews on Monday. You still going in on Saturday?"

"It'll be a short morning. Invoices only. Maybe we can find some time for a quick hike, or even a bike ride around Lake Pleasant."

"Consider it done. We'll work around each other's schedules."

It took a bit of maneuvering, but Marshall and I were able to enjoy some decent weekend time before Monday morning came with a vengeance. It started with a call from my mother first thing, as I was getting dressed. Marshall had already left for the fitness center and then the office.

The words flew out of my mother's mouth. "Roxanne's going to be released. Not enough evidence to make that arrest stick. For now. Cecilia found out from the phone tree for the Tappers. She couldn't wait to call me."

No. Waiting simply isn't in their vocabulary. "That's good news, huh? I hope she called Nate. He was planning on visiting her at the jail. It'll save him a trip downtown. Did they tell Roxanne to get a lawyer?"

"Cecilia didn't say. But if you ask me, those deputies don't have a strong-enough case. I saw an episode like that on *Law and Order.* It was a rerun, and—"

"Never mind. It doesn't matter. I really should let Nate know. I'll catch up with you later."

"Wait! Myrna called me last night. She can't go to the Model Railroad Club meeting with me tomorrow night because of her hemorrhoids. She can't sit that long. Has to take sitz baths with Epsom salt."

Ew! "Too much information, Mom. Much too much. Didn't you say Louise plans on going to the Railroad Club with you?"

"She does. But she can't go tomorrow either. She's giving a presentation at the Sunshine Bird Club. Said she'd go to the next meeting, but we can't afford to wait until Thursday. And forget about Herb. He's not going until Thursday. Something about a beer special at Curley's on Tuesday nights. So, like I was saying, the Railroad Club meets twice a week. Tuesdays for the G track and Thursdays for the H/O track. I looked it up on their website. Shirley got the letters wrong."

Big surprise there . . .

"Anyway, I thought because Marshall is so busy, you'd be able to join me. It would look too suspicious if I walked in by myself."

"And it won't look suspicious if I go with you? I'm not even a resident."

"It doesn't matter. We'll both act very, very interested in trains."

"*You* can act very interested in trains because I'm not going to the Model Railroad Club as part of your Operation Agatha."

"Fine. Then maybe you'll consider taking Streetman to the park this week so you can get the lowdown from Cindy Dolton."

I took a long gulp. It was the age-old game of "pick your poison," and my mother was a master at it. True, Cindy Dolton, with her cute little dog, Bundles, was a wealth of information when it came to the local scuttle-butt, but having to contend with Streetman when he got into one of his amorous moods was a situation I wouldn't wish on anyone.

"Okay. You win. What time is the meeting?"

CHAPTER 10

"So, Marshall was okay with the idea of you infiltrating the Railroad Club?" my mother asked when we pulled up to their meeting room at the R. H. Johnson Recreation Center the following evening.

"I'm not infiltrating. This isn't a covert operation, for crying out loud. If anything, I'm fact-finding." *Fact-finding? Who the heck was I kidding? It'd be nothing but gossip and innuendo.*

"What facts have he and Nate uncovered?"

"You know I'm not at liberty to share that kind of information with you. Even if I did know, which I don't."

"Ha! The two of them and those deputies haven't budged from square one. Poor Roxanne. Someone's probably filling out the paperwork already to stick her in the Perryville Prison for Women."

"She's not back in jail and she certainly hasn't gone on trial yet. Hopefully it won't get to that point."

I parked my car in the large lot in front of the complex and my mother and I walked across the small, interior courtyard to the club room. Large, potted agaves and cacti framed the walls of the courtyard and small pole lamps gave off an eerie glow. The large hanging sign in the shape of a train made the Railroad Club room impossible to miss.

"Looks like this is the place," I said. "We might as well go in."

My mother opened the door and stepped inside. A huge model railroad encompassed three of the four walls, and it rivaled anything I'd ever seen in department-store displays. In the center of the room were a few rows of wooden chairs and, with the exception of three or four of them, they were all occupied. A large refreshment table took up the fourth wall, and it was filled with all sorts of yummy-looking cookies and cakes.

A short, gray-haired lady wearing a striped railroad hat and a matching apron greeted us from the small table where she was seated. "Grace Svoboda. Welcome. Please sign in. It's so nice to have visitors at our monthly meetings. Of course, we meet every week, but that's only for work time and train runs. You'll love this club. And our dues are very reasonable. Twenty dollars for the year, and that includes refreshments. Tonight is G track. That stands for Garden track or Garden scale. Ours are the larger trains. Like the one at Beardsley Rec Center. Of course, you've got your N track and your O track, but those aren't as popular. H/O track meets on Thursdays, and four times a year we have a full meeting of the club in the social hall. Oh goodness. Don't let me forget to tell you—twice a year we have our Midnight Run at Beardsley. Of course, it's not really at midnight because none of us would be awake for that. It runs at dusk and it's lots of fun. Great popcorn, too."

"Um, sounds wonderful," I said.

Grace smiled. "Naturally, G track is my favorite. Even if you're H/O scale operators, you should stay for the meeting. It's always informative, and afterward we mingle, eat wonderful treats, and run the trains."

We thanked her and took the only two seats next to each other. First row, smack dab in the middle. The five or six ladies who were in attendance—aka the Choo-Choo Chicks—looked nothing like the harlots, men-chasers, husband-hunters, or wanton women Roxanne had told the book club ladies about. These women were more Betty Crocker than Betty Boop.

My mother must have been thinking the same thing because she grabbed my wrist and whispered, "Maybe it's that H/O part of the club with all those gold diggers and trollops."

I was barely seated in my chair when she gave me a nudge. "When the meeting's over, you take one side of the refreshment table and I'll take the other. Find a way into conversations and see what you can dig up on Wilbur. Try to be discreet."

"Try to be discreet?" Look who's talking.

The person who chaired the meeting, a tall, dark-haired man in his late seventies or maybe even early eighties, spoke briefly about the loss of their president and the unfortunate circumstances surrounding it. He told the club members they were now "up for community scrutiny" and needed to be circumspect in their words and actions.

"Good advice." I gave my mother a look and hoped she'd figure out the reference to being circumspect.

The meeting moved on with a brief comment about the vice president taking over until the election in November, and discussion about an expansion plan for the G-scale track.

"I wonder if that's the expansion project Aunt Ina told me about," I whispered to my mother. "Wilbur got into an argument with a club member about it and threats were made."

"Shh. I know. Your aunt told me. It was one of Louis's musician friends."

Next on the agenda was some potluck dinner they were planning for May and a mind-numbing essay someone wrote about train layouts. If the meeting lasted any longer, Myrna wouldn't be the only one with a sore butt.

Finally, the meeting was adjourned and everyone headed straight for the refreshments.

"I'll take the right-hand side." In an instant, my mother was off. Meanwhile, I bent down to pick up my bag as the gentleman sitting next to me beat me to it and handed it to me.

"Welcome to the G-scale crew. It's nice to see new faces around here. I'm Bob Burdock."

"Sophie Kimball. Phee. Everyone calls me Phee."

"Good to meet you, but this is my last meeting until next year. My wife and I leave for Edmonton next week. Probably just in time, too."

"In time? Oh, Edmonton. Canadians. I know you're only allowed to be out of your country for a certain number of months if you want to maintain your health insurance."

"Oh, that's not it, but you're right about our health insurance and the time limitation in the States. What I meant was the murder. Wilbur Maines. Things are going to get awfully messy around here, eh?"

"I'm not sure I understand."

"Everyone's talking under their breath and pointing fingers. Personally, I didn't have a problem with Wilbur, but I was in the minority."

"If so many people had issues with him, why was he president of the club?"

"Because no one else wanted to do all the grunt work. Late-night repairs when the outdoor track wasn't working, trips to Hobby Bench for supplies, phone calls to vendors . . ."

"I get it."

Bob darted his head left, then right. "Granted, the guy was a bit of a snoot, but I can't imagine anyone killing him for that reason. It had to be something much more personal. I plan to tell that to the investigator I'm meeting with tomorrow. Nate Williams, from Glendale. Ever heard of him? Doesn't matter. Seems everyone I know in the club is being questioned. I'd be mighty surprised if it turned out to be one of us. Eh?"

"I, um . . ."

"Oh no. Bart and Eugenie are elbowing into the far end of the table. That's where the good brownies are. Excuse me, will you? Nice meeting you, Sophia."

Sophia. Well, close enough.

I stood and walked to the left side of the refreshment table, glancing at the crowd to determine where and what my mother was doing. Apparently, it hadn't taken her very long to join two other women and a man. They were off to the side, chatting in a small circle. I selected a butter cookie from one of the trays and listened to the conversations going on behind me. Wilbur's unexpected death was the hot topic. I would have been surprised if it wasn't.

"You never know about marriages," someone said. A man's voice. "One minute it's all hunky-dory and the next minute there's a corpse on the living-room floor with a butcher knife in the chest."

"That's not what I heard." This time it was a tall, pencil-thin woman with short, gray hair who spoke.

"I'm just saying, Evelyn, that's how these things happen. We all know Wilbur's body was found at our railroad exhibit." The man again.

Then, another man's voice. "Think the wife got tired of his running around?"

I couldn't very well stand in front of the refreshment table like a statue, so I turned around. The minute I did, all conversation stopped.

"It's okay," I said. "The whole community's talking about it. Um, at least that's what my mother tells me. She lives here. I'm visiting. She's the lady with the burgundy top, off to the right."

"Why, that's Harriet Plunkett!" the woman exclaimed. "I've gabbed with her a few times at the dog park. Before her dog got put on probation. Anyway, I love that radio show of hers. Especially when she and that other lady have to share air time with that fisherman. I didn't know Harriet was interested in model trains."

Oh, you'd be surprised at what's she's interested in. "She, um, well, she's always checking out new endeavors." *And scuttlebutt.* "What a shame about your club's president."

"Personally," she said, "I don't think it was his wife. It would have been much easier to poison him at home. Although she probably had good reason. The man was one step away from being a hoarder. What woman's going to put up with that?"

Suddenly, I remembered the conversation at the Mexican restaurant, when Lyndy and I were cajoled into joining my mother and her friends. The women had mentioned Wilbur being a pack rat.

"He didn't hoard stuff in their house, Evelyn," one of the men said. "I've been in there. On club business. It was around Halloween. As I recall, Grace was there, too, along with Montrose Lamont. You can ask them. Besides, Wilbur had at least four storage units in Surprise. Behind Sam's Club. That's where he kept his railroad stuff. I've been there, too."

I was shocked. Four storage units? That must have cost the guy a fortune. When Marshall and I made our move, we rented a temporary storage unit, and that was costly enough.

"All those storage areas for railroad stuff?" I asked.

The man nodded. "The guy was a collector. What can I say? He had railroad memorabilia, as well as extra tracks and circuits, you know."

I didn't know, but I still nodded vigorously, as if I had a clue. "Maybe someone wanted something and he didn't want to part with it." Then I was sorry I'd opened my mouth. In less than three seconds, I had joined the Let's-speculate-about-Wilbur-Maines's-death club. I was supposed to pick up gossip, not spread it around like manure.

"Could have been those Trane motors and control boards he had in there," the taller of the two men said. "My guess is, they were worth at least a few thousand dollars. But if that was the case, whoever killed old Wilbur would have done it by the storage units. Not out in the open."

Then Evelyn spoke. "Why kill someone over old circuit boards and motors?"

Then both men spoke at once.

"Maybe he sold someone a rotten board."

"My money's on the wife. The news said they found a tap shoe at the scene. None of us are dancers, that I know of. And don't those tap shoes have heavy metal cleats on the bottom?"

Evelyn let out a loud breath, reached past me, and grabbed a snickerdoodle. "Wilbur was a player of the worst sort. Dallied around with some of our own Choo-Choo Chicks, from what I've heard."

"WHAT?" both men exclaimed in unison.

Then the shorter one spoke. "Look around. The women in the G-scale are all old enough to have been his mother."

Evelyn was nonplussed. "I'm not talking G-scale. When was the last time any of you went to an H/O meeting? *Those* are the women I'm talking about. It wouldn't surprise me a bit if he made a promise to one of them and jilted her. Nothing like old-fashioned revenge."

Then she looked at me. "Sorry. I'm afraid we're not making a very good impression. I'm Evelyn Watross.

Why don't you find your mother, and I'll give you a quick tour of our railroad museum? It's in the alcove off to the left."

"I, er . . ."

"Oh look! Harriet's headed this way. Just wait until you see the special memorabilia we've got on display. You'll be speechless."

Trust me. I already am.

CHAPTER 11

The model railroad museum consisted of a few show-cases and wall-to-wall posters of model train exhibits from all over the world, including a dazzling display from a model railroad club in Japan.

Showcased were old circuit boards, old motors, and even older train tracks, in addition to dioramas of train layouts. Housed in between the displays were photos of club members going back to the mid-1970s.

"Fascinating," I said.

My mother bumped my shoulder and mouthed, *"Did you find out anything?"*

At that moment, Evelyn, who was standing across from us in front of another showcase, let out a scream that sent at least five or six men from the other room into the museum area.

Given the decibel level of Evelyn's shriek, I was surprised the entire club didn't empty into the room. "It's gone! It's gone! Our precious replica of the Golden Spike is gone! Someone broke into our showcase and stole it!"

My mother and I rushed to the other showcase to see what Evelyn was bellowing about. I figured there had to be broken glass and wondered why we didn't spot it when we entered the room. The showcase was intact, and to the untrained eye, everything looked fine. There were old photos of the Transcontinental Railroad interspersed with headshots of former Sun City West Model Railroad Club presidents dating back to 1979.

In the center of the showcase was an empty space where I imagined the Golden Spike replica had once been. I tried to take a closer look but got jostled by the five or six men who had rushed into the room.

Suddenly, one of them shouted, "You scared us for a minute, Evelyn. Look at the edge of the showcase. There's our Golden Spike. It's resting against the wood frame. That's why you didn't see it. Damn near gave us a heart attack. That thing is irreplaceable."

I bumped my mother on the arm. "You don't think it's gold-plated or anything, do you?"

She shrugged. "How should I know what these clubs spend their money on?"

"The Golden Spike should *not* be resting on its side against the wood frame," Evelyn said. "Someone must have moved it and didn't put it back properly. See for yourselves. It rests upright with those tiny tacks holding it in place. It didn't wind up against the showcase by itself."

"Who would want to move it?" Bob Burdock from Edmonton asked. "Unless someone took it out for a closer look, or maybe to show it to someone else. Quite the piece of memorabilia, that spike. Eh?"

My mother pulled me aside while Evelyn and the men continued to discuss the spike situation. Thankfully, my mother kept her voice low. "Memorabilia? You'd think they were in possession of the real Golden Spike. Didn't that thing wind up in a museum somewhere?"

"Uh-huh. The Cantor Arts Center in Stanford, California."

"How on earth would you know that?"

"Kalese's seventh-grade history paper on the Transcontinental Railroad. I'm also quite familiar with the last days of Pompeii, if you're interested."

"Honestly, Phee."

At that moment, I turned to see Evelyn put her hands on her hips and glare at the men. "That showcase is kept under lock and key. No one's supposed to go near it."

"Give it a break," one of the men said. "The key's taped to the bottom of the showcase and everyone in the club knows it."

To prove his point, the man bent down and moved his hand under the showcase. "It's here. I can feel the key under the tape. Might as well unlock the showcase and put our spike back where it belongs—in the center of the display."

With that, the man pulled the key out from under the showcase and waved it in the air. The showcase had to have been built at the same time the original Golden Spike was pounded into the ground. It was one of those ancient wooden showcases where the lock was built into the frame.

It took the guy all of five seconds to release the mechanism and lift the glass front. "Anyone want to take a close look at our bad boy before I put it back?"

"Nah," someone else said. "We all know what's engraved on it."

"Our newcomers don't know." Evelyn took a step toward my mother and me. "Our Golden Spike is made from heavy-duty steel with twelve-carat gold plating. Of course, it's much smaller than the original spike, but it's quite formidable, and the shape parallels the original, right down to that little flattened curve on the top. And like the original, our spike has names engraved on it: all the club's past presidents. When one president retires and another one takes office, we bring it to the jeweler to be engraved with the name of the last president. It's a tradition that—Oh dear! Oh goodness! The spike . . . We need to have Wilbur Maines's name engraved on it."

The man who held the spike placed it back where it belonged in the showcase. "We'll let the finance committee know at our next full meeting. It *is* the finance committee that handles those sorts of things, isn't it? Can't remember who took care of it last time. Wilbur's been president for God knows how long."

A grumble of "Yeah, yeah, finance committee," was clearly audible as the man locked the showcase and reached under it to reaffix the key. "Tape's still good. Hmm, one would think it would have been all dried up, but I guess the glue on it was good."

Evelyn and the men continued to chatter about related topics, including bargain transparent tape versus a brand name and who was in charge of the finance committee.

"Now would be a good time for us to leave," I said to my mother. "I think we've seen and heard enough."

"True, true. We'll pick up more scuttlebutt on Thursday, when the H/O scale meets."

"Huh? What? What do you mean *we?* I'm not coming back on Thursday. Myrna's Epsom salt soaks should have worked by then, and how many bird presentations can Louise give? Bring one of them. Herb, too, for that matter. They signed up for Operation Agatha, not me."

We thanked Evelyn and started to exit the building when the greeter lady, Grace Something-or-other, stopped us. "Don't you want to stay for workshop time?"

Suddenly, I felt a frog in my throat. "Workshop time?"

"Oh yes," she said. "Once the meeting and the refreshments are over, our club members move into the workroom behind that door to your left. That's where they work on their models and attend to any repairs that need to be made. And, of course, our evening will conclude with the running of the trains."

I wondered why I hadn't noticed that door before, but, in all fairness, it had been closed when my mother and I first entered the club room.

My mother took a step toward the exit before turning to the woman. "It certainly would be interesting to watch the club members work on their models and run the trains, but I can't leave my dog alone in the house for too long."

Unless there's a giant sale at Sher's Clothing.

"Oh, I completely understand," she said. "We once had a terrier that would gnaw on the legs of our kitchen table if we left him alone for more than an hour. Wound up having to hire a pet sitter for him. Of course, that was years ago and back in Iowa."

"Thank you again for your hospitality," I said.

The woman smiled. "Don't forget, the H/O scale meets Thursday. I won't be here, but they'll have their own greeter to welcome you. Please consider joining us and becoming a Choo-Choo Chick."

"Sure thing."

I couldn't close the door behind me fast enough. My mother was already four or five feet in front of me and moving across the courtyard, as if we had to catch a train, not look at models of them.

"Why the sudden rush?" I asked.

"Oh, I'm not in a rush. I just needed for us to get out of hearing range. Tell me, what did you find out?"

"Not a whole lot that we didn't know before, but I did learn Wilbur had a few storage units in Surprise for his memorabilia and heaven knows what else."

My mother motioned for me to move closer and whispered, "I've got you beat. I found out he was planning on leaving Roxanne for one of those fly-by-night Choo-Choo Chicks in the H/O scale group. This is horrible. It gives poor Roxanne an even stronger motive for murder."

"Which Choo-Choo? I mean, woman. Which woman? Did you get a name?"

"No. Only a vague description. The club members who told me about it heard it secondhand."

"Secondhand? More like third or fourth hand."

"Only one way to find out—at Thursday's meeting."

"Good! You, Myrna, and Louise can have a wonderful evening playing Miss Marple. Maybe Herb can even dress up as Hercule Poirot. I intend to sit at home, watch TV, and eat popcorn."

"Are you sure?"

"Absolutely."

CHAPTER 12

I should have known there were no absolutes in this world. Especially when it came to sleuthing and my mother. However, in this particular case, I couldn't blame her. Nope. That particular pleasure was reserved for my fiancé, who thought it would be a good idea for me to go to that H/O scale meeting.

"That's incredible, hon," he said when I got home later that night. "You found out more information snooping around that club meeting than Nate and I could extract from the club members during our interviews. Face it, when people are off guard, or feel as if they're in a safety zone, like their club's meeting room, they're more likely to divulge information. Imagine what you'll find out the day after tomorrow."

"Seriously? You want me to attend another railroad club meeting? Two in the same week?"

"If we want to find out more about a possible woman who was having an affair with Wilbur, then yes. And didn't you tell me one of the women you met tonight even insinuated as much?"

"Um, yeah. Evelyn Watross. She was the one who had a coronary when she thought their precious Golden Spike replica was stolen."

"It's just a meeting. It'll be over in no time."

"Boy, you're going to owe me for this. Dinner at the P83 Entertainment District in Peoria. Restaurant of my choice."

"Done."

He gave me one of those cute, irresistible looks of his, and I wound up planting a kiss on his lips. So much for sticking to my guns as far as my mother was concerned. I phoned her a little while later, telling her I had changed my mind.

"I knew you'd come to your senses, Phee. One of those H/O harlots has to be the woman who that scoundrel was seeing. And most likely the murderess."

"Mother, you can't keep referring to them as man-chasing tramps or, worse yet, murderesses. I'm sure they're delightful, normal women, just like the ones we met tonight."

"I'll reserve my opinion for when I get to the meeting. Call me if anything comes up."

The next day, Marshall was out of the office more than in, having to handle a few of his smaller cases as well as continue interviewing the Rhythm Tappers at the posse station. Same deal for Nate.

At midday, Augusta received a fax from Deputy Bowman with Wilbur Maines's autopsy report. Also included in that fax was a background sheet listing prior employment and other pertinent information, including address, phone number, and a recent credit report. True, the confidential fax was clearly sent to Mr. Nate Williams and Mr. Marshall Gregory, but as Augusta said, "I can't help it if the papers slip out of my hands and I have to put them back in order. I have to read the words in order to do that."

"You could just look at the page numbers," I told her.

That was before we both broke up laughing.

"Read it for yourself, Phee. The men will probably tell you what's in it anyway. Besides, Mr. Williams is a detective. He'll know I've already looked at it the minute I hand it to him."

Maybe it was my accounting background, but my eyes immediately fixated on the credit report from Experian. "No outstanding debts as far as I can see, but holy moly, the guy sure owes—or should I say *owed*—a lot of money to creditors. Of course, this report doesn't show his income. That does make a difference."

Augusta leaned back and tapped the desk with her index finger. "Maybe they were drowning in debt and the missus decided to do old Wilbur in so any insurance monies could be used to pay off those debts. Then she could go off and live the good life."

"Good grief, Augusta! We're trying to figure out if anyone *else* might have had a motive to kill the guy, not give Roxanne another one!"

"Let me see that again. I didn't take a close enough look at where the guy used to work."

I handed the document back to Augusta and watched the expression on her face as she perused it. It went from wide-eyed and noncommittal to a deep furrow.

"Hmm. Wilbur worked for Sherrington Manufacturing

in Dubuque, Iowa. Stone's throw from my neck of the woods in Wisconsin. Sherrington. That company's been in business since before I was born. Appliance parts, I think. I'm not sure. Seems I remember reading something about them. Huh. Embezzlement? Scandal? It couldn't have been food poisoning, like those processing plants . . . For the life of me, I can't remember what the heck it was."

"Does the fax say what Wilbur did at Sherrington?"

"Nope. Only gives his dates of employment. After he left Sherrington, he went to work for Catapult Construction Equipment in Des Moines. Nothing here to indicate he ever worked for railroad companies, or toy companies that made trains, for that matter. Guess building those model trains was a hobby, not the result of being around them."

"I didn't see anything, other than his credit card debt, that would raise an eyebrow. It wasn't as if he owed money to the Mob."

"Hate to say it, Phee, but it doesn't look good for the wife. I mean, other than the banks, who would have cared if he owed money?"

I shook my head. "Argh. Brings us back to the age-old motives of love and revenge. Geez, I hope I'm wrong. I really, really hope I'm wrong or I'll never hear the end of it from my mother."

"Want to take a peek at the autopsy report as long we're looking this thing over?"

"Give me a second. How about I grab our sandwiches from the fridge in the breakroom and we can go over it together? Good thing we both brought our lunches today, huh? I rarely do that."

Augusta grimaced. "I try not to. It's too much work in the morning, and who feels like making a sandwich the night before? Only reason I've got one is because it's left over from a giant sub."

I smiled and darted across the room to retrieve our lunches.

"We're not expecting anyone for another half hour, so pull up a chair," Augusta said.

The two of us studied the autopsy report as if we were about to take a quiz on it. Augusta, with her hand under her chin, and me leaning my head against the elbow I propped up on her desk.

"Phooey," she said. "Nothing here we don't already know, except for lots of medical mumbo jumbo."

"Blunt force trauma all right. If I've read this carefully, the prior electrical shock he got wasn't even as strong as a Taser, but enough to stun him long enough for the murderer to deliver that blow. Crime of opportunity or what?"

"Maybe old Wilbur wasn't working on that circuit board alone. Maybe he had company. After the wife dropped him off. It's feasible, you know."

"Anything's feasible. It's evidence we need. Darn it, those deputies are looking for corroborating evidence. Meanwhile, Nate and Marshall are hoping they'll find something that will point to another player."

I stretched my arms and rolled my neck. "Hmm, if what you say is true, maybe it could explain those glue drops on some of the rocks. Of course the lab hasn't positively identified the substance yet, but what else could it be?"

"Clear nail polish?"

"Yeesh. Another piece of evidence that could incriminate Roxanne. I'm going to stick with the glue theory for a minute. Suppose someone was working with Wilbur on that circuit board and maybe something in the board needed to be glued together."

"Glue? On a circuit board?"

I shrugged. "Maybe."

"Oh what the hell," Augusta said. "That's what we have Google for. Give me a minute."

Twenty seconds later we learned glue is definitely used on printed circuit boards, the same kind as the ones those model railroads use. But it has to be heated up and used with a glue gun.

I tossed the autopsy report toward Augusta and stood. "Crap. Maybe it was clear nail polish after all."

"Doesn't mean it was Roxanne's."

"Let's hope you're right. Well, this was a most enlightening lunch. I'd better get back to work."

The next hour and a half flew by. I was so engrossed with my spreadsheets I literally jumped when the phone rang.

Thank goodness it was Augusta. "There's a Ms. Cecilia Flanagan here to see you."

"Huh? Cecilia?"

"Yes. Ms. Cecilia Flanagan."

"Is she by herself, or is my mother lurking around with her?"

"Herself."

Then I heard Augusta speak with Cecilia. "Miss Kimball will be right out to see you."

I couldn't for the life of me imagine what Cecilia could be doing here. In a quick second I saved my files and stepped out of my office. Cecilia, dressed as usual in shades of black and white, stood next to Augusta's desk holding a small shoebox.

"Sorry to bother you, Phee, but before I drove all the way back to Sun City West, I needed someone's opinion about the tap shoes I bought. The only store that sells them in this area is right around the corner from your office, so I hoped, if it wouldn't inconvenience you, you'd take a look."

Then she turned to Augusta. "Maybe you could look as well."

I hastily introduced Cecilia to Augusta. After the usual nice-to-meet-you pleasantries were done, Cecilia explained she had to buy her own pair of tap shoes for the Rhythm Tappers.

"It's like bowling shoes," Cecilia said. "They have pairs we can borrow, but ew! Who wants to be wearing someone else's shoes?"

Then she opened the box. "The standard shoes are beige with ribbons across the ankles. All of them come with some sort of silvery glitter on them. I just don't know. I selected a pair with the least amount of sparkle, but they're still so . . . so . . . flamboyant."

"My mother said you tap-danced in school. Didn't you wear the same kind of shoes?"

"Oh no. Back then they were plain. Muted black, if I remember correctly, just like the shoes we had to wear for school. In fact, we weren't allowed to wear shiny, patent leather shoes. Our teachers said that boys could look at those shoes and see under our skirts."

Augusta's jaw nearly hit the ground and I had all I could do to prevent myself from bursting out laughing.

"Your shoes are fine," I said. "The perfect blend of performance and style."

Cecilia covered the box and tucked it under her arm. "That's a relief. It's just that, well . . . when I put them on, I don't feel like me anymore. Next thing you know, I'll be lining up to join those Choo-Choo Chicks for a wild ride at the Model Railroad Club."

CHAPTER 13

"Stepping out of one's comfort zone may be a good thing," I said. "Besides, all the tappers will be wearing glittery shoes, so you'll fit right in."

"I hope this won't last for long. I mean, I hope Wilbur's murder gets solved before the tap dance recital. That's coming up in a few weeks. The Spring Fling Thing tickets are already on sale. They'll probably stick me in the chorus line. Hopefully the line in back and not the front line. At least I don't have to worry about a solo part."

As soon as she uttered the words "solo part," something flashed across my mind. "Roxanne's a good dancer, from what I've heard. Does she have any solo parts?"

Cecilia nodded. "And how. It's all everyone talked about at our practice session. They gave her solos to Candace Kane after the deputies carted poor Roxanne off."

The laugh lines around Augusta's mouth widened. "Candace Kane? As in Candy Kane?"

"Uh-huh."

"Sounds more like a stripper than a tap dancer, if you ask me."

"Geez, Augusta," I said.

"Well, I call 'em as I see 'em."

"You may not be far off," Cecilia said to Augusta. "Judging from what I've seen, Candace Kane really lives up to her name. Very striking and over-the-top."

" 'Over-the-top' as in looks or behavior?" I asked.

"Both. Of course I can only vouch for the looks part. The behavior part was kind of implied during a few hushed conversations that took place in the changing room. Anyway, you think these shoes will be all right? I can always special order a muted pair, but they'd cost me more, and I'm not sure if the Rhythm Tappers would want me to wear a different kind of shoe. Dear me! I wish I never told your mother I'd do this for Operation Agatha."

"The shoes are fine. You'll be fine. Trust me, they won't stand out. No one will even notice. It's not like the costumes."

The moment I said "costumes," Cecilia face turned ashen.

"Oh no. I never thought about the costumes. I simply can't wear anything frivolous or suggestive."

Augusta shot me a look and then turned to her computer monitor, as if she was expecting some breaking news to appear on the screen.

I took a step closer to Cecilia and gave her a pat on the shoulder. "I doubt you'll have to worry. Chances are they'll pick a movie theme from Walt Disney or something." *That, or the opening number from* Chicago.

"I hope you're right, Phee. Anyway, I'll insist on dancing in the back row."

"Good plan," Augusta shouted out.

This time I shot *her* a look.

Cecilia thanked us for taking the time to comment on her tap shoes and walked toward the door.

"Um, one quick question," I said before she left our office. "This Candace Kane . . . do you think she's the type of person who'd have ulterior motives? You know, to weasel the solos away from Roxanne?"

Cecilia furrowed her brow. "I have no idea, but some of the other women thought she was a little too eager to snatch those solos."

"With a name like Candy Kane, I wouldn't be a bit surprised," Augusta said.

"Oh. That's not her maiden name. Her maiden name was Toplinsky. Candace Toplinsky. Some of the women said she married Barry Kane just so she could get a snazzy last name."

"Harrumph," Augusta muttered. "Much easier to have one's name legally changed than to wind up marrying for it and getting stuck washing someone's dirty old socks and the like."

"I suppose," Cecilia said. "Well, I'd better get going. Thanks again."

I walked her to the door and closed it behind her. "Really, Augusta? 'Washing someone's dirty socks?'" Then I let out a laugh.

"Glad you think it's funny. But don't come crying to me when Marshall's socks pile up on the laundry room floor."

"I'm not worried. The guy's pretty conversant with the mechanics needed to turn on a washing machine."

"That Cecilia Flanagan is quite the conservative ditty, don't you think?"

"I think she was a former nun, but my mother says no. Nun or not, Cecilia gave us something to think about. I mean, as far as exonerating Roxanne goes."

"What do you mean?"

"We now have another suspect in Wilbur's death—Candace Kane. What if she bumped him off and set up Roxanne to take the fall so she could get the solo parts in that tap-dancing show? I know, I know. It's a weak theory. Maybe even borderline ridiculous, but at least it throws another suspect into the mix other than Roxanne."

Augusta shook her head. "Too complicated. Why didn't she just do away with the competition and call it a day?"

"Too obvious. Maybe this Candace Kane is quite the diabolical little planner. Nate and Marshall always say people have killed for less."

"You're going out on a limb, Phee."

"Argh. I know you're right, but it's the only branch I have. We've got to find out if those drops are glue or polish or something else."

"*We*?"

"Yes, *we*. I can get my mother to do some snooping around. Those women all seem to use the same nail salon in Sun City West, so it might not be so hard. My mother can always tell the technician she wants her nails to look like Candace's and see what happens."

"Better hope this Candace doesn't like black or dark purple nails. Look, I know I was the one who mentioned nail polish to begin with, but does that stuff glop up or does it run all over the place? Never use the stuff. I like my fingernails just the way they are, so I can press down on them and make sure the blood's still running. And don't get me started on toenails."

"'Press down and make sure the blood's still running'?"

"Why do you think they make you take off your nail polish if you have surgery? One quick look and they'll know if you're dead or alive."

"Uh, I think I'd know without pressing down on my nails. But I don't use polish either. I get them manicured and buffed." Then I pressed my left index finger on top of Augusta's desk and stared. "Yep, blood's still running."

"You can thank me."

"Honestly, Augusta, this whole case looks like a slam dunk for the prosecution. We need to ferret out any possible suspects and, other than that very weak motive for Candace, I've got nothing. Zilch."

"Didn't you tell me you found out Wilbur had a few storage units in Surprise?"

"Uh-huh. Some guy in the Railroad Club mentioned it."

"Maybe our victim was dealing in stolen goods. Or worse yet, drugs. Or even worse than that, stolen drugs. Every other night someone in Phoenix is murdered over drugs."

"I don't think Wilbur was dealing in drugs. Stolen or otherwise. Besides, the guy from the club said he'd been to Wilbur's storage units and it was all railroad stuff. Like old circuit boards and motors."

"Maybe Wilbur didn't show the guy all his storage units. Begs the question, doesn't it?"

"Possession of tangible goods that someone else wants can be a motive for murder, I'll give you that much. But like the guy said last night, if that was the case, the murder would have taken place by the storage units, not the model railroad exhibit."

"It could have been unfinished business."

"Ugh. Speaking of unfinished business, I'd better get back to work. It's getting late."

Marshall called me at a little before five and said he'd head straight home from the "interviews that got him nowhere."

"I've been sitting so long," he said, "I'll be a candidate for muscle atrophy. Mind if we make sandwiches and I can head to the fitness center?"

"No problem. I want all your muscles to be in top shape."

He left the house at a little before seven, and I decided to call my mother to see if I could persuade her to stop by the nail salon.

"I'm in the middle of *Family Feud*; call me at seven thirty."

"Can't you DVR it or something?" I asked.

"I can, but I like to watch it in real time."

"It's not real time. It's prerecorded."

"It's real time for me. I'll talk to you in twenty-five minutes. Unless they caught Wilbur's murderer. Did they catch Wilbur's murderer?"

"No."

"Okay. Twenty-five minutes."

Good thing Marshall was at the fitness center or he would have been blown away by my conversation with my mother. Then again, he was getting used to her.

When I was certain Steve Harvey had signed off for

the night, I called back and gave my mother the rundown on Cecilia's visit and the feeble nail polish theory Augusta and I had come up with. And while Candace wasn't a suspect as far as the sheriff's office was concerned, she had garnered a spot on my radar.

"Myrna and I have nail appointments on Friday. It's not our regularly scheduled day, but Myrna's cleaning lady had to change her schedule, so Myrna had to change ours."

"So you'll try to find out what kind of nail polish Candace Kane uses?"

"I'm not an amateur. If Candace Kane isn't one of their customers, I'll find out where she goes. These nail technicians all know one another."

"Find out what Roxanne uses, too. Just in case."

"For her sake, I hope it's bright red."

"Okay, then. I'll give you a call tomorrow. We can finalize what time to meet at the Railroad Club again."

"Herb plans on being there, too. He said something about refreshments."

"Oh brother."

"Refreshments are the last thing on my mind, Phee. We'd better turn up a few more suspects or Roxanne will need to tap her way out of whatever correctional facility she winds up in."

It wasn't just the nail polish theory that plagued me. It was the bizarre combination of clues that didn't make any sense, except for the Phillips head screwdriver that could be used for fixing a circuit board. Poor Marshall—the minute he got back from his workout I shared my frustration with him.

"Hey, that's par for the course, hon, as far as clues are concerned. Nothing seems to make sense at first and then, suddenly, there's a connection and it all seems to fit. Re-member that case in Goodyear a while back and the only piece of evidence was some sort of tiny plastic fiber? The police thought it might have come off a bottle label or something, but after extensive testing in the lab, they con-cluded it was a false eyelash. Once they got that far, they were home free. The killer used fake eyelash extensions, and one of them got dislodged during the altercation."

"I don't think this is going to be that easy."

"That's why the old-fashioned methods tend to pro-duce better results."

"Questioning and nagging people to death?"

"Uh-huh. Eventually someone caves, although I don't expect that to happen tomorrow night when you scout out the H/O scale meeting."

"Terrific. And while I'm doing that, Herb will be scouting out the food. Unless—oh my gosh—the women. He'll be checking out those women, and if what I heard from the attendees at last night's meeting even holds an ounce of truth, those women are bound to catch Herb's eye. You know what a Don Juan he pretends to be."

Marshall laughed. "Oh yeah. He might turn out to be the best secret weapon Operation Agatha has. That is, if he can concentrate long enough to eke out some informa-tion from them."

CHAPTER 14

"Look," my mother said when we pulled into the parking lot in front of the Model Railroad Club. It was déjà vu all over again. "That's Herb's car. He must be inside the Railroad Club room already. No, wait. He's just getting out of the car. Quick. Pull up next to him. I want to talk to him before he sets foot in there. I didn't get a chance to call him today."

I pulled up next to Herb's car and my mother all but slammed into him with my passenger door as she got out. The two of them were wedged next to each other in the narrow space between the cars, but that didn't stop either of them from speaking as if they were in a stadium full of spectators.

By the time I got out of my seat and walked to the front of my car, my mother finished with her definition of discretion as it pertained to what she expected from Herb.

"For heaven's sake, Harriet," he said. "I'm not about to go in there and grill those people as if they were being ushered into the Fourth Avenue Jail. I know how to be discreet."

"Good. Drop little hints and coax them into sharing whatever they may know about Wilbur locking lips with one of the Choo-Choo Chicks. Oh, and see if you can find out about Candace Kane, too."

"Who? Who's Candace Kane? Was she having an affair with Wilbur?"

"Oh, I must have forgotten to clue you in. She's one of the Rhythm Tappers, and I don't know about an affair. I'll tell you later, when we have more time. Meanwhile, we'd better get a move on. The meeting's going to start in a few minutes."

The three of us started for the door as another car pulled into the lot and took one of the available spots in the next row over.

"That's Myrna's car," my mother said. "She went out and bought a super fluffy, fleece cushion for her rear end."

"That's too much information, Mom," I whispered.

Herb turned to face Myrna's car and then looked back at me. "What's too much information, cutie?"

"Hemorrhoids," my mother answered. "And don't you say anything to Myrna."

"No problem. Don't need to hear the details on that one."

"You and Phee go inside and save us seats. I need to have a quick word with Myrna and Louise."

I glanced at the building and then turned to my mother. "Didn't you just tell me the meeting was about to start?"

"Myrna, Louise, and I can talk while we walk."

"That'll be a first," Herb muttered under his breath.

"Fine. We'll save some seats. Hurry up."

Herb held the door for me as we entered the club room. Same setup as Tuesday night, including the refreshment table. And, like Tuesday's meeting, this one was a full house, too. Surprisingly, my mother must have walked fast because she was right behind us, along with Myrna and Louise.

"Remember," my mother whispered to Herb, "don't ogle the women."

He shot her a look and said hello to the greeter. Unlike sweet little Grace Svoboda at the entrance, the H/O greeter looked more like the security detail at a biker bar. Heavyset man, mid-to-late fifties, dark beard and mustache, dark T-shirt with denim vest, and jeans.

"Welcome, folks. I'm Walker Scutt, but everyone around here calls me BS, short for Big Scuttie. Glad you decided to stop by our H/O meeting to check things out. Always good to get new members. You *do* run H/O scale, don't you?"

I took a step forward, moistened my lips, and smiled. All the while thinking about the guy's nickname. Who'd want to get stuck with a moniker like that? "To be honest, this is a new endeavor for us."

As soon as I said that, Myrna nudged me.

"I'm Phee, and my mother and I attended the G-scale meeting on Tuesday. These are our friends, Myrna, Louise, and Herb." Then I waved offhandedly at them.

Big Scuttie slid a sign-in sheet toward me and handed me a pen. "Forget G-scale. Once you get to know us, it'll be H/O scale all the way. Sign in and grab a seat. After the meeting, we'll make a dent in those refreshments and work on our trains."

Louise handed Big Scuttie the pen when she finished signing in. "I was so terribly sorry to hear about your president. That must have been quite a shock for the club, let alone the community."

Big Scuttie slid the paper off to the side. "Wilbur had his quirks, that's for sure, but to off him like that takes a cold-blooded killer. Hope they catch the murderer pretty soon, because this whole thing gave us a black eye. What with all those sheriff interviews, people around here think it's one of us."

"Um, that kind of goes without saying," I said. "The sheriff's office always questions the people who worked with or knew the victim."

"They can question all they like, but I seriously doubt it was one of us H/O scalers. Now, G-scale. That might be another story. Not to go shooting off my mouth, but there's been a bit of tension regarding the expansion plan. No secret Wilbur favored us H/Oers, and the expansion plan was for G-scale. Still, I'd hate to think a Model Railroad Club member was responsible for knocking off the president of our club."

Just then we heard a man's voice. "Take your seats, everyone. The meeting's about to start. You can gab later."

"That's Montrose Lamont," Big Scuttie said. "Long story, but Wilbur put a restraining order on the guy. Doesn't matter now. Montrose is back in business and will get tonight's agenda going. Nice meeting all of you."

The only row that was empty was smack dab in front of the room like last time, but at least we'd all be next to one another. As I motioned for the others to join me, I noticed Herb had already cozied up to a platinum blonde in the last row. Mentally, I rolled my eyes. "Herb's already seated," I muttered to my mother and ushered her into the row. I plopped down on a hard, straight-backed wooden chair next to hers and watched as Myrna put her newly purchased car/chair cushion on her seat. She sat down as if someone had put a dozen eggs on the chair. Louise sat next to Myrna, but not before turning around in her seat. I figured she wanted to take in the crowd.

A lanky, dark-haired man with a pencil-thin mustache shuffled some papers on the small podium in front of him. "Welcome, everyone. For those of you who don't know me, I'm Montrose Lamont and I drew the short straw to conduct tonight's meeting. Heh. Heh. The full club meeting for both G and H/O scale will be run by the vice president until we can elect a new president. The date will be sent to members via email. Again, for those of you who are new to the club, our former president, Wilbur Maines, passed away recently."

"You mean was murdered, don't you?" someone shouted.

Montrose touched the tips of his mustache. "I was trying to refer to his death in generic terms, but yes, according to the news, he was killed. Unless, of course, he clocked himself in the head because, as we all know, Wilbur just *had* to do everything by himself."

"Yeesh," I whispered to my mother. "No love lost there."

"Now then," Montrose said, "following the secretary and treasurer reports, we have some old business to attend to and one new business item that came to my attention yesterday. Let's begin with the secretary's report, shall we?"

For the next ten minutes or so I daydreamed about everything ranging from my food shopping list to possible motives for Wilbur's murder. Occasionally, I'd return to the actual meeting agenda, but the reports were so boring my mind kept drifting off. The only comment I did catch was about the upcoming Midnight Run that Grace Svoboda mentioned the day before. It was a few weeks away. At least that was what I thought I heard Montrose say. Before I knew it, he had moved on.

"Under new business, folks, there's only one item on the table. It's our precious Golden Spike. I got a call yesterday from Evelyn Watross over in G-scale."

No sooner had he mentioned her name than collective groans from the audience could be heard all the way to Cleveland. The groans were followed by people shouting things like, "What did the old bat want?" and "Now what's the old biddy complaining about? We changed the brand of toilet paper for her last month."

"Quiet down, all of you. I'm getting to it." He took out a piece of paper and studied it for a minute. "Seems someone moved our Golden Spike out of its position of honor in the showcase and had it resting up against the side of the frame. No one is supposed to take that precious spike out of the showcase or move it around without prior authorization from our board."

"Oh brother," someone said. "That woman needs to get a life."

Montrose sighed. "No matter how any of you may feel about Evelyn, the matter of the Golden Spike being moved is a serious one. If anyone has any information regarding this indiscretion, please see me privately. And that includes the responsible party. Even with good intentions, that spike is not to be moved."

Just then, a bald man wearing a bright orange shirt

raised his hand. "How do they know it was one of us? Could have been one of their own G-scalers."

Montrose glanced at the paper and cleared his throat. "Knowing Evelyn, I'm certain she addressed that section of the club with the same severity. Now then, if we don't have any further business, I suggest we adjourn the meeting so we can enjoy the refreshments and run the trains."

In the blink of an eye, the meeting ended and the only thing I heard was the sound of chairs being moved as the crowd made its way to the refreshment table.

"I guess no parliamentary procedure, huh?" I said to my mother.

"That's only for the general meeting with both sections. Grace Svodoba explained that to me on Tuesday. These are considered work sessions."

"Oh. Good to know. Say, other than that platinum blonde sitting next to Herb, I don't see any of those eyebrow-raising women at this meeting. The one over by the window looks like she could double for Whistler's mother."

"Look again. This time at the door to the restroom. Three women just came out and are headed for the refreshment table. Oh goodness. I simply love that ash-blond color on the tall one with the tight, black sweater. And her wine-colored highlights are fantastic. I'd look good with that color combination, wouldn't I, Phee?"

I looked at the tall blonde and then at my mother. "I, um, er . . ."

"I need to find out who does her hair."

Who does her hair? We're supposed to find out who Wilbur Maines was seeing. "Mom, I don't think—"

My mother shot over to the refreshment table before I

could finish my sentence. Suddenly, I realized I was the only person still standing in front of my chair. Everyone else had gathered by the refreshments. Well, everyone except Herb. He and the platinum blonde were still seated and, from the looks of things, the poor woman was trapped.

Without wasting a second, I bolted over to where Herb and the woman were seated.

"Hi!" I said to the woman. "I'm Phee Kimball and I'm a visitor. I see you already met Herb. He's my mother's neighbor, and he's also visiting the club tonight."

"Vickie Owen. Nice to meet you. My late husband was an avid model train conductor. I used to attend all the meetings with him, so when he passed away a few years ago, I decided to join the club. The people are friendly, the programs are interesting, and it gives me something to do. I don't play golf, I can't sing or dance, and I'm terrible with knitting. And as for card-playing, well, that's not up my alley either. But I can paint a bit and assemble the small parts for the train layouts and even the circuit boards. Believe it or not, it's lots of fun. Up until I joined, I really didn't have a whole lot going on."

Herb nudged Vickie with his elbow. "A woman with your looks? That would surprise me."

I immediately kicked him in the ankle. "Maybe we should get to the refreshment table while there's still food on it."

Herb started to say something, but to be on the safe side, I gave his ankle another kick.

CHAPTER 15

In the thirty or so seconds it took Herb to rub his foot, Vickie and I raced to the refreshments.

"Thanks for saving me," she said. "He's a nice man and all that, but I got the impression he was hitting on me. And frankly, he's not my type."

"Oh, you got it right, but Herb Garrett is more talk than action and yes, he really is a nice guy."

"Well, that's more than I can say for some of the men who started knocking on my door when I became a widow."

"I don't mean to be intrusive, but was Wilbur Maines one of them?" *Intrusive? I all but hit her over the head with a sledgehammer.*

"Funny you should mention that. Wilbur locked lips with just about every woman at this H/O meeting. Except for Olga Loomis, over by the window."

I turned to look and, sure enough, it was the woman I had pegged for Whistler's mother. Olga had a paper plate in her lap and it was piled high and deep with food.

"Olga's an expert when it comes to fixing circuit boards. Next to her, I'm skill-less. You'd never know it just to look at her, but she used to work for one of those circuit board manufacturing companies back east. Come to think of it, so did someone else in this club, but for the life of me, I can't remember who. Anyway, you'd better grab a bite to eat before it's gone."

"Thanks. It was nice meeting you."

"Likewise."

I helped myself to a small plate of cheese and crackers. Off to my left, Herb's plate was beginning to rival Olga's. He had found another woman to annoy, only this one appeared to be interested in his advances. I watched as she gave his shoulder little pokes in between fluffing her reddish-blond bangs.

"Psst! Phee!" The voice came from directly behind me, and I spun around to see Louise balancing two plates of food. "One of these is for your mother, but I can't find her anywhere. She went off to talk to some woman about hair color and asked me to fill up a plate."

"Oh brother. Just put down the plate on one of the chairs. She's got to be somewhere in this crowd. Were you and Myrna able to pick up any info on Wilbur?"

Louise shook her head. "No. But I did pick up some scuttlebutt about Big Scuttie and one of the Rhythm Tappers."

"Not Roxanne?"

"No, a woman by the name of—"

All of sudden we heard a loud bang. It was the entrance door hitting the wall as a man the size of a small tanker stormed into the room. "I'm looking for a guy who goes by the name of BS. And that's no BS. Where is he?"

"Uh-oh," Louise murmured, "this could get ugly."

Could? More likely will.

"He's in the workroom," someone yelled.

I took my iPhone from my bag and slipped it into my pocket in case I needed to dial 9-1-1 in a hurry. Then I followed the lumberjack into the workroom, along with half the crowd from the refreshment table. Within seconds, the decibel level in the room climbed.

Sure enough, Big BS, or whatever, was bent over a small table that resembled my cousin Kirk's junk drawer when he was twelve. Lots of pieces of parts that could have belonged to anything. Big Scuttie looked up to see what the commotion was all about.

That was when the guy gave him a shove and shouted, "You getting it on with my wife, buddy?"

"I don't know what the heck you're talking about. Let alone who your wife is."

At that moment my mother appeared at my side. "Fuchsia-toned berry blond over caramel. There's a new color, too. Called *bronde*. Sort of brownish-blond. What's going on? Everyone made a dash for the workroom while I was in the ladies' room."

"I'm not sure. The guy in the NAU sweatshirt thinks Big Scuttie's hooking up with his wife."

"Who's the wife?"

"I don't know, Mom. They didn't hand out a Playbill."

"Do you think it could be one of the Choo-Choo Chicks at tonight's meeting?"

I shrugged. "Like I said, I have no idea."

"What's going on, Harriet? I had to elbow my way over here." It was Myrna, with Louise in close proximity.

I looked around, and the only one I didn't see was Herb. I imagined he was in his glory, stuffing himself at the refreshment table or continuing to flirt with the second woman he met tonight.

"Something about one of their wives cheating with the other guy. Isn't that right, Phee?"

"I'm not exactly—"

A loud crash, and whatever it was I planned to say never materialized. The NAU sweatshirt guy knocked over BS's chair, and the two of them were inches away from fisticuffs. I reached into my pocket for the phone when a bunch of men tried to pull them apart. That only made things worse.

Positive the situation was going to escalate, I pushed 9, followed by the first 1.

That was when Olga Loomis cut through the crowd like a knife into soft butter. "You will stop this instant!" Then, if that wasn't enough, she stomped her foot on the floor and placed herself between the two men.

I slipped my phone back into my pocket.

The once-chaotic scene appeared more like a tableau, with everyone holding perfectly still. At least for three or four seconds.

"Now then," Olga said, "what is it you two hooligans are fighting over? And before either of you opens his mouth, we will begin with having our unidentified visitor introduce himself."

The man who resembled a Mack truck cleared his throat, and the moment he gave his name, I gasped.

"Do you know him?" my mother whispered. "I didn't hear his name. Don't tell me you know him."

The accuser pulled out a cell phone and shoved the

screen in BS's face. I wasted no time edging behind them to get a good look at the screen.

"Now do you recognize her?" he asked Big Scuttie.

"Nope. But that's Roxanne Maines standing behind you in the photo. I recognize her. Recent widow of the late Wilbur Maines, who was the president of our Model Railroad Club."

"Can't say that I knew him personally, only by reputation. And not a good one either. Geez, I shouldn't be speaking ill of the dead," the accuser said.

I ushered my mother closer. "If I'm not mistaken, he already did."

"Shh. I want to hear more."

Unfortunately, the only thing my mother and the rest of us got to hear was Olga chastising the men for "engaging in business that had nothing to do with the Model Railroad Club."

Seconds later, Big Scuttie's accuser left the building and Montrose made an announcement about the next general meeting.

"I never found out the man's name," my mother said. "Everybody was too busy talking. I couldn't hear."

I groaned. I'd seen the photo on the cell phone and I couldn't ignore it. "Barry Kane. The man's name is Barry Kane. Are you satisfied?"

My mother, Myrna, and Louise exchanged looks and shook their heads in unison.

"Who's that?" my mother asked.

"*That,* or I should say *he,* happens to be Candace Kane's husband."

"The nail polish Candace Kane?" my mother continued. "*That* Candace Kane?"

"How many Candace Kanes do you know?"

Louise crossed her arms over her chest and let out a breath. "Well, we don't know. What are you keeping from us, Harriet?"

"I'm not keeping anything. Cecilia stopped by Phee's office to show her some tap shoes she bought from the store around the corner and told Phee that Candace Kane, who happens to be in the Rhythm Tappers, will be taking over Roxanne's solo dances."

"Goodness," Louise went on. "That must be the scuttlebutt I overheard. This Candace Kane could have killed Wilbur and set up Roxanne to take the blame. I've seen movies where the rising starlet does that."

I gave Louise a pat on the arm and looked around to make sure we weren't close enough to anyone to be overheard. "Um, yeah. We kind of thought of that, too, but it's a very, very sketchy theory. Too much Hollywood and not enough solid motive. Look, we can't stand here gabbing. We either need to get back to the outer room and mingle or call it a night."

My mother looked around the workroom, then headed to the outer room. "Seems to me we're not going to find out much more than we already know at this point, so we might as well leave. The Homey Hut's still open, if anyone wants to stop for pie."

I widened my eyes and gave my mother a look. "Stop for pie? We all but cleaned out their refreshment table. I'm thinking Herb's still at it because he isn't in here."

Sure enough, there was no sign of Herb in the outer room.

"Maybe he's using the restroom," my mother said. "It wouldn't be like him to up and leave without saying anything to one of us."

Myrna adjusted her tortoiseshell glasses, stood on tippy-toes, and looked around. "If he was with a woman, he might leave. Not like he has to get permission from us."

"It's common courtesy, that's all," my mother replied.

Louise gave her a nod. "Maybe he's in the parking lot. He could be having a conversation with a woman in the parking lot. More private than in here. I'll go look. Meanwhile, one of us should probably thank Montrose or Big Scuttie for their hospitality."

"I'll do the honors," I said. "Besides, I want to sneak over to the entrance and snap a photo of the sign-in sheet for Nate and Marshall. I did the same thing on Tuesday when Grace Svoboda wasn't looking. And yes, I'm sure the deputies gave them the complete club list, but there could be other visitors here tonight who aren't club members."

Louise left the club room, presumably to locate Herb in the parking lot. Meanwhile, Myrna continued to fiddle around with those tortoiseshell glasses of hers. "I swear, Phee, you missed your calling. You should become a detective."

"It's not about the pie." My mother ignored Myrna's comment. "We need to reconnoiter."

I shuddered. "'Reconnoiter' as in a military operation?" *God help us.*

"No, like in chew and digest everything we found out up until and including tonight."

"Oh, as in pile it on with more rumors and innuendos?"

"Those rumors and innuendos usually have a solid foundation, Phee. So, Homey Hut or what?"

"Fine. But only for a quick cup of coffee. Oh, here comes Big Scuttie. I need to thank him."

For a man who'd almost had a physical altercation with someone twice his size, Big Scuttie seemed as nonchalant as anyone.

"Thanks for letting us visit your club tonight," I said. "It was very, um, enlightening."

"Anytime. You know, your mother and her friends don't have to latch on to a particular scale when they join. The club operates both G and H/O, but I'm sure they already knew that. Maybe you can convince them to join. We're really quite a nice club, even if someone did knock off our president."

"Um, I know you mentioned something about Wilbur favoring the G-scale expansion. Is that how you and Mr. Lamont wound up with restraining orders?"

"Whoa! How'd you find out about that? Wait a minute . . . wait a minute. Don't tell me—Evelyn Watross. I swear, that woman is in to everything. Look, it's no secret. Montrose and I were against Wilbur's favoritism and made no bones about it. So, he used his authority and booted us out of the club. Montrose threatened to get even, and that's when old Wilbur filed those restraining orders. A week or so later, the board found his action to be illegal and we were reinstated into the club."

"I understand."

"I'm pretty sure Montrose and I are going to wind up as persons of interest in Wilbur's death on account of those restraining orders, but honestly, murder isn't up our alley. If you ask me, I'd be looking at his wife. Or whoever his beneficiaries were. Wilbur had a regular money stash in those storage units of his. Do you have any idea what some of those antique trains are worth? Not to mention everything else the guy hoarded."

Again with those storage units . . . Guess the G-scale people weren't the only ones who knew about them.

"I, er, well . . . no, not really. Anyway, I should get going. Thanks again, Mr. Scutt. It was a most interesting evening."

"You bet."

By the time my conversation with Big Scuttie had ended, my mother and her friends had already left the building. I figured they were waiting for me out front in the parking lot. What I didn't figure was that we'd have two more suspects cropping up before the night was over.

CHAPTER 16

"Hurry up, Phee!" My mother was standing next to my car with Myrna and Louise. "Herb's going to meet us at the Homey Hut. He's been out here talking to some woman. She just left. Anyway, Herb tried to talk us into going to Curley's Sports Grill, aka Curley's Bar, and even offered to buy the first round, but Myrna nearly clobbered him, so he agreed to have coffee instead."

"That's right," Myrna added. "Don't need to sully my reputation."

"Okay, fine, whatever . . . my mom and I will meet you over there."

Ten minutes later the five of us were seated at one of the larger round tables. New blue-and-white tablecloths had replaced the old ones. Other than that, the cutesy décor hadn't changed since the last time I was there.

"Good!" Herb said. "Lots of real sugar packets. I never know what chemical crap is in the blue, pink, or yellow ones."

"That's why I use a substance called mannitol," Louise said. "It's a natural derivative and helps with balance. In fact—"

My mother propped her elbow on the table, made a fist, and rested her head on it. "Enough with the sugar substitutes. We came here to go over whatever information we were able to find out from the meeting. And goodness, Herb, could you possibly have flirted a bit more?"

"That wasn't flirting. Although the thought did cross my mind. I was covertly gathering intel."

"So, what did you find out?" she asked.

At that moment the waitress arrived for our orders. That took another two or three minutes as the women bantered back and forth regarding pie fillings. I opted for coffee only, along with Herb, who planned to head to Curley's as soon as we were done here.

"Pie doesn't go well with chicken wings and that's what I'm getting at Curley's," he announced once the waitress left.

"So," my mother continued. "What did you learn?"

Herb leaned back in his large captain's chair and stretched his arms. "More than one of those Choo-Choo Chicks had a motive for murder. Wilbur made promises to at least two of them, according to Estelle. That's the lady I conversed with."

"Did you get their names?" I asked.

"I wasn't born yesterday. Of course I got their names. I couldn't very well stop to write them down while I was talking to Estelle, but I'll do it right here. Someone hand me one of those small napkins. Mine got wet from the water glass."

I reached across the table and handed Herb a napkin. He studied it for a minute and then took a pen from his pocket. "Let's see . . . Oh hell. I'm not sure I remember their last names."

"It doesn't matter," my mother said. "Phee took a photo of the sign-in sheet. Plus, she can get her hands on the club list."

Herb scrawled on the paper and handed it to my mother. "Here you go–Tracee and Grace."

I gasped. "Not Grace Svoboda. Good grief."

Herb shook his head. "Nope. That wasn't one of the last names. I'm sure. Hmm, give me a second . . . Oh yeah. Kimbur and Pearl. Or was it Kimpur and Burl?"

"Forget it." I tried not to raise my voice. "That's a big help. Really, it is."

The rest of the time at the Homey Hut was spent discussing jilted women and the best tactics for revenge. Herb left while the women were on their second cups of coffee.

"Let me know what you find out." He pushed himself away from the table. "If one of those Choo-Choo Chicks turns out to be the killer, I'm taking the credit for solving the murder."

Not if Bowman and Ranston have any say in the matter. They get credit for everything, no matter what.

True, Nate and Marshall had the list of Model Railroad Club members, but with Herb's newfound gossip—for lack of a better term—they might be able to use it to their advantage as far as the questioning went.

When I got home later that night, Marshall was absolutely exhausted. "I picked up a chicken salad sandwich for you at Quick Stop in case you were hungry after that meeting. I thought about baking brownies or something, but I'm totally wiped out," he told me.

"The interviews?" I walked over to where he was sitting and kissed him on the forehead.

"Not so much the interviews, although we're making a dent in the list, but that simple missing-necklace case I picked up a week or so ago seems to have mushroomed into something much larger. Turns out it was a one-of-a-kind piece of jewelry with an encrypted message on it. The client wouldn't tell me that at first, but finally revealed the truth. If that necklace falls into the wrong hands, it could jeopardize national security."

"National security? Like one of those espionage novels?"

"Hard to believe, huh? Anyway, I caught a decent lead on it, but it's involved. Nate's helping me out with this one. It means we'll be driving to Tucson tomorrow, and we might wind up staying the night. Hope you're not too upset with the last-minute plans."

"No, of course not. That's your job. But please tell me you and Nate aren't putting yourselves into a really dangerous situation."

"I know this may sound like something straight out of the Cold War, but honestly, it's just detective work at this point."

"Promise me you'll send for the big guns if it turns out to be something much worse."

Marshall smiled. "I'll call for the militia. And Homeland Security. Oh, and to be doubly safe, I'll call your mother and borrow Streetman. He still snaps at people, doesn't he?"

"Very funny. And only when he's stressed."

"Oh my gosh, I've been so centered on my own schedule, I didn't even ask you how it went tonight at the Railroad Club meeting. And, by the way, I plan to keep my promise about taking you out for dinner at one of those P83 restaurants off of Bell Road."

"I'm holding you to it. Well, here's the condensed version: boring business meeting, good refreshments, a verbal altercation with the second holder of Wilbur's restraining order, and two names of women who might have been jilted by our man of the hour."

"Whoa! Why don't you get comfortable, eat your sandwich, and give me the details? My head's spinning and I wasn't the one who had to sit through the meeting."

"Or the Homey Hut. That's a whole other story."

Forty minutes later, with only crumbs remaining from my sandwich, Marshall had the unabridged version of the night's events.

"It doesn't seem as if there was enough animosity about those restraining orders to result in murder, but Montrose and Walker aren't off the hook. Especially where Bowman and Ranston are concerned. As for those Choo-Choo women, Nate and I will have to revisit our interviews with them."

"So you met Tracee and Grace?"

"Nate must have. I don't recognize the names offhand. Gee, I wonder where this Barry Kane character got his information about the wife getting it on with Walker. Oh, and I'm calling Walker by his given name because I just can't bring myself to refer to someone as 'BS.'"

"Who knows where this stuff comes from? The gossip seems to be never-ending, but Cecilia did say Barry's wife was, um, well, 'over-the-top' in looks and behavior. Of course, that was gossip, too. Yeesh."

"It'll all get sorted out, hon. It just takes time and persistence."

"And patience when you're dealing with possible affairs, accusations, and lip-locking."

"Yep, but for the next two days I'll be more Daniel Silva than Dashiell Hammett."

"Just be careful."

The next day was as mundane and uneventful as could get. At least until four. That was when the lunacy began. And naturally it involved a phone call from my mother, with Augusta heralding it along.

"Phee," she announced from her desk, "your mother's on the phone. I'm transferring the call. I know you can hear me. Your door is open."

Wonderful. Not only can I hear her, but half the population in the greater Milwaukee area can.

If I thought Augusta was loud, it was nothing compared to my mother. "How soon can you get off work and drive to the R. H. Johnson Social Hall?"

"What? Why? And I'm working until five."

"Cecilia just called from the Rhythm Tappers' practice session. There's a situation."

"What situation? What's going on?"

"Candace Kane injured her ankle. Tripped over something. Not a break, but a bad sprain. She's at the urgent care center on Meeker Boulevard."

"Sorry to hear that, Mom, but it's not a situation. People sprain their ankles all the time. I'm sure it will heal."

"You don't understand. The Tappers want Cecilia to take over for Candace, and Cecilia hasn't stopped hyperventilating."

"Let me get this straight. They want Cecilia. Cecilia Flanagan. The woman who hasn't performed a tap dance since the fourth grade? Is that what you said?"

"Yes. Apparently, Cecilia is more talented than any of us imagined. But unless they plan to let her perform in an ankle-length skirt and a long-sleeved blouse, she won't do it."

"Can't they give the solos back to Roxanne? That would be the easiest solution."

My mother was adamant. "They can't take that chance. Roxanne could be arrested any minute now. That's the other reason I called you. We need to get into Wilbur's storage units to see what that old buzzard was hiding. It might point to his real killer and exonerate Roxanne."

"Or it might get both of us arrested."

"Not really. Roxanne has the keys and all but begged for my help. She called me right before Cecilia did. But first, we've got to talk some sense into Cecilia. We need her to remain undercover in the Rhythm Tappers. It's part of Operation Agatha."

I felt like banging the receiver on my desk but stayed calm. "Cecilia's not in the CIA. She's snooping around, that's all. And as for Roxanne . . . that could mean a whole lot of trouble."

"Well, Cecilia won't be able to snoop if they boot her out of the Rhythm Tappers. And Roxanne is convinced we'll find evidence in those storage units that will point to the real killer. Shirley's on her way to the social hall right now to talk some sense into Cecilia, but you need to get over there, too."

"Why? Give me one good reason."

"Cecilia trusts your judgment."

Wonderful. I'm not even sure I trust my judgment at this point. "Five fifteen. That's the earliest I can make it. And it means giving up my afternoon break." *Which I probably spent already on the phone . . .*

"Fine. The rehearsal goes until six thirty. Plenty of time."

In whose world?

CHAPTER 17

"I didn't know they added a ventriloquist act to the show," my mother said as we walked into the social hall. "Look over there. Someone's practicing with two puppets."

"Take a closer look, for heaven's sake. That's not *someone*, it's Cecilia, and those aren't puppets, those are her tap shoes."

Cecilia was seated by herself while nine or ten ladies practiced a routine from *Aladdin* in the middle of the room. In the opposite corner of the room, four or five women were painting large poster boards with backdrops of minarets and camels.

"I thought Shirley was supposed to be here," I said.

"Oh, I forgot to tell you when I got in your car. Shirley called me. She was here, but then left. It's Friday night and she's going to a fish fry with some of her church ladies. Wanted to know if we cared to join her, but I wasn't sure when we'd finish up with Cecilia, so I said no."

Thank God. "Good. I want to get home and kick off my heels. Come on, let's see if we can convince Cecilia that ankle-length clothing went out with the suffragettes."

All things considered, the conversation didn't go as badly as I thought it would, even though my mother and I could have used a tad more tact. A tad? Who was I kidding? If we were at the UN, we would have set diplomatic relations back at least four decades. Frankly, I blame it on the fact I was tired and hungry. Two things that don't bring out the best in me. As for my mother, it was anyone's guess.

"It's a harem outfit, Cecilia," my mother said. "Those balloon pants go all the way down to your ankles."

"But the top cuts off at my belly button. My belly button!" she wailed.

I took a breath and blurted out the first thing that came into my head. "Buy one of those body-shaping tops and paint a belly button on it. From a distance, no one will know the difference."

"She's right," came a voice from behind us.

I turned to see a tall blonde with a figure that belonged on the cover of a fashion magazine. And the last time I saw her was in our office.

"Roxanne!" my mother said. "You didn't mention you were coming here."

"I absolutely had to come." Then she took a step toward Cecilia. "Harriet's right. We'll figure out something with the costumes, but you need to take my solos. My life depends on it."

Cecilia clasped the tap shoes to her chest and let out a sigh that reminded me of one of those pining women in an old Gothic movie. "I suppose I could talk Shirley into making my costume."

The tension in the back of my neck began to dissipate. "Good. Then it's all settled. Guess I'll be on my way home." Then I realized how abrupt I was and immediately turned to face Roxanne. "I'm Phee, Harriet's daughter. Nice to meet you."

Before Roxanne could respond, my mother took her arm. "Phee and I will be happy to help you check out those storage units."

For an instant words couldn't form in my mouth, and I wound up muttering something like *I what?* but that didn't stop my mother from continuing.

"We should do it sooner rather than later. You know, before those detectives get a search warrant for them."

Roxanne nodded. "You're right. We should go tonight. After dark. The place is open twenty-four hours. Wilbur used to go at all hours. It's a Friday night, and I doubt many people will be checking out their storage units. I've never been there, but I'm sure they have lights in and around those units."

"They'll also have surveillance." I hoped to deter my mother and Roxanne.

Like a flash, Cecilia put her tap shoes on the floor and sat bolt upright. "You'll need to go incognito. I'm sure Shirley must have some old wigs floating around somewhere. And doesn't she handle the costumes for the Stardust Theater?"

I shot her a look that would freeze a can of nitrogen. "I'm positive she can't go loaning out costumes from the theater."

That didn't stop Cecilia. "Hmm, good point. But Shirley also handles the costumes for her church plays, and I know for a fact she's working on a few of them right now. They're probably piled up in her spare bedroom."

"I'm calling her right now," my mother said. "If we time this right, we can stop by her house when she gets done with that fish fry. That'll give us enough time to grab a bite somewhere and let Streetman out to do his business."

"And then what?" I asked. "We all dress up as if it's Halloween and sneak into those storage units?" *Thank goodness Marshall and Nate are in Tucson.*

Cecilia bent down and picked up her tap shoes again, this time tucking them under an arm. "Not all of us. I can't go. I mean, I have other obligations tonight. I need to stay here and practice, for one thing."

"It's best you don't go," my mother said. "Four of us would be too unwieldy."

As opposed to three of us bumbling around?

I started to respond, but my mother had already placed the call to Shirley and had her on the line.

"That's right," my mother said, "we need to go in disguise. What? Uh-huh. Uh-huh. All you've got are wigs from *1776* and some biblical outfits? Yes, I'll hold on for a minute."

"Shirley's checking with some of her church ladies. They're still at the fish fry."

"Geez, I hope she doesn't tell them what we're about to do," I said.

A few seconds later Shirley was back on the line with my mother, but all I heard was "Uh-huh, Uh-huh, it'll have to work. We'll be at your place in an hour and a half."

The next few minutes were spent with my mother giving Roxanne directions to Shirley's house and me tapping my foot on the floor, a reaction from sheer frustration.

"Come on, Phee," she said. "We'll let Streetman out and grab a quick bite at Starbucks."

"Starbucks? What about Bagels 'N More? You always go to Bagels 'N More."

"Not tonight. People gossip in there. Someone might overhear us."

The sheer irony of her remark didn't go unnoticed, but I bit my lip and didn't say a word.

"So we're all set. Cecilia, I'll call you later if it's not too late."

Roxanne thanked Cecilia for being a sport and told my mother and me we were her last hope before the system moved her "farther down the dungeon."

At that point I would have opened the castle gate myself and given her a good shove.

As planned, my mother and I arrived at Shirley's house ninety minutes later. It was dark, but the solar walkway lighting, coupled with solar dragonflies, bumblebees, and assorted flowers illuminated the area like a runway at Sky Harbor Airport.

Roxanne was halfway up the walkway and turned when she heard our voices. "Aren't these LED lights amazing? I always wanted Wilbur to install something like that, but he was too busy to find the time. Actually, if the truth be known, he was too busy with his model trains and, well . . . I don't need to say it out loud. Frankly, ours was a marriage of convenience."

I couldn't believe Roxanne had chosen that particular

moment in time, when we were standing on Shirley's walkway, to give us the definitive lowdown on her marriage.

"It's really none of our business," I said. "People marry for all sorts of reasons."

"In my case it was a matter of being well taken care of. I wanted to live a financially comfortable life. A respectable life. I rationalized I didn't need passion when there was a roof over my head and a steady income."

By now we had reached Shirley's front door, and I couldn't ring the bell fast enough.

Shirley opened the door and ushered us inside. "I've got the costumes. This is almost like one of those Hallmark Mysteries on TV. Come on in. Can I get you anything to drink? Tea? Coffee?"

"We're fine," my mother said. "We need to get a move on because I don't want to leave poor Streetman alone for too long after dark."

I nabbed her elbow. "You left the big-screen TV on for him in the living room and the small one in the bedroom. And you left most of the lights on."

My mother ignored my comment and followed Shirley into the living room.

"We really appreciate this," Roxanne said to her. "I can't thank you enough."

"Don't go thanking me yet. You haven't seen the costumes or the wigs. Follow me. I've got them piled up in the spare bedroom."

Seconds later the three of us stared at the mound of clothing on Shirley's guest bed. From bright fuchsia and puce linen to material that featured polka dots and stripes, I had no idea what we were looking at.

"These are some leftover costumes from our tribute to

Annie, Carnival!, Fiddler on the Roof, and *Seven Brides for Seven Brothers.* Of course we didn't do the full productions, only featured numbers."

I bit my lip. "So, um, essentially nineteen-thirties attire, circus costumes, old Russia, and the pioneer west."

"Mmm-hmm. The outfits from *Annie* are your best bet. They're rather bland and nondescript. Not at all eye-catching. Now then, the wigs are a different story. I've got Princess Olga from *Carnival!* and some striking red and silver wigs."

"Striking is the last thing we need," my mother said. "We're trying to go incognito, not look like a Las Vegas sideshow. What about babushkas and aprons from *Fiddler*? That might work."

"On what planet?" I moaned. "We're going to call more attention to ourselves. Someone might think we're the cleaning crew."

Roxanne picked up one of the wigs and studied it. "I doubt anyone will be there. We're taking a precaution, that's all. Especially if we do get picked up on any of those security cameras."

"Come to think of it," my mother said, "the only one who really has to worry is *you*, Roxanne. You need to disguise yourself completely."

Shirley handed Roxanne a pair of the ugliest brown pants I'd ever seen and a long, beige cardigan. "Try these on. They'll cover up that figure of yours and you won't need a wig. Maybe a cloche, and I've got all kinds of them."

Roxanne put the clothing over her form-fitting outfit and looked at herself in the full-length mirror behind the bedroom door. "I look like I'm ready to panhandle."

"Good," Shirley said. "Now all we need to do is find you some shoes. You can't wear heels with that getup."

With that, Shirley pulled out a box from the closet and handed Roxanne a pair of saddle shoes. "These were left over from our tribute to *Bye-Bye Birdie* six years ago. I almost forgot about them. If they're too loose, we can stuff them with paper."

Roxanne tried on the shoes and walked across the room. "I hate to say it, but these are really comfortable. Guess I've been wearing heels for too long. I forgot what flats feel like."

"Okay, then," my mother said. "We can get going."

"Aren't you going to make an attempt to conceal your identity?" Shirley asked.

My mother shook her head. "What? And ruin my hairdo? I'll keep a low profile. Besides, going incognito was Cecilia's idea, not mine." Then she looked at me. "You should probably put on some fake glasses, and maybe a hat, Phee. You don't want to take a chance they have a security tape running."

"I don't want to take a chance, period!" *Yet here I am.*

CHAPTER 18

Shirley found a pair of dark, oversize glasses that looked as if they belonged to one of those cartoon minions. The glass was missing, but from a distance no one could tell the difference.

"If you pull your hair into a bun and wear these," she said, "no one will recognize you."

She handed me a rubber band and some bobby pins, and I reluctantly did what she said.

"Go for contacts if you ever need long-distance glasses, Phee," my mother said. "At least you can take reading glasses on and off."

I glared at her and mentally rolled my eyeballs. "I suppose we should be on our way if we expect to tackle those storage units."

We thanked Shirley and walked to our cars. It had

been agreed that Mom and I would take my car and Roxanne would drive her own.

"We should park our cars by Sam's Club and walk over." Roxanne clicked her car door unlocked. "In case the storage facility has outdoor surveillance. They'd be able to identify our license plates."

I shrugged. "Um, I hate to tell you this, but Sam's Club has security cameras all over their parking lot."

Roxanne didn't say anything for a second or two. Then, all of a sudden, her face beamed. "We can park in front of that little dessert shop in the strip mall. It's off to the side and no one will notice. The place closes at five. Same goes for the nail salon next to it. And I doubt they have cameras. We'll walk across the parking lot and be at the storage facility in minutes."

"Works for me." I adjusted the ridiculous glasses, which wobbled on my nose.

Just then, Shirley came running out of the house with a satchel the size of a carpetbag. "Take this, Roxanne. In case you need to remove anything. You know, like important papers or something. I stuffed some extra plastic garbage bags in there, too. In case you needed to cart off more stuff."

"I'm not even sure what we'll find," she said. "But I'm optimistic we'll find something."

Me too. Mice. Spiders. Scorpions. We'll find something all right.

We thanked Shirley again and drove directly to Stow and Store on Bell Road, by the 303 interchange. I had a nagging feeling things weren't about to go as planned. Maybe it was Roxanne's ridiculous disguise, or my mother's overly zealous attitude about tonight's venture. I'd been through enough of these escapades to know better, but, after all, it *was* my mother, and I couldn't let her and Roxanne tackle this job without my help. Thank God Marshall and Nate weren't around to stop me.

As decided, we parked in front of the little dessert shop and walked across the parking lot to Stow and Store. It was a huge, two-story complex that reminded me of a prison. Tall, windowless, and drab. With the exception of neon signs that indicated the business name and flashing lights that read "Open 24 Hours," there was nothing inviting about the place. No shrubbery, no palm trees, no bushes, no nothing. The one redeeming feature, however, was the lighting. Pole lamps seemed to be everywhere, and the main entrance had two enormous coach lights on either side of the door.

"I've got the key to the front door," Roxanne said. "At least I think it's the key to the front door. It's the only one without a number on it."

I held my breath and waited while she put it in the lock and gave it a turn.

"Keep your head down," my mother whispered. "We might be standing underneath a camera."

I didn't say a word and waited to see if this would be a wasted trip or not. In less than two seconds I got my answer. The door opened without fanfare and the three of us stepped inside the building. At first glance it looked like a labyrinth of narrow corridors with corrugated metal garage doors of all sizes. Next to each door was a large number. Dim fluorescent lighting completed my original impression of a prison, and I half expected to see an arrow pointing to cell blocks.

"Wilbur's units must be on the second floor," Roxanne

said. "According to the keys, they all begin with the number two."

Terrific. Nothing like a creepy stairwell to make the night complete or, worse yet, a questionable elevator.

"We're better off using the stairwell," my mother said. "No sense taking a chance with the elevator."

Roxanne walked a few yards in front of us, where two corridors met. "*If* we find a stairwell. It's like a maze in here and the only signs I see say 'Exit.'"

I shifted the carpetbag from one arm to the other and caught up to Roxanne. "Chances are the stairwells are by the exit signs. Come on, let's get this over with."

At that moment my phone vibrated. It was a text from Marshall. Actually, more of a note, because neither of us was conversant with texting lingo. **Sorry so late, hon. Crazy day and even crazier night. No time to chat but Nate and I are fine. Hope you're having a relaxing night. Call you tomorrow. XXs.**

"Excuse me a second," I said to Roxanne and my mom. "I need to send a quick text."

Wonderful evening. Miss you. Stay safe. XX too. *Relaxing evening . . . if he only knew.*

"Marshall?" my mother asked.

"Uh-huh. And I'm not breathing a word about this to him." *Not yet anyway.*

The three of us walked to the nearest exit sign and, sure enough, there was a door to a stairwell adjacent to it. Concrete stairs, drab gray handrails, and a sign that read, "No Smoking."

When we got to the second floor, it looked just like the one below us. Narrow corridors that seemed to branch out in all directions.

"This is a nightmare," Roxanne said. "It's going to take us all night to find those storage units."

I rolled my eyes and pointed to a faded sign on the wall. "Look! Just like in hotels. There are arrows indicating the numbers. What's the first key number, Roxanne?"

Roxanne fumbled with the keys for a second. "Two-seven-seven-eight. The next one is two-seven-eight-zero. They must be next to each other."

"What about the other two?" my mother asked.

"Two-three-six-nine and two-four-eleven. We'll be traipsing all over the place."

I sighed and shook my head. "Well, we'd better start somewhere. According to this sign, we're closest to two-four-eleven. Let's go there first, okay?"

Not waiting for anyone to object, I charged down the corridor to 2411. It appeared as if there were three garage door sizes in this complex—small, medium, and large. Number 2411 was large, and I had a suspicion the other three units would be as well.

Roxanne used her key to unlock the unit. Then, using the handle, she lifted the door and stepped back. None of us had thought to bring a flashlight, but the one on my iPhone was all we needed until we could locate the wall switch.

I expected the unit to have one low-hanging light bulb like the ones in those interrogation rooms on TV, but I was pleasantly surprised to find the unit well-lit with four inset light bulbs. What I wasn't pleasantly surprised to see was the floor-to-ceiling stacks of boxes everywhere. So many, in fact, that only one person at a time could wedge between them in the tight space Wilbur had left.

"We can't possibly stop to open all these boxes," I said. "Besides, judging from what I can see from here, they all look as if they came straight from the manufacturer. They've got the company logos plastered all over them, and the boxes look fairly new."

Roxanne walked sideways in the narrow space and eyeballed one of the columns. "Phee's right. The boxes are unopened. Give me a moment. I'll try to turn around and see what's behind me."

While Roxanne maneuvered inside the storage unit, I put the satchel on the floor by the unit's entrance and waited. Meanwhile, my mother took a step forward and nudged a box off to the side. "This one says 'Bachman,' and underneath it reads 'Broan motor.' The one next to it says 'Nutone fan motor.' I don't think we're going to find anything incriminating in this storage unit, Roxanne, unless, of course, your late husband was dealing in stolen goods. And there's no way to tell offhand."

I shook my head. "It's a tremendous amount of inventory to be stolen. And from where? Wilbur didn't work for any of those companies."

Roxanne dusted something from her shoulder and stepped outside the unit. "I'll tell you where he got that stuff from–our savings. No wonder we couldn't afford trips to Hawaii like everyone else. Maybe Wilbur enjoyed looking at boxes of gears and fan blades, but I would have liked to see a white sand beach."

I picked up the satchel and flung it over my shoulder. "I don't think we're going to find anything in this unit that's going to give us a lead as to who might have killed your husband. Maybe we'll have better luck with the next one."

Ha! Who was I kidding? Number 2369, which was located around the corner on a different corridor, was also piled high and deep with boxes, but, unlike the motors and gears in the first storage unit, this one boasted an endless supply of model railroad landscaping material. You name it—fake grass, fake earth, molds, foam, tunnels, grass mats, and boxes marked "hardscape," whatever that was. The good news was, two people could stand next to each other in this unit without fighting for breathing space.

The three of us took turns perusing the boxes in case we "missed something," according to my mother. I was the last out of the storage unit when I glanced at the lineup of boxes marked "foam." I must have missed it at first glance, but not this time. It was marked, "Foam Track Glue," and I suddenly froze.

"What's the matter, Phee?" my mother asked. "Did you see a mouse? My God! Is there a mouse in there? We should have brought Streetman with us."

Perish the thought. "No. No mouse. But there's a box marked 'Foam Track Glue.' Maybe that's the stuff that was on those rocks, not nail polish. And maybe foam track glue doesn't require a glue gun, like the stuff they use for printed circuit boards."

"Glue guns? Circuit boards? What are you folks talking about?" Roxanne asked.

I bit my lip and spoke softly. "When Deputy Bowman placed you under arrest, did he mention the evidence they found at the crime scene?"

"He mentioned my tap shoe. Good grief. I haven't used those tap shoes in years. I'm far too advanced for full cleats. I thought I disposed of those old shoes months ago, but lo and behold, there was one of them in my closet. The mate to the murder weapon. Bowman couldn't believe it either. He said he originally thought Wilbur's death was due to shock from some sort of electrical malfunction, but the coroner's report said otherwise. Why? What does this have to do with glue guns?"

"Probably nothing," I said, "but the tap shoe wasn't the only evidence at the crime scene. They found a screwdriver and some rocks with a coated substance that might have been glue or even clear nail polish."

Roxanne immediately held her hands in front of her face. "If it was clear nail polish, I'm off the hook. I only use shades of coral or red. Do you think the gooey substance might have come from that foam track glue? The boxes here are still sealed, but any of those Model Railroad Club members probably have the stuff in their garages."

I nodded. "Could be. Anyway, we need to get going. It's late already and we still have two more units to check out."

"Did they find out where that screwdriver came from?" she asked.

I shook my head. "I don't know. Why?"

"Most seasoned tap dancers carry screwdrivers around with them. Especially if they're going to practice. Those cleats loosen all the time and have to be refastened constantly. I don't go anywhere without my little Phillips head. Here, see for yourself."

She opened her bag and began to move her hand around. "Oh no. This can't be. It's missing. My screwdriver is missing. So help me, God, if the screwdriver they found by Wilbur's body happens to be the one I use for my tap shoes, I'll be arrested and tried for murder before anyone can blink an eye."

CHAPTER 19

"We won't let that happen," my mother said. "We've got two more storage units and we're bound to find something. Come on. Lock this one up and let's get going."

Roxanne didn't say a word. She closed the corrugated garage door, locked the unit, and followed my mother and me to the corridor where the wall arrows pointed to the unit numbers.

Numbers 2778 and 2780 were down the corridor to the left. By now I was exhausted. Unfortunately, unless Wilbur had stored a few comfortable chairs in one of those units, I wasn't going to get any rest anytime soon.

We started down the corridor toward 2778 just as I thought I heard footsteps somewhere else on the floor. "Shh! You hear that? We're not the only people in here tonight. Those footsteps seem to be coming from the corridor adjacent to this one. We'd better walk softly, just in case."

"In case what?" my mother asked. "I'm pulling out my Screamer if anyone makes an unwanted move toward me."

The Screamer was a small device Myrna had purchased when she was positive there was a killer lurking around the Stardust Theater. My mother and the rest of the book club ladies did the same. So far, my mother's device had only been activated by accident, and the result was that Streetman peed on her floor.

"Other people are going into their units, too." I said. "We don't want to be noticed, that's all. Put away that device before you set it off by accident."

Then my mother turned to Roxanne and showed her the Screamer. "You really should buy one of these. No one should be without one."

"Enough with the Screamer," I said. "Keep moving."

We trudged down the corridor to number 2778, where we discovered Wilbur had amassed so many cartons of HLW Power Packs that he could have started his own business. Only he hadn't. At least as far as Roxanne knew. Apparently, the rumors of Wilbur being a hoarder were more than substantiated by tonight's find.

"This is awful," Roxanne said when we left 2778 and went to the unit directly across from it. "I was hoping we'd find something. Anything. Anything at all that would get me off the hook."

Expecting more of the same in unit 2780, I resigned myself to the fact that Roxanne better have a damn good attorney. The key went into the lock effortlessly and Roxanne lifted the large garage door, but instead of finding mounds of cartons from every model railroad manufacturer in the business, we found ourselves staring at a rusty, four-drawer file cabinet shoved against the wall, a rickety wooden chair, and eight or nine water-stained cartons marked MISC.

"Maybe we'll find what you need in here," my mother said to Roxanne. "Those cartons look as old as the hills, and there aren't many of them. Might as well see what's inside."

What was inside those cartons wasn't worth the time it took for us to go through them. At least not in my mind. They were jam-packed with old motors, wires, gears, and a few unopened bottles of Mega-Steam Smoke Fluid. I remembered Big Scuttie mentioning something about using pine and peppermint smoke fluid for train demonstrations because it smelled better than the regular old oil the club used. Again, no earth-shattering findings. That left the rusty file cabinet, and without a key we'd be out of luck.

By now I felt as if I'd taken a thirty-three-hour flight to Singapore, but instead of looking forward to a classy hotel and fabulous Chinese cuisine like the characters in *Crazy Rich Asians*, I'd be lucky to get home to a TV dinner and a Coke. It was jet lag all right, but without the rewards. I could tell my mother was tired, too, because she wasn't as talkative as usual.

"Maybe you can look around the house for the key," she said to Roxanne, "and we can come back then."

Roxanne walked over to the file cabinet and stared at it. "It'll be too late." Then, without saying another word, she dragged it out from the wall, one side at a time. Surprisingly, the woman had more strength than I'd realized. "I know my husband's tricks. He always kept an extra key to his desk by taping it underneath the front drawer.

File cabinets, even old relics like this one, come with two sets of keys. I'm sure he's got one taped behind it."

Without waiting for my mother or me to respond, Roxanne reached in back of the file cabinet and bent down. "I knew it! I knew it! We hit pay dirt and it better pay off." Like a madwoman, she unlocked the top drawer and pulled it out. "I have no idea what this crap is, but it better mean something. Looks like a bunch of file envelopes with numbers on them."

I walked to where she was standing and peered into the open drawer. "Maybe you should pull out the other three drawers to see if anything stands out." *Or how much paper crap there really is.*

"Good idea." Roxanne pulled out the other three drawers one at a time and shrugged. "The bottom one's a bust. Look! Nothing but old copies of *Model Railroader* magazine and some old railroad calendars dating back at least a decade."

"What's in the middle two?" my mother asked.

"Third one down has unused file envelopes, and lots of them."

Then she reached into the second drawer down. "Well, I'll be darned."

"What? What?" my mother all but yelled. "What did you find?"

"Some old photos from when Wilbur used to work for Sherrington Manufacturing in Iowa. Goodness. He had a full head of hair back then."

"That's it?" I asked. "Old photos?"

"Uh-huh. And old paper clips and pens. Probably dried up by now." Roxanne shoved the photos into my hand. "Looks like office photos. All taken the same day, judging by the clothing they were wearing. Wilbur was in middle management back then. Got promoted from his engineering position."

I glanced at the faded color photos and handed them back to her. Nothing earth-shattering, but still better than no photos at all. Then, I reached out my hand again. "You know, maybe there's someone in your late husband's past who could have been responsible for his death. We should look these over. Along with those numbered file folders from the top drawer. Think they can all fit in the satchel?"

Roxanne pulled out a hefty handful of folders and gave them to me. "They'll fit. Cram them in."

True, there were only nine or ten folders, but they were cumbersome. I had just shoved the last one into the satchel when I heard footsteps again. Closer this time. "We should really get out of here. No reason to stay."

In seconds Roxanne pulled the garage door down and locked it. Then, two things happened at once. The sound of the air circulating in the building stopped and everything went dark. Make it three things. My mother screamed.

"The power went out, that's all." I hoped she wouldn't scream again. "I've got the flashlight on my iPhone. We'll have enough light to get down the stairwell and out of here."

My voice might have sounded calm, but the truth of the matter was I was shaking like the proverbial leaf. Thoughts of deranged killers popped into my head like the ones that appeared in every *Halloween* movie. I pictured one of them waiting for the opportunity to land blows on our heads and send us flying down the stairwell. Oddly enough, that sounded better than being stuck in a dark elevator. Although I doubted the elevator door would even open.

Then I had an idea. "I'll stand with my back to the stairwell and inch my way down while the both of you walk in front of me."

"Why?" my mother asked. "What good will that do?"

I wasn't about to mention killers or maniacs, so I went with something that sounded almost logical. "Better lighting."

As it turned out, I didn't need to use my phone. The stairwell had backup lighting. Dim, but visible enough. I figured the building must have a backup generator of sorts for emergencies like this one.

"Probably an electrical outage," I said as we walked down the stairs. I was the last one down, with Roxanne in front, followed by my mother. I still plastered myself against the wall, moving sideways and glancing up from time to time to make sure we weren't being followed.

"Probably an electrical outage?" my mother repeated, only this time as a question. She followed it with, "As opposed to what? Someone who deliberately turned off the power so they could do to us what they did to Wilbur?"

I kept my voice low. "Don't be ridiculous. No one even knows we're here. Except, of course, for Cecilia. And Shirley. And probably the book club ladies by now."

When we emerged from the stairwell the corridor was pitch-black. I supposed only the stairwells required emergency lighting.

"No problem," I said, "I can manage my iPhone and this satchel."

Suddenly more footsteps sounded from the rear of the corridor where we were standing. Footsteps and a dry cough that sounded vaguely familiar. Whoever it was must have found another stairwell to the ground floor. Again, those dry, coughing sounds. It was too familiar.

Where had I last heard a cough like that? "Come on, ladies, let's move quickly."

I could see the illuminated "EXIT" sign a few yards away, and another corridor that opened up into ours. The coughing came from behind us and seemed to be getting louder. Worse yet, it was joined by the sound of someone clearing their throat. Not one of those polite, muffled sounds, but one of those incessantly annoying, phlegmy sounds I associated with waiting rooms in doctors' offices.

"Hurry up!" I shouted, this time not worried about keeping my voice low.

The "EXIT" sign was fast approaching, and if we hurried, we could be out in the open before whoever was behind us caught up. I aimed the phone's flashlight straight ahead and kept moving. Roxanne and my mother were in front of me, but even though they walked at a brisk clip, it wasn't fast enough to escape the thundering footsteps behind us. Or prevent the catastrophe that followed seconds later. Too bad the Three Stooges couldn't have used it in one of their routines. And worse yet, I couldn't line up the events in order if I wanted to because everything blurred.

"I'm here for you!" It was a raspy man's voice, and not altogether unfamiliar.

Then Roxanne screamed. Louder than that device my mother carried with her. Someone bumped into me and I dropped my phone. The only light was that "EXIT" sign, and it was a good five or six yards in front of us.

I wasn't sure exactly what happened, but when I bent down to retrieve my phone, the person who was at my back stumbled and fell over me. The fake glasses slid off my face and most of my hair had slipped out of the rubber band.

"It's Wilbur's killer!" Roxanne screamed.

"Where? Who? Damn it. I'm not running in the dark." It was another man's voice, but not up close. *Thankfully.* Again, a voice that wasn't totally unfamiliar.

"Where's that satchel?" my mother bellowed. "Hit him over the head with it, Phee! Now. While he's on the ground."

I couldn't have hit anything or anyone if I wanted to. The satchel was looped around my arm, and it was as cumbersome as could be with all those files stuffed into it. Besides, I was fumbling to find my phone.

"If you can't hit him, kick him," my mother continued. "Before his accomplice gets here."

"I'm almost on the ground. How can I kick someone when I'm on the ground?"

Whoever was a few feet from me on the floor let out a moan I thought would never end. And when it did, it was followed by softer groans and a few expletives.

Judging from the huffing and puffing emanating from the corridor, the person belonging to the second voice was fast approaching.

"It's a gang!" Roxanne shouted. "Let loose with your Screamer, Harriet!"

CHAPTER 20

Thank God my mother never got the opportunity to push that Screamer button or we'd all be lining up for hearing aids. While I struggled to locate my phone, the man who tripped over me tried to stand and, in doing so, stumbled into me again. It felt like a giant beach ball rolling over my back, and that was when it dawned on me. I only knew one person with a stomach like that—my mother's neighbor, Herb. I hoped I was right.

Without wasting another second trying to find my phone, I stood up and gave the man a light shove. "Is that you, Herb?"

"Of course it's me. Couldn't you hear me yelling? Kenny too."

Hmm, that explains the other familiar voice. It's Kenny.

"What the heck are you doing here?" I swear, my voice all but bounced off the corridor walls. "And whatever you do, don't make a move or you'll step on my phone."

"Herb?" my mother asked. "I can't see you in the dark. For crying out loud, why are you stalking us? It's okay, Roxanne. It's only Herb and his pinochle buddy Kenny."

My eyes were slowly getting adjusted to the dim light from the "EXIT" sign. Enough for me to bend down again and locate my phone. "We thought you were someone else."

"Killers," Roxanne said. "You took ten years off my life. And why did you cut the power to this place?"

"Cut the power? Kenny and I nearly fell down a staircase when the power first went out. Damn backup power doesn't boot up right away."

"You can say that again." Kenny had finally made his way to where we were standing. He was taking deep breaths, as if he'd recently emerged from an underground spelunking expedition and not a stroll through a storage facility. "And this is the last time I'm doing a favor for you, Herb. It's bad enough I'm going to have hell to pay with my wife for bolting out of the house."

"Will someone please tell me what's going on?" The tone in my mother's voice was sharp and shrill.

"Um, maybe we can do that once we get out of here. Come on, I've got my phone and the flashlight's working. It's only a few feet to the exit door."

One would think that under the circumstances the four of them would have been more than happy to exit the building and continue the conversation outside. But oh no. Not this crew. My mother accused Herb of being snoopy and he accused her of not recognizing the heroic gesture he'd made by entering the building in the first place.

"What on earth are you talking about?" she asked.

To which Herb replied, "Ask your friend Cecilia. This is all her doing. She remembered reading somewhere about people being attacked in parking garages and figured the storage facility might belong in the same category. So she called me to go check on you. I told her I didn't have a key to the place, so I couldn't check on you if I wanted to. Then she insisted I call all the pinochle guys in case one of them had stuff stored in here."

"Yeah. And lucky me," Kenny said. "We've got my mother-in-law's old dining room set on permanent storage because the wife couldn't bear to part with it but didn't want it in the house."

I wondered how many people purchased storage units for the same purpose and cringed. It seemed like an awful waste of money, but then again, who could put a price on sentiment?

For some reason I caught a second wind and tried to usher all of them out of there. "We can talk outside. In the parking lot. Under the parking lot lights."

I edged past my mom and Roxanne and opened the exit door. Complete darkness. Not a single parking lot light in view. "This is a side door. Maybe the lights are on out front."

My mother, Roxanne, Herb, and Kenny stepped outside. I heard the loud thud of the door closing behind them. "Uh, look at Bell Road. And the little strip mall. No lights there either. Or at Sam's Club, too, for that matter."

"Oh my God!" my mother shrieked. "Look to your

left. Down the road. Blue and red flashers. Lots of them. Must be at least four or five police cars. It could be a manhunt for all we know."

I stared at the distant flashing lights. "A manhunt? Since when does the power go off for a manhunt? Probably a bad traffic accident. We're right by the three oh three. Lots of rollovers involving speeders. Hold on. I can pull up a news app on my phone."

Before anyone could say a word, I tapped the breaking news app for channel 15. "Someone hit a pole and knocked out the transformer. Power is out from the three oh three past Sunrise Boulevard to our east. West of the three oh three is fine. Must be a different transformer."

"West of the three oh three has power?" my mother asked.

"Uh-huh."

"Good. We can all go to Wendy's. They stay open until midnight. It's the least I can do for poor Streetman. He won't be as upset when I come home late if I bring him a nice, juicy hamburger."

Then Kenny chirped in, "A nice, juicy hamburger sounds good. Count me in. Come on, Herb. Your car's around front. It's not *that* dark, and the way I see it, you owe me."

Herb groaned. "Hmm. Seems Harriet owes us both."

My mother stomped her foot. "I didn't ask you to sneak into the storage facility to spy on us."

"Spy on you? More like providing you with a security presence."

"Some presence. I nearly had heart failure back there."

"Enough!" I shouted. "No one owes anything. Let's get hamburgers and get this over with."

"Someone's a little testy tonight," my mother whispered.

"That's an understatement," I replied.

Herb and Kenny walked around front to where Herb had parked his car while my mother, Roxanne, and I walked back to the little dessert shop for our cars. A few minutes later we were sharing one of those large, six-person booths at Wendy's.

Looking out the window, I saw the westbound traffic was moving smoothly, but the eastbound lanes on Bell Road were creeping at a snail's pace. I prayed the situation would improve by the time we were done with our burgers.

"I can't believe you ordered the Baconator," my mother said to Herb. "I don't know how you can get that thing in your mouth."

He gave her a look and took a giant bite. "That's how it's done," he replied when he finished chewing. Then he leaned across the table to Roxanne, who was seated directly in front of him, next to my mother. "Did you find what you needed, or will we be visiting you in the Perryville Women's Prison? Looks like someone already sent you the uniform."

"Herb!" my mother snapped. "Can't you see Roxanne's beside herself already? And it's a disguise, if you must know. You don't need to make things worse."

"Geez, it's just a little gallows humor."

"I liked it better when you were biting into that burger."

"It's okay, Harriet," Roxanne said. "I know what a horrible situation I'm in. Maybe there's something in those folders that can help, but I don't want to take them home with me. If the sheriff's deputies show up again, I don't want them to get their hands on them. Not until I know what information Wilbur was keeping. Maybe Phee can take them with her."

The last thing I needed was to be in possession of evidence that could either incriminate or exonerate someone that my boss and my fiancé were investigating, along with the Maricopa County Sheriff's Office. Then again, Nate and Marshall were in Tucson and not expected back for at least a day.

"I'm off work tomorrow," I said. "That should give me plenty of time to peruse these files. How about I drop them off at my mom's when I'm done? I really shouldn't have them in my possession either."

My mother took a sip of her Coke and nodded. "How about Phee drops them off on Sunday and you can stop by to see what she's discovered? Let's say around three thirty. I'm doing brunch with some of the ladies from mah-jongg. Three thirty should work for you, too, Phee. Won't it? You'll be back in plenty of time for dinner with Marshall."

"Aren't you jumping the gun? It's not 'what I discover,' it's 'if I discover.' Big difference. For all we know, those files could be Wilbur's model train set inventories. We didn't have time to take a close look."

"Ain't nothing stopping you now," Kenny said in between bites of his double cheeseburger.

I looked around the restaurant and, other than a table with two teenagers in the back of the dining area and one with a young couple and a baby, the place was pretty empty. "Fine. But only a quick look."

The clasp on the satchel was tight, and it took me a second to open the bag. I pulled out one of the numbered file folders and opened it. "Uh-oh. This looks like a copy of an official company letter of reprimand for someone dating back three decades."

"Read it," Herb said. "I want to hear the juicy details."

I shoved the letter back in the folder and put it in the satchel. "I most certainly will not. Whatever this information is, it's personal and only of use to Roxanne if it relates to her situation. And before you even ask, I'm not mentioning the name of the company."

"Out of state, huh?" Herb asked, but it sounded more like a statement than a question.

Roxanne took a swallow of her drink and fiddled with her earrings. "Please don't tell me those folders are all letters of reprimand for company employees. What if Wilbur was blackmailing them?"

"Then it would give one of them a darn good motive to kill him." Kenny's voice was loud, but fortunately no one from the other tables seemed to notice.

I shook my head. "If those people already received letters of reprimand from their employer, blackmailing them wouldn't do any good. It doesn't make sense." Without wasting a second, I shoved the folder back in the satchel and leaned over to put it on the floor.

"That's all you found?" Kenny asked. "Those folders?"

"There were a few old photos in there," Roxanne said, "but I doubt they'll amount to anything."

Herb propped an elbow on the table and leaned in. "Old photos as in boring old photos, or old photos as in something more speculative?"

"Oh, for heaven's sake," I groaned. "Old office photos. Are you satisfied?"

"Might as well show Herb and Kenny the photo of Wilbur when he had hair," Roxanne said. "It can't possibly do any harm."

I opened the satchel again and looked inside. The photo we had seen earlier was adjacent to the side of the satchel and easy for me to grab. "Here. See for yourself."

Herb took the faded photo and squinted. "You're right. Boring as hell. And no names written on the back. It's just four men sitting at a conference table full of paperwork. Hmm, no wonder they all look so miserable. Especially the guy with the suspenders. Who wears suspenders anymore?"

"That photo was taken a long time ago and lots of men wear suspenders. It's now considered hip and stylish," I said.

Herb took another look at the photo. "And uncomfortable. I'm all about comfort. Are all the photos this dull?"

There were only three or four more, and I fanned them out on the table. "See for yourselves. Same room, same men, but at different angles. Oh look, there's a sign hanging over the watercooler behind the table. It says, 'Happy Birthday, Mavis Gear!' It must have been a birthday party."

"More like a funeral, if you ask me," Herb said. "And who's Mavis Gear? I don't see any women in those pictures."

Roxanne picked up the photo with the birthday sign and chuckled. "Mavis Gear is a specialized gear that Sherrington Manufacturing developed while Wilbur worked there. It was way ahead of its time, according to Wilbur. Goodness. That was so long ago. At least thirty years, and the patent expired after twenty. I imagine Sherrington's developed much more efficient gears by now."

"Roxanne," I asked, "was Wilbur one of the engineers who developed that gear?"

"He was part of the team; why?"

"Duh!" Kenny exclaimed. "Because your late husband might have been privy to some trade secrets that cost him his life."

CHAPTER 21

Roxanne gathered her food wrappers, cup, and napkins into a neat pile. "That was a long, long time ago, and I hardly think it had anything to do with Wilbur's demise. I'm no expert on homicide, but it seems to me blunt force trauma isn't a means that someone would use to extort trade secrets. Anyway, I'm exhausted and need to get home. Thanks, Harriet. And you, too, Phee, for coming here tonight. I'll see you Sunday afternoon."

Just then, Herb's annoying, dry cough reemerged, and Roxanne looked directly at him. "Thank you, too, Herb. And Kenny. It was very valiant of you to give up your evening to check on our welfare."

Herb puffed out his chest and leaned back. "Any time."

When we left Wendy's the eastbound traffic was moving slowly, but moving. All of us cut through Sun City

Grand on Sunrise Boulevard and crossed over Route 60 into Sun City West. Roxanne continued down R H Johnson Boulevard, with Herb and Kenny in the car behind her. I figured Herb had to drop Kenny off before returning to his house across the street from my mother's.

"Would you like to come inside and give Streetman his hamburger treat?" my mother asked when I pulled into her driveway.

As much as I would enjoy feeding hyenas at the zoo. "Um, no. It's really late. Maybe tomorrow. If there's any left."

She unlocked the front door and flashed the porch light twice. A signal we had used since I was a kid. Then I drove directly home, my mind spinning with all sorts of possible motives for Wilbur's death.

It was eleven fifteen when I got inside and tossed my clothing into the laundry bin. I took a peek at the landline blinker in case Marshall had decided to phone home instead of calling my cell, but the blinker was unlit. His earlier text did say he'd call me in the morning, but I had hoped to hear his voice, even if it was brief.

In spite of what he and Nate told me about the precautions they took when they were working a case, I still worried like crazy. Especially when that case involved a possible matter of national security.

Too tired to concentrate on any real work and too wired to sleep, I took a hot shower and curled up in bed with a V. M. Burns dog-themed mystery. Cute dogs. Normal dogs. Nothing at all like Streetman, but then again, she wrote fiction.

At some point I must have fallen asleep, because the ringtone on my cell phone jolted me awake and I had to untangle myself from the sheets to reach for the phone.

"Hey, hon. Did I wake you? I know it's early, but Nate and I have to hit the road in a few minutes."

"You have no idea how good it is to hear your voice. Is everything okay?"

"We're still standing, if that's what you mean. Hey, don't worry. It's a complicated case. I'll text you when I can. Don't expect me home until late tomorrow. If anything changes, I'll call. Miss you like mad. Did you have a nice evening yesterday?"

If by "nice" you mean did I enjoy rooting through old storage lockers and nearly mangling Herb and Kenny in a dark corridor? Then the answer is yes. "It was fine. We can catch up when you get home. Be careful."

"You too. Love you, hon."

There was no sense getting into all the minuscule details from last night's escapade. They'd hear enough once they got back from Tucson. Meantime, it gave me the morning to look over those folders to see if I could glean anything pertinent from them.

When Marshall said it was early he wasn't kidding. It was six fifty-three, according to my phone. That usually meant another hour of shut-eye on weekends, but I was too energized to get back to sleep. I made myself a cup of coffee and popped a bagel into the toaster. Then I scanned my news apps to see if there was any breaking news out of Tucson, but none as far as the media was concerned. Good.

Once I rinsed out my coffee cup I removed the linens from the bed and tossed them in the wash. Usually Marshall and I dealt with laundry on Sundays, but I wanted to get this over with. An hour later, with the house picked up and fresh sheets on the bed, I sat down to review Wilbur's folders.

There were eleven of them in all and, like the first folder with the letter of reprimand, these all contained similar epistles. A few folders had more than one letter. Some were counseling memos, others were clearly letters of reprimand, and one was a letter of termination. I felt as if I had intruded on someone's most personal, most private correspondence, and frankly, that was precisely what I'd done. Even though these letters were written decades ago, they still carried the same weight and tone as if they'd been penned yesterday.

The question that immediately sprang to mind was obvious: What on earth was Wilbur Maines doing with them? According to Roxanne, he was an engineer and later promoted to manager, not a Human Resources director. I couldn't help but wonder if he used those letters for his own nefarious reasons. Kenny thought Wilbur might have been sitting on some valuable intel regarding the company's Mavis Gear, but I was banking my money on something much worse. Extortion.

For simplicity's sake, I pulled up a spreadsheet on my computer and listed the people's names and reasons for the correspondence. It read like a who's who of high school infractions. The only thing missing was smoking in the boys' room. And with the exception of one name, no one else on the list had been terminated.

Albus, G., continued tardiness
Betsley, V., inappropriate comments to coworkers
Dennison, C., sloppy work performance
Elitsky, F., excessive absenteeism without valid
    reason
Hammermeyer, A., poor attitude
Jenko, J., insubordination

Norton, C., insubordination
Ortiz, A., unauthorized use of company equipment
Rouzoni, G., petty theft
Tartantian, T., intellectual property theft,
    terminated
Vidlesson, M., continued tardiness

Only two folders caught my attention: A. Ortiz's unauthorized use of company equipment and T. Tartantian's intellectual property theft. I immediately read the first letter and laughed. Apparently, Angela Ortiz used the office Xerox machine to make a copy of some recipes. I wondered what disgruntled employee turned her in to management.

Thomas Tartantian's letter was no laughing matter. In clear and succinct terms, he was terminated for piracy. The letter began with a legal explanation of intellectual property and went on to provide a detailed explanation of intellectual property theft. Next came the documentation that substantiated Mr. Tartantian's termination. According to Sherrington Manufacturing, Mr. Tartantian knowingly took "property protected by the intellectual property laws."

I read the letter three times and thought about Kenny's comment at Wendy's. Could Wilbur have been privy to trade secrets, and that was what cost him his life? Then why wait a few decades to kill the guy?

My gut feeling told me this was a much more personal deal, but I wondered if Nate and Marshall would have an entirely different take on the matter. Now wasn't the time to text Marshall. He and his boss were immersed in a much more compelling situation. Instead, I decided to call Lyndy to see if she would be interested in grabbing an early dinner somewhere so I could unload all the stuff spinning around in my head. I figured if she was up and about, she'd answer her cell phone.

"Hey, Phee. You must have read my mind. I was going to give you a call this afternoon. I'm dying to find out how that murder investigation is coming along. I've got a zillion errands to run, but we can do a late, late lunch or early, early dinner. Call it whatever you want."

We decided on a neat, little sushi and steak place that had a happy hour beginning at three. And while I was no fan of sushi, their tempura was unbelievable. It was late afternoon and the place was pretty full. Saturdays were like that around here. Unlike back home in Mankato, where dinner was eaten at a proper dinner hour and lunch was served midday.

"I never thought I'd be right on the money with my theory about how the guy died." Lyndy reached for a pan-fried dumpling and took a small bite. "How awful. I mean, the electrical shock and then WHAM! Getting hit over the head. Are they still pretty sure it was the tap shoe?"

"Bowman wasn't so sure at first. He was convinced it was death by electrocution until the coroner's report agreed with you—blunt force trauma inflicted after the guy was stunned. Now he's touting the tap-shoe theory. Face it, other than the Phillips head screwdriver, there's not much to go on. Not that the screwdriver was used as a weapon, but it may be corroborating evidence. Worse yet, Roxanne's petrified it's her screwdriver."

"Really? *Her* screwdriver?"

"Yeah. Seems tap dancers are always screwing the loose cleats back on their shoes. Often enough, according to Roxanne, that they carry those screwdrivers in their bags. Anyway, last night when we foraged through those storage units I told you about, Roxanne went to look for her screwdriver and couldn't find it. She was certain it was in her bag."

"Yikes. If it turns out the screwdriver at the crime scene is hers, that will cinch it, won't it?"

"I'm afraid so. I don't think she killed her husband, but I'm not a Maricopa County detective. They go strictly by the evidence."

"What do Marshall and Nate think?"

"They're hoping to find other evidence once they get back from that case in Tucson."

"Did that friend of your mother's ever find out any-thing from those Rhythm Tappers?"

"Cecilia Flanagan. And the answer is no. Not yet. And get this. The woman who replaced Roxanne sprained her ankle, and with that Spring Fling Thing coming up pretty soon, the Rhythm Tappers gave those solos to Cecilia. Cecilia Flanagan. Can you imagine?"

"Wow! She must be in her glory."

"Uh, I wouldn't exactly describe it that way. Cecilia in her glory would be reading a book in the library with her black cardigan sweater buttoned all the way up to her neck."

Lyndy laughed and grabbed another dumpling. "We're awful. Talking like this."

"Yeah, but at least it won't go any farther than this table. One good thing about this whole murder case is the fact that my mother has stopped nagging me about the wedding. True, I want the case to be solved and Roxanne exonerated, but if I could keep my mother's attention on something other than the upcoming nuptials, it would be fantastic."

"I think it was smart of you and Marshall to go low-key on it."

"Yeah, I'll save the blushing bride days for my daughter, if and when she ever decides to tie the knot with someone. Frankly, I'm still twitching over my Aunt Ina's wacky wedding, and that was what? Two years ago. Yeesh."

"Tell me, what's your next step? On the investigation, not the wedding."

"I really need to dig up the background on Thomas Tartantian. If Wilbur had anything to do with the guy's termination, or if Wilbur was extorting money from him, it would be a darned good motive for murder. Much better than some model railroad aficionado upset because the club's expansion plans didn't call for the gauge size they liked or, worse yet, the jilted Choo-Choo Chick theory."

"I liked the jilted Choo-Choo Chick theory."

"Forget it. This one's much more substantial." I took a sip of my Coke and nabbed a batter-dipped shrimp from the tempura tray. "You know, on second thought, maybe I should drop this gem on Marshall's lap. He and Nate have access to all sorts of databases that are only available to licensed detectives."

"Or you could get a head start with one of those fourteen-dollar-and-ninety-four-cent background check companies and go from there."

"Drat. You know me too well."

CHAPTER 22

As tempted as I was to plunk down the lousy fourteen-plus dollars on a cookie-cutter background check late last night, I decided to hold off until I spoke with Roxanne later today. My mind was fuzzy from the bizarre circumstances surrounding her husband's death and the ever-growing suspect list comprised of Choo-Choo Chicks, model railroad aficionados, and possible jealous Rhythm Tappers who coveted Roxanne's solos. To top things off, a new list of suspects emerged: the recipients of reprimand letters from Wilbur's former place of employment. And why on earth he had copies of those letters was one conundrum I didn't feel like dealing with on a Sunday morning.

Instead, I took a polar-bear plunge with the other brave souls in Vistancia's pool. Polar bear in Arizona terms, that was. The pool might have been heated to eighty-seven degrees, but the outdoor temperature of sixty-four felt like sixty-four below zero.

I rationalized it was good for my physical and emotional well-being. If I didn't, I would have had to admit I was nuts. Even for a former Minnesotan, who once thought nothing of wearing cutoff jeans and cotton T-shirts in fifty-degree weather.

When I returned from the pool I stuck a chuck roast in the slow cooker and ate a handful of pretzels. At least there would be a decent meal waiting for Marshall when he got back. *If* he made it back that afternoon. The last conversation I'd had with him didn't sound too promising, and so far no calls or text messages. Normally, I'd reach out to him, but it sounded as if the last thing he and Nate needed was an interruption.

My head had cleared and I decided to give the reprimand letter list another look-see. This time I read all the letters and reached the same conclusion as before. The only letter that mattered was Thomas Tartantian's. And geez, who was turning these people in? Not that I condoned pilfering rubber bands or some extra paper clips, but honestly, the way the reprimand letters read, one would have thought the culprits walked off with the office Nespresso machine.

I put the folders back in a neat pile and was about to grab a snack when the phone rang. Marshall! Without even bothering to check the landline's caller ID, I picked it up and offered the cheeriest of hellos before I realized it wasn't Marshall.

"It's Aunt Ina! You sound chipper today, Phee. And you'll be even happier when you hear what I'm about to tell you."

Define "happier." "Um, hi, Aunt Ina. What's up?"

"You know that clarinet player who got slapped with the restraining order? Montrose Lamont? Well, Louis had a gig with him last night, along with some other men, and afterward, when he'd had enough alcohol to loosen up, he told Louis he'd seen Wilbur Maines paying off someone by the name of . . . hold on a minute, will you . . . LOUIS! What was that man's name? Big Scootie? Big Scottie? What? . . . Oh, I'm back, Phee. Sorry about that. The man's name—and it must be his nickname—is Big Scuttie. Maybe Wilbur was being blackmailed, and when he couldn't pay up this Big Scuttie murdered him."

"Golly, Aunt Ina, I'm not sure—"

"You and Marshall can thank me later."

"Did Uncle Louis happen to find out where this transaction took place?"

"Hold on. LOUIS!!!"

I held the receiver away from my ear and waited.

Aunt Ina was back on the line in a nanosecond. "He must have gone into the bedroom. No sense having you wait on the line. If I find out, I'll let you know. I was going to call Roxanne and tell her myself, but I didn't want to get her hopes up."

"Good idea. Good thinking."

"Well, I'd love to stay and chat, but Louis and I are going to an art reception in Scottsdale this afternoon. A new artist from Berlin, who only paints while naked, with his eyes closed. Fascinating oil paintings, although Louis finds the colors somewhat disturbing."

I find the whole idea disturbing and I hope he doesn't plan on giving a demonstration. "Okay. Have a wonderful time. And thanks for calling."

My aunt's revelation put a whole new spin on a motive for Wilbur's death. But I seriously doubted Big Scuttie was the one responsible. The fact that Wilbur was seen handing the guy money could have been anything. Railroad club business, money owed for something Wilbur purchased from Big Scuttie, or even a gambling debt. For all any of us knew, Wilbur could have been one of those serious card players who got in over his head. I'd certainly come across a few of those. I made a mental note to ask Roxanne if Wilbur owed anyone a substantial sum of money. However, I never got the chance when the three of us met at my mother's house later in the day.

"Forget the file-folder information," my mother announced as soon as I got in the door. "We'll get to it later."

Roxanne was seated in one of the floral chairs and Streetman was under the coffee table. Upon closer inspection, I realized my mother had set out an assortment of juices and a tray of cheese, crackers, and pepperoni. No wonder the dog was poised and at the ready if something were to drop.

I waved hello to Roxanne and turned to my mother. "What do you mean?"

Before my mom could answer, Roxanne motioned me over to the chair next to hers. "I can't believe I'm such a dunderhead. People will be convinced I murdered my husband. The file-folder info can wait. Wilbur's celebration of life can't. Not if I want to keep my head above water. I was in the process of planning a celebration of Wilbur's life to be held at the Railroad Club room this week and it never happened. When that Neanderthal of a deputy put me in handcuffs I completely forgot about the memorial plans. I've done nothing! Absolutely nothing! Everyone will be convinced I'm a cold, calculating black widow."

I reached for a cracker and was about to put it in my mouth when Streetman got up on his rear legs, circled around, and whined. I wondered if that was the "doggy dance" my mother had told me about. "Fine, you can have this one, but only this one." I gave him the cracker and then leaned toward Roxanne. "No one will think that. Lots of people don't have funerals or memorials for their loved ones." *They take the money and run.* "People will understand." *They won't.*

She shook her head. "Not in this case. I've got to get that celebration planned and completed by week's end and I hardly know where to begin."

My mother sat on the couch and proceeded to put a few pepperoni slices between two crackers. "Now do you see why the folders have to wait? We've got to get Wilbur's celebration planned immediately. And whatever you do, don't let your aunt Ina in on this or Roxanne will wind up with some New-Age, hippie-dippie thing that will leave all of us in a state of shock."

"No problem there," I said.

"Roxanne's going to contact Grace Svoboda and Evelyn Watross at the Railroad Club tomorrow. They're the ones who manage the room. Once she gets a definitive date and time for next week, she can give that to the caterer."

I snatched another cracker and closed my hand around it, hoping the dog wouldn't notice. Unfortunately, he did. Streetman got up on his hind legs and twirled around a few times. Then he whined. I acquiesced and handed him the cracker. "What caterer?"

"Well, that's what we're trying to work out, Phee," my mother said. "We need to decide. Bagels 'N More always puts on a nice spread, but so does the Homey Hut. Then you've got the usual fanfare from all those chain restaurants, not to mention private caterers."

"Um, I really don't want to sound sexist, but that club is mostly men, and they'll probably be happier with pizza and wings as opposed to bagels and spreads." *Or worse yet, those little cucumber sandwiches from the Homey Hut.*

"I think Phee makes a good point," Roxanne said. "Besides, pizza is easy, and one of those restaurants won't need a lot of lead time. A week should be fine. They can also bring the soft drinks. I'm not supplying alcohol."

My mother nodded and stood. "Let me get a pad and pen to write this down." She walked toward the kitchen.

"While we're waiting," I said to Roxanne, "maybe I can read you the list of names from those folders and you can tell me if any of them jump out at you."

"I, er . . ."

"I'll read them off fast. Here goes."

From Albus to Vidlesson, I read off the names as if it was a high-school honor roll. Roxanne furrowed her brow and didn't make a move. "Tartantian. I remember hearing that name. It was a long time ago. Wilbur was on the phone with someone, and at first I thought he said, 'tarantula.' I asked him about it when he got off the phone and he said, 'Not tarantula, Tartantian.' He told me it was a guy who worked in his office. That's all I know."

Just then, my mother returned with her pad and pen. "I suggest Florencia's Pizza on Camino del Sol or Ray's Pizza on Grand."

"I'll call for prices and confirm," Roxanne replied. "Now what? I've never planned a celebration of life before."

My mother put the pad on the coffee table and moved the pen around in her hand. "Think of it as a birthday party without the cake or games."

"Uh, what my mother means is, someone speaks about the deceased's life and then other people say some nice things. Sometimes there's a slide show or a PowerPoint presentation."

Roxanne opened her mouth slightly, but no words came out.

I decided to keep going. "Sometimes someone plays the guitar or sings a song. Then everyone eats."

Finally she spoke, but her words were choppy, and it sounded as if she might cry. "All I envisioned was a quiet little get-together with food. Not a production with slides or, worse yet, some computer thing."

"See what you've done, Phee," my mother whispered. "You've upset her."

"I, I . . ."

Roxanne wrung her hands and sighed. "It's okay, Harriet. Phee didn't upset me. This whole mess has taken its toll on me. I can't get to sleep without spraying lavender mist on my pillow. And even then, I lay in bed wondering if that horrid deputy is going to break down the door to arrest me again."

"Um, I've been to a few of these memorials or celebrations"—*some worse than others*—"and keeping it simple is a good idea. Maybe just a big poster board with photos of Wilbur and some fond memories. You don't need a fancy program." *Or, heaven help us, a singer. Why did I even mention that?*

Roxanne took a sip of her juice and nodded. "Maybe Grace or Evelyn will think of something when I speak with them. Maybe even a farewell train run in Wilbur's honor."

"Good," I said. "Glad that's all settled. Anyway, about those file folders and the photos, I was wondering if—"

"I knew anything about those people?" Roxanne asked. "Because I don't. Wilbur never shared office information with me. Or *any* information, for that matter. Otherwise I'd have a darn good idea which Choo-Choo Chicks he was messing with. Listen, I know this is an uncomfortable situation for you because your boss and fiancé were hired to assist the Maricopa County Sheriff's Office. But I'm willing to take my chances if you are. I didn't kill my husband and maybe, just maybe, someone in one of those file folders did."

My throat suddenly felt tight. "Are you asking me to share this with them?"

"Only them. The people in the file folders. Not those dreadful deputies."

There were only eleven file-folder names. Not that daunting of a task to see if any of them now resided in the area. And even though the offenses were minor, I was a firm believer in that old adage, People have killed for less. I was also a believer in Ricky Ricardo's often-quoted words, "Lucy, you've got some 'splaining to do." And once Marshall got home, I'd have lots of 'splaining to do myself, beginning with the storage unit escapade and culminating with a new to-do list for the Wilbur Maines investigation.

CHAPTER 23

Given what little Roxanne knew about her late husband's business, I doubted she would have known anything about money crossing hands between Wilbur and Big Scuttie. I put that thought on the back burner and instead tried my own hand at matching my mother's Sun City West phone book directory with the eleven names from the file folder. My mother couldn't shove the directory at me fast enough when I left her house. "Here, this will get you started."

At least it gave me something to do while waiting to hear from Marshall that evening. It wasn't like him not to text or call, and by early evening I was more than worried. I was one step away from letting my imagination run away with every nail-biting crime-show episode I'd ever seen.

At last, somewhere between Clarisse Dennison (sloppy

work performance) and Arnell Hammermeyer (poor attitude), the phone rang, and this time it wasn't my aunt Ina.

"It's me, hon. Hope you weren't too worried." The tension I felt evaporated instantly at the sound of Marshall's voice. "What a stupid thing to say," he continued. "I'm sure you were, but Nate and I were literally on the chase since we got to Tucson. Long story short, it's over. Can't tell you too much over the phone, just that we're staying at the Hampton Inn in Marana and we'll be back tomorrow midmorning. Can you bring a shirt and a pair of pants to the office? I feel as if mine are glued to me."

"Sure, but if it's any consolation, my clothes are covered with Streetman's hair. Another long story, but it can wait. You must be exhausted."

"Brain-dead is more like it. I'm too tired to even eat. Maybe later, but I intend to take a shower and a long nap that may turn into a night's sleep. Boy, do I miss you. I'll call or text you once we're in earshot of Phoenix. Nate and I want to get into the office as soon as possible. Only I have a better reason than he does."

My face warmed and I smiled. "Your 'better reason' feels the same way. Get a good night's sleep."

The next day I learned more about the missing necklace and why it had gone from a simple theft to a matter of national security. The client, it seemed, wasn't straightforward with Nate at first, but when she realized it was the only way to make sure the necklace didn't fall into the wrong hands, she had to own up.

Handmade out of eighteen carat gold, the low collar necklace was comprised of a number of leaves, each with its own pattern of veins, creating a stunning design. Upon closer inspection, it was the backside of each leaf that made the necklace irreplaceable and dangerous.

Encrypted into each singular leaf was a binary code that unlocked portions of our defense system's central computers. What the client had neglected to tell Nate was that her father worked in top security at the Pentagon. He'd had a goldsmith encrypt the code into the necklace in the event the other means of safeguarding the information was destroyed. And he gave the necklace to his daughter for safekeeping. When the goldsmith was found dead in his Arlington, Virginia, condo, the father contacted his daughter to ensure the necklace was still secure. That was when she realized someone had broken into the hidden safe in her Paradise Valley, Arizona, home and immediately sought out help from Williams Investigations.

Nate was able to pick up a strong lead that sent him and Marshall to Tucson, where, for the next two days, the situation played out like a cat-and-mouse game until the thief/possible terrorist was apprehended.

"I'll give you and Mr. Gregory credit for that," Augusta said when Nate finished recounting their weekend. "But Phee's business Friday night in that storage facility was just as exciting."

"What business? What storage facility?" Nate and Marshall asked at once.

I glared at Augusta and pushed the blue button on the Keurig for my coffee. "I was going to get to that. Once you guys had a chance to settle in."

"I'm pretty settled," Nate said. "How about you, Marshall?"

"Settled as they get. Might as well spill it, hon."

For the next five minutes I explained everything, beginning with Roxanne's insistence we check Wilbur's storage units before the deputies got a search warrant and ending with Herb's rotund stomach rolling over my back like a beach ball in the pitch-black corridor. I wasn't sure how to gauge the reactions on Nate and Marshall's faces until they both broke up laughing.

"I'm honestly speechless," Marshall said. "Stunned and speechless."

Nate put his hand under his chin and shook his head. "Hell, I'm still trying to get that picture of Herb out of my head."

"So you're not upset? At that fiasco I got talked into participating in?"

Marshall took a step closer to me. "Not the best move, to be in a storage facility at night, but considering you were with your mother and that arsenal of self-defense products she keeps in her bag, you were probably safe. But holy cow, please don't do it again."

"Unless you come up with better disguises," Nate added.

"Ugh. Don't remind me."

Augusta sat up at her desk and put her hands on her hips. "Tell them what you found. Go on, Phee. It's evidence, isn't it?"

I looked at her and shrugged. "I wouldn't call it evidence, but it *is* something."

I went on to explain about the photos and letters of reprimand we found in folders that were housed in one of the storage units. "Minor stuff if you ask me, like tardiness and petty theft. But one of those people, Thomas Tartantian, may have had a good motive for doing away with Wilbur. Thomas was terminated for intellectual theft. Product piracy. That's a major big deal and a motive for murder if Wilbur was blackmailing him or something. Of course, those letters date back decades."

"Tell them the rest, Phee," Augusta said.

Nate widened his eyes and continued to rub his chin. "There's more?"

"Uh-huh. I got the Sun City West phone directory and looked up all the names on the off chance one of those people retired here, but no such luck. Still, it's decent evidence, isn't it? That someone other than the wife had a burning motive for murder."

Nate and Marshall exchanged glances before Marshall spoke. "I wouldn't exactly call it a burning motive, but it could be something. Maybe Wilbur threatened to blackball one of the employees. Why would he have those letters of reprimand in the first place? Wasn't he a manager or something?"

"A manager and an engineer," I replied.

"Look, I wouldn't get my hopes up about those folders if I were you. Or Roxanne. Especially Roxanne."

By now my coffee had finished brewing and I reached for the cup. "What do you mean?"

"We got a text from Bowman this morning. The Sheriff's Office has even more reason to believe she was the one who murdered her husband. I was about to tell you when we got off talking about the necklace and then the storage-locker incident. Sorry, hon."

My hand shook and the coffee almost spilled. "What reason?"

"Oldest one in the book," Nate said. "They learned Roxanne took out a substantial insurance policy on Wilbur, and she's the only named beneficiary."

"That doesn't mean anything. Lots of spouses have insurance policies on each other."

"Yes, but this one was fairly recent. Less than six months ago."

I was so flustered I forgot to put milk in my coffee and the first sip burned my lips. "Is that all? The insurance policy?"

Again, Nate and Marshall looked at each other, and Nate continued. "One of those silent-witness tips came into the office. The woman claimed to have overheard a conversation between Roxanne and Wilbur that took place in front of the social hall as Roxanne was on her way to a Rhythm Tappers rehearsal. It was a few days before his body was found."

"Hurry up with it, Mr. Williams," Augusta said, "I'm not getting any younger."

"Hmm, that was pretty much what Roxanne told her husband, but with a different pronoun. According to the silent witness, Roxanne told Wilbur, 'Keep up your shenanigans and you won't live to see me tap another dance. In fact, the only tap you'll see is from the bottom of my shoe on its way to your head.'"

I put my cup on Augusta's desk for fear of dropping it. "Yeesh. That does sound bad, but it could have been anything. People make all sorts of meaningless threats in the heat of the moment. Heck, we overheard her say something about kissing the pavement when she was in this office."

Augusta moved my cup away from the edge of the desk. "That was before her husband wound up dead. With her tap shoe. You may have to give up the ghost, Phee."

"Please don't tell me those deputies are going to arrest her again. The corroborating evidence is hearsay. Okay, and maybe the insurance policy. But still . . ."

"Take a breath," Marshall said. "We're dealing with it. Sure, Bowman and Ranston want to move quickly, but Roxanne's not going anywhere."

Augusta leaned in the chair and straightened her back. "Unless it's the Fourth Avenue Jail."

I gulped. "Tell Bowman and Ranston you have new evidence. Those files. Stall. Please."

Marshall squeezed my shoulder. "We're trying."

"You know," I said, "the poor woman is in the middle of planning Wilbur's celebration of life. They can't put her behind bars until they hold that event. It's next week. Roughly nine days from now. Depending on getting the Railroad Club room. Those deputies simply can't lock her up. Not now."

Nate groaned for what seemed like the longest time. "I'm afraid they can, but we'll see if we can get them to hold off for a week. No promises. Celebration of life, huh? Sounds like one of those memorial services to me."

"It is," I said. "Hopefully without the music and slide show."

CHAPTER 24

It was slow moving as far as the next few days went.
Nate and Marshall continued with their suspect interviews as well as their regular client business, only now
they had eleven more names on their list—the ones from
those reprimand letters.

I concentrated on my bookwork and managed to
dodge my mother's phone calls until I ran out of excuses.
At one point I felt like making a recording that said, "No,
they haven't discovered who the real killer is yet."

"I can't keep telling your mother you stepped out of
the office, Phee," Augusta said on Thursday afternoon.
"You need to think of something else. And by the way,
she said to tell you to turn on your cell phone because she
thinks your landline isn't recording her messages."

"Ugh. I suppose I'll have to break down and call her."

Just then, the office phone rang and I jumped. *Not my mother?* I mouthed to Augusta.

"Nope. Your aunt Ina. Says she remembered something."

I rolled my eyes and walked to my desk. "Tell her I'll pick up in a second."

Aunt Ina's voice was at its usual decibel level—bellyaching loud. "Phee! I'm so sorry it took me this long, but Louis and I have had the most hectic schedule this week. Anyway, about that payoff Montrose Lamont witnessed; it happened in the little courtyard in front of the Railroad Club. Not out in the open, mind you, but in one of those tiny alcoves. The only reason Montrose spotted it was because he had just come from the admin building to pay his yearly Rec Center fee. He dropped the receipt on the way out and it blew across the courtyard. When Montrose picked it up he spotted Wilbur and that Big Scootie."

"Scuttie. And when? Morning or afternoon?"

"Louis didn't say. It's a payoff, I tell you. A payoff. That should be more than enough information for Marshall to crank up a notch on the questioning. Didn't you say he and your boss were interviewing all the suspects?"

"Not all. Deputies Bowman and Ranston are also interviewing a few names from that list."

"Tell them to take a shortcut and twist Big Scuttie's arm."

"I'm sure they'll—You know what, Aunt Ina? That's a really good idea. Excellent, in fact. I'll let Nate and Marshall know right away. And be sure to thank Uncle Louis."

"Anytime, Phee. We're always here for you. And your mother. Not so much the dog, but don't tell her that."

I chuckled and ended the call. When it came to my aunt Ina I'd learned it was much easier to agree with her than to get into any long discussions. Too bad the same couldn't be said for my mother. Somehow I always felt the need to prove my point, even if it didn't matter in the long run.

An exchange of money could have been anything, but maybe Aunt Ina had a point. Marshall was out of the office, but Nate had finished up with a client a few minutes before, and I heard him talking with Augusta. I popped my head out the doorway and called to him. "My aunt Ina has some information about Wilbur Maines."

"Information or rumor?" Nate asked.

I walked over to Augusta's desk, where he was standing, and told him about Montrose Lamont's eyewitness account of money being handed over to Big Scuttie.

"Could've been anything," Nate said. "I already interviewed Walker Scutt, but I don't have a problem calling him back in and leading with that. He might not be intimidated because I'm not law enforcement." Then he turned to Augusta. "How does my early morning schedule look?"

"First appointment at nine forty-five."

"Good. You've got the list of those Model Railroad Club members. See if this Big Scuttie is willing to meet with me over coffee tomorrow morning. Say eight fifteen at the Bell Road/Boswell Starbucks between Sun City West and here. Tell him I'm buying."

Augusta shook her head. "The Dunkin' Donuts in Surprise is cheaper, you know."

"I know. And it's a virtual petri dish for gossip. No one cares at the Starbucks. They're all too busy with their laptops and cell phones."

"It'll be worth it, Augusta," I said, "if Nate can find out what was going on between them."

"I'll give it my best shot." With that, he returned to his office.

As it turned out, Nate's "best shot" got him the information he wanted, but it was pretty much useless.

"Whoopee," Nate announced the next morning when he returned to the office, having met with Big Scuttie. "Ever hear of a Lionel Number Six Empire Express Set?"

I had just finished making copies of some expense sheets when he came through the doorway. "I've heard of Lionel trains. They've been popular forever. Why?"

Augusta turned away from her computer monitor and faced Nate. "Not to sound snippy, Mr. Williams, but I bet there isn't a kid who hasn't."

Nate brushed what might have been crumbs from his shoulder and leaned his arm against the file cabinet. "For your information, the Lionel Number Six is a built-to-order steam locomotive that sells for upward of two grand. That's right, ladies, two grand. And the so-called payoff Lamont witnessed was Wilbur sealing the deal with Walker. Seems our Big Scuttie had a connection with someone in the company and was able to purchase that train for a measly sixteen hundred dollars. What a bargain."

I turned off the copier. "So that was it? Wilbur bought a train set?"

"Uh-huh. And a very pricey one, I might add, bargain or no bargain."

"I'm sorry. I shouldn't have sent you on Aunt Ina's wild-goose chase."

"No, you did the right thing. We've got to follow every stinking little lead until something breaks. That's how it goes in this business. Besides, the coffee was decent. Anyway, your fiancé and I will take a crack at the names on those reprimand letters. You never know. By the way, is he back yet from meeting with Bowman?"

"Any second now," Augusta chirped in. "He called a few minutes ago."

Marshall had driven to the posse station in Sun City West to compare notes with Deputies Bowman and Ranston, but I suspected he really went in order to prevent them from arresting Roxanne. Wilbur's celebration of life was scheduled for next week, and it would look awful if his grieving widow was behind bars.

All of us in the office knew Deputy Bowman had the strongest need for closure than anyone on the face of the earth, so it was no wonder we were on edge waiting for Marshall to get back. My mother had phoned last night to tell me Grace Svoboda reserved the Railroad Club room for next Wednesday and Florencia's Pizza would be catering the event.

"That's only six days away if we count today," I said. "Certainly Bowman can wait another six days."

"Look at it this way," Nate said. "Celebrations of life can be held anytime."

"Not if they find Roxanne guilty and give her fifteen to twenty years."

"Whoa. Slow down. Even if she is arrested, it doesn't mean the investigation stops. Face it, the more corroborating evidence the better, and we're in the business of finding evidence, so who's to say we won't find the real killer? Williams Investigations isn't off the case yet."

I bit my lower lip and took a breath. "'Yet' as in this could take a long time or 'yet' as in 'any day now they'll throw you off the case'?"

The thud from Augusta's elbow hitting her desk made us turn to face her. Her grin was as wide as the Cheshire cat's. "'Yet' as in 'Look who's about to come through the door and end this guessing game.' I caught sight of your soothsayer when I spotted him parking his car across the street."

The door hadn't even closed behind Marshall before we barraged him with questions. All at once, so he didn't seem to know who to answer first.

"Is Roxanne off the hook for a week?"

"Fourth Avenue Jail again?"

"What did you tell Bowman?"

"Any other leads?"

"Don't tell me they found more incriminating evidence. Did they?"

And finally, Augusta's final two cents. "Say something already!"

Marshall walked over to the box of tissues on top of the file cabinet, took one, and waved it in the air. "That should answer everyone's questions."

All of us groaned at once, including Augusta, but in retrospect, I think she was clearing her throat.

"This is really bad," I said. "Really, really bad. Maybe we should call Grace Svoboda and cancel the celebration of life. And Florencia's catering, too."

Nate looked at Marshall. "Where's Roxanne? Still in Sun City West or on her way to—"

"Bowman hasn't placed her under arrest yet, but he plans to do it ASAP. I tried talking him into waiting a few more days, but he refused."

"That man is as obtuse as they get," I said. "Do you think we should warn her?"

Nate and Marshall shook their heads.

Then Nate said, "We're not her lawyers and we can't appear as if we're going behind Bowman or Ranston's backs. Roxanne's a big girl, and she'll deal with it. I gave her the names of some decent criminal defense attorneys when I last spoke with her. I'm sure by now she's contacted one of them."

"So now what?" I asked.

"We do what we always do: question the suspects, review the timeline, and look for discrepancies." Marshall wadded up the tissue and tossed it in the trash. "And in this case we hope to prove Bowman and Ranston wrong."

For the rest of the day I expected the phone to ring with the bad news. I figured it would either be my mother at the brink of hysteria or Roxanne. What I didn't count on was a call from Cecilia at a little before four.

"Oh my goodness, Phee, I'm so sorry to bother you, but I honestly don't know what to do. I found someone's small jewelry pouch after today's rehearsal in the social hall. I was the last one out of the building because I stopped to use the ladies' room, and by then everyone had gone. About that pouch . . . it was the kind with a drawstring, only it wasn't one of those gauzy ones; it was more like a linen material."

I thought she'd never get to the point. "I'm not quite sure how I can help you. Isn't there a lost and found in the administration building?"

"That's not the point. Oh heaven help me, I'll need to spend my weekend in confession."

"For what? Finding a little drawstring pouch?"

"I didn't just find it, I opened it. I had no business opening it, but I figured it had to belong to one of the Rhythm Tappers. I wanted to see if I could find a driver's license or recreation card, and that's when I saw it."

"Saw what? What did you see?"

"It was a gold charm on a necklace. No house key or anything. Only a charm in the shape of a train, and on the back it was engraved, 'You chug and tug in all the right places. W.M.' Don't you get it? 'W.M.' That has to be Wilbur Maines. How many train-shaped charms with W.M. engraved on them can there be?"

"Forget about the charm for a minute. What did the license say?"

"There was no license. Or rec card. And the pouch was too small for a cell phone."

"That's it? You found a charm on a necklace?"

"I rooted through it like a vandal. Trust me when I tell you I'm on the ladder down to hell."

My eyes rolled around so much in my head I wondered if I'd ever regain focus. "Listen, your discovery may be an important clue. A clue! If it means what I think it does, then those Choo-Choo Chicks may not have been the only ones Wilbur was messing around with. Is there a manufacturer's tag on the pouch?"

"Give me a minute."

I held the phone and waited. I could swear I heard Cecilia sniveling and catching her breath in the background.

"I'm back," she said. "The pouch is robin's-egg blue, by the way, and there's a tiny little tag that says 'DB Jewelry Co.' If I'm not mistaken, Kohl's had lots of those pouches on sale not too long ago. They sell them in batches."

Kohl's, Walmart, Target . . . "Listen, I have an idea. Don't turn the pouch in to the admin office. Call them when you get home and tell them you found a jewelry pouch and it was too late to drop it off. Have them post a 'found' notice in their office and on their website. Give them your phone number and direct the owner to call you and identify what's inside the pouch."

"Then what?"

"Then you can find out who Wilbur was really seeing, but whatever you do, don't give them your address. Better yet, have them meet you someplace that's really busy, like Bagels 'N More, and don't go alone. Get my mother or one of the book club ladies to join you."

"You can say it, Phee. You think the owner of that little bag with the gold train charm might be the scorned lover who killed Wilbur."

"Um, that's not exactly what I was thinking, but—"

"I'll get Myrna to come. She just bought a new and improved Screamer. It's five times louder than the original. And I'll get Louise Munson, too. She has a can of Mace she keeps under her sink just in case. I'll tell her to bring it. And I might as well ask . . ."

I broke in before Cecilia finished. "Try not to make it a spectacle."

Those were my famous last words. I should have known better.

CHAPTER 25

"What can possibly go wrong?" I asked Marshall that night at the Irish Wolfhound's all-you-can-eat fish fry in Surprise. "Cecilia will be surrounded by the book club ladies, complete with their online self-defense purchases. It's not like the owner of that pouch is about to wield a weapon."

"True, but knowing those women, something's bound to go wrong. Did you tell them not to make any accusations about an affair or, worse yet, Wilbur's murder?"

"I told Cecilia. Besides, we don't even know if the owner will come forth. It's not as if they were missing a cell phone or a credit card. The only valuable thing in that pouch was the charm, and for all we know, it could be a cheap, gold-plated thing. Cecilia wasn't specific."

"Guess it's a waiting game, huh? Honestly, the list of

possible suspects keeps growing, like those weeds in our yard. First thing tomorrow I intend to spray the daylights out of them. Then it's off for what I hope will be the last of my interviews with three of the Rhythm Tappers who've been unavailable up until now."

"At the office or the posse station in Sun City West?"

"The posse station. Say, you're working tomorrow morning. How about I drop you off and pick you up when I'm done? It should be around twelve thirty, or one at the latest. No sense taking both cars. We can grab a bite and get our food shopping over with at Costco."

"Not quite as romantic as dinner and a movie, but yeah, it works for me."

I reached under the table and gave his knee a squeeze.

"Speaking of romantic, you haven't told your mother where we plan to honeymoon, have you?"

"Absolutely not! Are you kidding? She'd find a way to suddenly take a vacation there, and she'd bring Streetman with her."

"I don't think they allow dogs."

"Oh, you'd be surprised at how she sneaks that Chi-weenie into places. She's got a number of assorted tote bags, each one larger than the one before."

Marshall popped a french fry into his mouth and grinned. "Your mother has a skill set that will never be replicated."

"Thank God."

The weekend flew by as if someone had pushed a fast-forward button, and next thing I knew it was late Monday morning and we were back at the office. Well, not all of us. While Marshall finished up his interviews on Saturday, Nate was at the posse station interviewing Grace Kimbur and Tracee Pearl, the two Choo-Choo Chicks who allegedly had affairs with Wilbur Maines, according to Estelle, the second lady Herb latched on to at the Model Railroad Club meeting. The first one, Vickie Owen, probably blocked his calls by now.

"This will be worth the trip over there," Nate said when he left for Sun City West. "Even if it's a bust where those women are concerned, I plan to pick up some decent bialys and cream cheese while I'm out that way."

"Get an extra half dozen," Augusta shouted as Nate was halfway out the doorway. "And a tub of cream cheese with chives."

I had just faxed an invoice to one of our clients. "Get plain cream cheese, too. I don't like chives in mine."

"Maybe the two of you would like to see a menu."

Augusta laughed. "Nah, Phee's been to Bagels 'N More so many times she can recite it in her sleep. As for me, I know what bagels and cream cheese are."

Nate ran his hand through his hair and groaned. "Fine. Plain cream cheese. Chive cream cheese and bialys. I think I've got it."

"Have a nice morning," I said, and then Augusta and I broke up laughing.

"Good thing that guy has a sense of humor," she said. "Another boss might can us both."

"I doubt it. We know too much."

"Think he'll have any luck with those Choo-Choos?"

"Something's got to give. Meanwhile, Roxanne doesn't have a clue in the world that Bowman and Ranston are poised to arrest her at any given minute. Not that she's living in La-La Land, mind you. She knows she's the only suspect right now, but she's convinced that won't be the case for much longer."

"Humph. Knowing those deputies, I'm surprised they didn't drag the woman into the posse station this weekend."

"Yeah. Me too. It's kind of like knowing someone is about to pop a balloon at a birthday party, yet when they do, everyone jumps."

"What about that gold charm you told me about Friday afternoon? The one Cecilia found in the social hall. Anyone come forth yet?"

"It's too soon. The admin building at the Rec Center is closed on weekends, so it won't go up on their lost-and-found notices until today. But once it does, news travels fast around that place."

"Your advice to her was good, by the way. Can't be too careful. Lots of kooks and nutcases out there. In fact, last week some woman got arrested in Walmart for driving around intoxicated in one of those handicapped carts. Customers said she deliberately tried to run them over."

"Geez. Well, if someone does call to claim the charm, Cecilia plans to meet them in a busy restaurant."

"The posse station might be better. And she should come armed."

"It's a gold charm, Augusta, not plutonium."

"Like I said, 'kooks and nutcases.'"

"Or ex-lovers. Come to think of it, that could be worse."

A second later the door to Marshall's office swung open and Evelyn Watross stepped out. I didn't even real-

ize she had been meeting with Marshall because I was sequestered in my own office most of the morning and hadn't
asked Augusta who was in Marshall's office.

The minute Evelyn saw me, she spoke. "Hi, Phee. I
hope that situation at the Railroad Club meeting the other
night won't deter you from visiting again. Or getting your
mother to join. But it was a most unsettling matter, and
that's why I decided to seek help from your firm. Oh dear.
Please don't tell anyone I was here. You can't believe
how fast gossip travels in some circles."

*Oh yeah. Fast enough to leave the speed of light in its
quake.* "Um, no problem. Williams Investigations has the
highest degree of integrity and discretion."

"Thank you." Then she looked at Augusta. "And you,
too, Miss Augusta."

"That's a thing around here," Augusta said when Evelyn left. "Adding the word 'Miss' in front of someone's
name. Makes me think of barmaids like Miss Kitty, if you
want the truth, but I suppose it's better than being too
overly familiar with someone you don't know."

"I kind of thought it was a Southern thing. Go figure.
So tell me, what was she meeting with Marshall about?
Do you know?"

"I only schedule the appointments."

"Since when?"

"Since she didn't tell me when she called last week."

"My door's open and I can hear you," Marshall announced. "Give me a moment before you jump to conclu-
sions."

Augusta crinkled her nose. "Next time we'll lower our
voices."

"I can hear that, too." Marshall stepped out of his office and went straight to the coffee maker. "It's nothing racy or eyebrow raising, if that's what you're thinking. In fact, it doesn't have anything to do with Wilbur's love life."

"Don't tell me it's a missing cat," Augusta said. "We had one of those a few weeks ago. Darned thing came back on its own."

Marshall stifled a laugh. "No missing cat. More like concern over something that could go missing: the Model Railroad Club's replica of the Golden Spike. Give me a minute. I'm going to need a cup of coffee."

He popped a K-cup into the Keurig and turned to me. "You were there, Phee, the night of that Railroad Club meeting. What was it? G-scale?"

I nodded. "Uh-huh."

The coffee began to pour into the cup and Marshall glanced at it. "The replica wasn't in its usual spot, and Evelyn was convinced someone had removed it and returned it without positioning it correctly. That's how she knew it had been removed."

"But it's back now," I said. "Why is she so worried?"

"Evelyn was in the club room last Thursday to tidy up. Apparently, different members come in to dust the displays. Ugh. I had to listen to her go on and on about why the computer keyboard minivacuums were best for sucking up the dust from the tracks. Anyway, when she went to polish, yes, *polish* the showcase that houses the Golden Spike, she noticed it had been moved again. 'It is off-center by at least an inch from the top,' were her exact words. But that wasn't what alarmed her."

"Your coffee's done, Mr. Gregory," Augusta said.

I raised my hand so Marshall couldn't make a move. "It can wait. Tell us what got her so upset."

"Fine. When she took a closer look at the spike, she realized it needed cleaning. Said the spike was usually polished, but when people held it, they got their body oils on it and that ultimately dulled the finish."

"Oh brother." This time it was Augusta who rolled her eyes.

"Anyway," Marshall went on, "Evelyn didn't have time to take care of the spike because a crew of painters had arrived. The club received a mini grant from the Rec Center for repainting the museum room and installing new shelves."

"That shouldn't take too long," I said. "That silly old spike can wait a few days."

"According to Evelyn, the room project will take longer than a few days. Seems those crews start a job, leave things all over the place, disappear for a few days, and then return only to work a few more hours. With paint cans and materials all over the place, she felt it would be unsafe to venture in there. Needless to say, she was distraught over the condition of the spike and even more concerned someone tampered with it. She's convinced they're going to steal it. I told her if they wanted to take it, they would have done it there and then. She disagreed. Insisted the would-be thieves were, and I quote, 'waiting for the right moment.'"

I couldn't believe what I had just heard. "All of this over a club mascot, or whatever it is. So now what?"

"Yeah," Augusta said, trying not to laugh. "Are you and Mr. Williams going to stake out the club room?"

"As a matter of fact, we are," Marshall replied. "But

via technology. I told Evelyn I'd set up one of those mini surveillance cameras. You can get them for less than twenty bucks at Walmart. If nothing else, it'll put her mind at ease. And she can always watch paint dry."

I took a step toward the Keurig and handed Marshall his coffee cup. "I'm glad Evelyn's mind will be at ease, but what about poor Roxanne?"

CHAPTER 26

About two hours later Nate returned to Williams Investigations with bagels, bialys, and enough cream cheese to last us a decade. Augusta announced his arrival the second he stepped foot in the door, and I immediately walked out of my office.

"I got plain, chive, and vegetable, if any of us wants to eat healthy," he said. "I drew the line at chocolate chip and cinnamon. Anyway, I'll put these in the breakroom and we can help ourselves. I, for one, am starving."

"Any luck with Tracee and Grace?" I asked.

Nate rubbed the back of his neck with his free hand. "Boy, do those gals kiss and tell. Seems old Wilbur was quite the lothario, but Tracee and Grace didn't take him seriously. They knew he was married, but get this— according to Tracee, 'At our age, we take any action that comes our way.' Good grief. That's not all. I spoke with them separately, and it seems they also heard something about Wilbur planning to leave his wife for another woman. But who? They had no idea."

"Roxanne certainly didn't," I said. "But if that rumor's floating around out there, Bowman and Ranston are bound to throw it in with their other corroborating evidence against her. Let's face it, the jilted wife motive for murder is pretty common."

Marshall stepped out of his office. "What's that I hear about jilted wives?"

Nate laughed. "Only Phee's concern that it's a motive for murder Bowman and Ranston might use."

"Heck, they'll use anything. Hey, I can smell those fresh bagels you're holding. I've got time for a quick snack and then I need to pick up a minicam with a motion detector alert for my phone. Evelyn Watross said she'd be at the Railroad Club room at three. The place should be empty then and there's no meeting tonight. And no one signed up for work time either. I should be in and out of there in no time." Then he smiled. "Surveillance to protect the Holy Grail. I'll explain while we eat."

The four of us sat around the table in our back room. The door was ajar in case anyone walked in, but we didn't have any scheduled appointments that afternoon. That didn't mean, however, we were off the hook as far as phone calls went.

No sooner had I taken a bite from my bagel when it rang. "I'll pick it up. I have a sneaky suspicion it's going to be my mother. She can always sense when something's up. Even if it's surveillance for a lousy Golden Spike replica."

Sure enough, Harriet Plunkett's voice reached across the phone line and straight into my ear. "What on God's green earth were you thinking when you told Cecilia to meet the person who lost that gold charm?"

"Um, hi, Mom. I guess you spoke with Cecilia, huh? For your information, I was thinking she could kill two birds with one stone: return someone's lost item and find out if they were having any sort of affair with Wilbur Maines. What's the big deal? I made it really clear she shouldn't meet that person alone."

"Oh, she won't be meeting that person alone because, for *your* information this time, she'll be meeting with three women in search of their little gold train charms."

"Three? Three women? Wilbur gave three women that charm?"

"Three that we know of. That scoundrel could've purchased those charms by the dozen."

"Oh my gosh. This is awful. Awful. Unless, of course, those charms were some sort of swag. You know, the promotional stuff vendors give away at events. Maybe this is nothing." *Who am I kidding? Not with that engraving on the back.*

"I don't think so. Cecilia took a close look at the charm with a magnifying glass and it's fourteen carat gold."

"Yeesh."

"You can say that again. Poor Cecilia. She was barely coherent the first time she called me, and I didn't know who it was. Her words were so garbled, all I heard was something that sounded like 'disaster.' I thought someone was having a stroke and told the person to call nine-one-one. When Cecilia called me back the second time and explained, it all made sense. At least she was more composed that time."

"That's good, I suppose. Did she arrange meetings

with them? It would probably be best if she met them on different days, or at different places."

"Too late for that."

"What do you mean?"

"Cecilia got so flustered she told each woman to meet her at Bagels 'N More the day after tomorrow. At seven in the evening."

"All of them at once? Can't she call and change the arrangements?"

"No. Because in all her flusterment—is that a word? It should be—well, needless to say, Cecilia neglected to get their names and contact info."

"Oh brother."

"Mark it on your calendar, Phee. In bold ink. You won't want to be late."

"Me?"

"Yes, you. This was your idea. Your brainstorm. You need to be there, along with the rest of us."

"Please don't tell me all the book club ladies are going."

"Even your aunt Ina. And you know how busy her schedule is. Mark it down. Seven this Wednesday. Let's hope it doesn't turn out to be a catfight. Next time run these things through me. I know how these women are."

"I, er, um . . ."

"Seven o'clock. Bagels 'N More. The day after tomorrow."

With that, the call ended, and I stood motionless at Augusta's desk. I couldn't get over the fact that three women all claimed to have lost a gold, train-shaped charm that was still in its little robin's-egg blue pouch. And worse than that, how were they going to react when they realized their precious memento wasn't one-of-a-kind?

"You look like you've seen the cable bill, hon," Marshall said when I returned to the breakroom. "Don't tell me it really was your mother on the phone."

I nodded and let out a long, slow breath. "You won't believe this. None of you will. The owner of the little blue jewelry pouch contacted Cecilia. But there's a glitch. Um, well, a real glitch, if you must know. Three different women called her."

Augusta nearly spat out a piece of her bagel. "Damn. The goings-on in those senior communities are worse than the reality TV shows."

"They *are* the reality shows," I said. "Fortunately, no one has chosen to film there."

Marshall walked to the mini fridge and grabbed a Coke. "Whoa. Now Cecilia's stuck with three meetings."

I winced. "Not exactly." I went on to tell them how flustered and flummoxed Cecilia had gotten and how her state of mind had prevented her from thinking straight.

"Holy mackerel!" Augusta let out. "You mean to tell us all three women are meeting with her at once?"

"Oh it gets better. Trust me. Not just Cecilia. The entire Booked 4 Murder Book Club will be there. At Bagels 'N More the day after tomorrow. At seven."

Nate shuddered. "That's a scene I'd like to miss. Tell your mother to take copious notes and share them with us."

"She won't have to." Then I gave Marshall one of those what-can-I-do looks by widening my eyes and shrugging. "Because this entire thing was my idea, my mother laid on the guilt, insisting I be there."

"Hey, this may turn out to be a good thing." He returned to his seat and picked up the remains of his bagel. "It may bring us closer to discovering whether there was another woman who wanted to get even with Wilbur for cheating on her."

Augusta plopped her elbow on the table and leaned toward Marshall. "Cheating on her? The other woman? What about on his wife?"

"It's okay, Augusta," I said. "Remember, we're trying to exonerate the wife. We need to find the jealous, hot-tempered floozy who was really responsible for the whack on Wilbur's head."

A moment later Nate's cell phone vibrated and he pulled it from the pocket of his pants as if the thing was about to explode. "It's a text from Bowman. With a cc to Marshall. He and Ranston are on their way to arrest Roxanne."

"Really?" I said. "They couldn't wait a few more lousy days for the celebration of life? It's not as if Roxanne poses a threat to anyone."

"No, but Bowman's like a kid in a candy store. He got lab results back from the bottom of that tap shoe and the bottom of the screwdriver found at the scene. Not only was the screwdriver the exact size to fit the screws on the cleats, but both had trace elements of the same debris."

"Of course they did!" I shouted. "They were found on the ground. The ground. You know. Dirt."

Nate wiped his brow and rubbed his neck. "I can't give you the technicalities, but according to Bowman's never-ending text, the gunk found on the shoe and the screwdriver wasn't from dirt on the ground."

Augusta reached for the chive cream cheese container and grabbed a knife. "Guess that settles that. Maybe it's just as well Wilbur's tribute is on hold. It could have turned into a fiasco if more lip-locking women came out of the woodwork. The three of them who'll be meeting with Cecilia may be the tip of the iceberg."

I rolled my eyes and didn't say a word.

Marshall stood and put his napkin in the trash and the Coke can in our recycling bin. "Gotta meet with Evelyn. Don't look so glum. What's that old adage? It's not over until it's over, or something about a fat lady singing? When I'm done setting up the minicam, I intend to do some deeper delving into those eleven names you found in Wilbur's files. Jilted spouses are one thing, but long-term grudges make for motives, too."

He gave me a wink as he left the breakroom. A minute or so later I heard the front door to our office open and close.

"All that fuss for a memento." I looked at Nate. "Rox-anne's allowed one phone call. Think she'll contact our office?"

Nate shook his head. "More than likely her defense at-torney. She must have reached out to one of the names I gave her by now. Roxanne didn't strike me as one of those women who would be unprepared. Besides, I've worked with those lawyers. We'll get a heads-up. Trust me."

Funny, but when most people said, "trust me," it had the opposite effect. But not as far as Nate was concerned. If he had reason to believe something was going to come to fruition, he was usually right. And the heads-up he ex-pected came late in the afternoon with a phone call from Jane Ellis-Engle, Roxanne's criminal defense attorney. Her firm had an outstanding reputation in Phoenix, and I later found out Nate had done some investigative work for her in the past. That was the good news.

The bad news was that the Maricopa County Sheriff's

Office had a pretty solid case against Roxanne, beginning with the tap shoes. According to Jane, Roxanne insisted she hadn't used those tap shoes in years and, in fact, was pretty certain she had donated them to charity. However, with one shoe showing up in her closet and the other at the base of her late husband's head, it wasn't looking too good.

"Any chance we can visit Roxanne while she's at the Fourth Avenue Jail?" I asked Nate when he told Augusta and me about Jane's phone call.

"I knew you'd ask that. Excluding their legal counsel, inmates are allowed one thirty-minute visit per week. And only two people per visit. Marshall and I can't very well burn two ends of a candle, so it's best if we keep a distance. After all, we're still on interview duty as far as Bowman and Ranston are concerned. But there's no reason why you can't pay her a visit. Hours are from eight to eight, but I'd stay away from anything in the evening. Pick a morning and come in here late. It's fine."

"You know my mother will insist on joining me. And she'll find out, one way or the other."

"Harriet's pretty astute. Not a bad idea if she joined you. But make sure she knows dogs aren't allowed. And if she walks out of the house carrying a large tote bag, have her turn around and deposit the contents inside."

"No problem." *And lately it wouldn't just be the dog in the tote. It'll be Streetman with a boom box and dance music.* "Much as I might regret this, I'll give her a call and get it set up for tomorrow or Wednesday the latest. I'll let Marshall know. Hmm, I wonder how his research is coming along. I never asked."

Nate rolled his neck. "He logged into idiCORE before

he left to check on those eleven names. Between that and the TLO database, he's bound to pick up something."

"Too bad the rest of us are stuck with public records."

"I keep telling you, Phee, get your detective's license; then you can join the rest of us who get stiff necks from the tension."

"Not on your life. Bookkeeping and amateur sleuthing are all I can handle."

CHAPTER 27

"This is going to make for one long, miserable day," I said to Marshall as we left for the office on Wednesday morning. Marshall in his car, me in mine. "I'm picking up my mother at nine and we're heading over to see Roxanne. If that's not bad enough, I'll be taking part in a Monty Python show at seven."

"What?"

"I'm trying to be funny. It's the only way I'll survive the day. I can't even begin to imagine what tonight will be like when Cecilia's cadre of prize contenders shows up at once. I immediately thought of Monty Python, but even his comedy troupe couldn't come up with something like this."

"Relax, hon. Take it one thing at a time. First Roxanne, then Cecilia. Meanwhile, I was able to pull up some interesting, but not necessarily promising, leads on the recipients of those reprimand letters."

"Really? You think one of them might have had a genuine motive for knocking off Wilbur? I mean, it's been years, but still . . ."

"Nothing definitive yet, but I've got some calls to make and more digging around to do. By the way, I've been monitoring the Railroad Club's museum room, and so far nothing. I set up the motion detector to signal me if someone gets within a foot of that showcase. As far as I can tell, not even a dust mite's been in there. If nothing else, the minicam should give Evelyn some peace of mind for a while."

"Lucky Evelyn. She'll be the only one."

It was a little past ten when my mother and I signed in to the Fourth Avenue Jail. The building was even drearier inside than it appeared from the street. I seriously doubted the Count of Monte Cristo would've traded his abode for this one.

"Whatever you do," I whispered, "don't get into any conversations with the guards. I doubt they have a sense of humor."

"This is worse than the TSA. We're not the ones under arrest."

"Shh. They have to make sure we're not bringing in any contraband."

A few minutes later my mother and I were seated in a small room with a counter and two chairs that faced a closed window. Next to the window was a phone with an extra-long cord.

"Oh, for heaven's sake," my mother said, "you would think we were visiting a hardened criminal."

"Um, Roxanne has been arrested for murder, not shoplifting. We'll take turns talking to her on the phone."

In spite of the god-awful orange uniform Roxanne had on, complete with a black silk-screened "MCSO Jail" on the front, and I imagine an even larger one on the back, she looked pretty good. No bags under her eyes or anything. Even her hair was decently styled. She picked up the phone from her side of the wall and spoke to my mother. I couldn't hear what Roxanne was saying, so I gave my mother a little jab.

"Tell her we only have thirty minutes. Can't waste it on chitchat."

My mother turned to me. "The woman's distraught. I have to let her vent."

"Let her vent when we leave. Give me the phone."

My mother handed me the phone without a word.

"Roxanne, we don't have much time. I'm sure your lawyer will take care of all the legal stuff, and I know for sure Nate and Marshall are working like crazy to find the real killer. But I need you to think about that tap shoe for a minute. You said you were pretty sure you donated that pair to charity, and yet one of the shoes was in your closet. Are you sure it was that particular pair of shoes?"

"Of course I'm sure. That shoe had large cleats. Large cleats are used by beginning tap dancers, not seasoned dancers like me. We use tiny cleats at the tip of our shoes and the heel. I had no use for those shoes anymore, but they were in excellent shape for a beginner. Tap shoes are very expensive, you know, so beginners sometimes buy lightly used ones secondhand."

"Okay. Fine. What charity did you donate them to? Think back. Goodwill? Salvation Army?"

Roxanne shook her head. "I always donate to the Sun City West Resale Shop. It's by the posse station. Goodness. Our club alone gets over twenty new members a year, not to mention all those middle and high schoolers who take tap dancing lessons around here. Anyone could have bought them."

"Can you remember when you donated them? What month?"

"It was last fall. October maybe. Or November. I meant to do it sooner, along with other stuff I had stashed away."

At that point my mother jabbed my arm, and I figured she was anxious to get in a few words with Roxanne before our time was up.

"Hold on. I'll give you the phone in a minute." Then I asked Roxanne another question. "Did you or your husband drop off the donations? Do you remember?"

"I dropped them off. I remember distinctly because two of those Choo-Choo Chicks were volunteering there that day. I don't know their names, but I'd recognize them if I saw them again."

I wondered if those were the lip-locking ones Nate had questioned, but I kept mum on that topic. I held up my hand so my mother wouldn't snatch the phone from me and asked Roxanne one final question. "Was there anything on those shoes that could identify them as yours?"

"My initials," she said. "RM, hand sewn under the tongue of the shoe. Those were very expensive tap shoes at the time. What I don't understand is how one of them wound up back in my closet." *Because Bowman and*

Ranston will say they never left and you're making the whole story up.

"If we figure that out," I said, "we may be one step closer to nailing your husband's killer."

"Don't give her false hopes." My mother snatched the receiver and cleared her throat. "Wilbur's celebration of life can't take place without you. It would almost be an admission of guilt. Do you want me to contact the Railroad Club and Florencia's to postpone it?"

I couldn't hear Roxanne's response, but when my mother said, "No problem whatsoever, I'll take care of it," I knew the grand send-off would have to wait. Hopefully not indefinitely.

Suddenly the door to our visiting room opened and a woman's voice announced, "Five more minutes." The door closed before I could get a good look at the timekeeper. All I saw was the back of a gnarly gray uniform.

We said our goodbyes to Roxanne, told her not to worry, and got out of the Fourth Avenue Jail as if we were fugitives on the run.

"Do you think there were bedbugs in that room?" my mother asked as soon as the jail door closed behind us.

"Ew," I groaned.

As if on cue, both of us dusted off our clothing and gave our bags a good swipe, too. I ran my fingers through my hair as we walked toward the car and thought about it.

"Yes or no?" my mother asked again. "You know, they found bedbugs at Sky Harbor's Terminal Four and at the AMC Theatre in Peoria last year."

I shuddered. "Those places have upholstery furniture. In case you forgot, we sat on metal stools against a Formica counter. I seriously doubt bedbugs were nesting in there."

As logical as my reasoning was, I still couldn't get the image out of my head.

My mother was worse. "Check my back, Phee. Are there any bedbugs climbing on it?"

"No, none that I can see. They're not microscopic. If one of them was on you, it would be visible."

Again I dusted off my shoulders vigorously and patted down my legs. Two passersby paused to look at me, but I ignored them. "I think we're okay, Mom. Let's hit the road."

"As soon as I get home, remind to call Evelyn or Grace at the Railroad Club to postpone that celebration. I need to call Florencia's, too."

"Maybe that celebration won't need to be postponed indefinitely. Maybe tonight's meeting or whatever the heck you want to call it with Cecilia and those women will get us the results we need."

"The most it will get us is some woman admitting to an affair with Wilbur, not hitting him over the head with his wife's tap shoe."

"It's a start."

I dropped my mother off at her house and peeled out of there before she had a chance to invite me in for lunch again. "I've missed too much time from work already," I'd said. "I can't hang around. I'll grab a burger on the way back to the office and I'll see you tonight."

As soon as I reached the end of her block, I pulled over and called the office.

Augusta picked up immediately. "Please tell me you're not still at the Fourth Avenue Jail, requesting bail money or something."

"Very funny. Listen, are either of the guys in the office?"

"Mr. Williams is. Mr. Gregory left to meet with those deputies."

"Okay. Can you get Nate to the phone?"

"Hold on."

The line went quiet and I held my breath until I heard that familiar voice. "Hey, kiddo. How'd it go at the jail?"

"Remind me to stay on the good side of the law. Even when it comes to jaywalking. Seriously, Nate, I think I may be on to something and I'm going to be late getting back to the office."

"I'm listening."

"Roxanne said she donated those tap shoes to the Resale Shop in Sun City West last October or November. She remembered the volunteers who worked there that day and told us they were Choo-Choo Chicks but didn't know their names. Anyway, what if one of them *was* having an affair with Wilbur and he dumped her after leading her on to believe he was going to leave his wife for her? That would give the woman a motive for murder, wouldn't it?"

"It's one of the theories we've been playing around with, that's for sure."

"Okay, here's more. With Roxanne's tap shoes in her possession, not only would she have a motive, but a means as well. All she had to do was wait for the right opportunity or, in this case, create the opportunity."

"Why wait four or five months?"

"So as not to cast suspicion on herself if she was recently dumped. And here's the really diabolical part of the equation—set up Roxanne to take the fall."

"I see. But why are you calling me? Couldn't this wait until you got back to the office?"

"I want to make a stop at the Resale Shop to find out who their volunteers are and if they're the same ones who were working there in the fall. That'll be the easy part."

"And the hard part?"

"Finding out how the tap shoe got back inside Roxanne's house."

CHAPTER 28

The Resale Shop in Sun City West was a nonprofit enterprise created to support community families in need. It sold furniture, clothing, jewelry, and household goods. Housed in the same plaza as the posse station, it shared the same beige color and design. I figured the developer must have gotten a deal on paint.

A few cars were parked out front when I pulled up. Other than a really nebulous plan to get the information I needed, I walked inside totally unprepared to start the conversation. Fortunately, I didn't have to. A buxom brunette with dark leggings and a long, color-block tunic waved from across the room. It was only when she got closer that I realized she had to be in her seventies and not seventeen.

"Welcome! Are you looking for anything in particular?" she asked.

"Tap shoes." The words flew out of me like a belch.

"Hmm, we haven't had a pair of tap shoes in here for months. Maybe you'd have better luck at Goodwill."

"Um, I'm not in a big hurry. I just thought if you had a pair that was my size, I would buy them. I like to support this community. My mother lives here." *Oh why, why did I say that? Now she'll ask me for my mother's name. Unless she's been living under a rock, she's bound to know who Harriet Plunkett is.*

"Would you care to leave your name? If we do get a pair, we can call you."

"Uh, sure. That would be nice of you. Does a particular volunteer handle the shoes and clothing?"

The woman shook her head. "We all do a little bit of everything. But come to think of it, Tracee Pearl usually works with the clothing. I much prefer the household goods and jewelry. And everyone wants to handle the furniture. Ever since HGTV came on the air, we all like to think of ourselves as interior designers."

"Tracee Pearl, huh?" *I have to be subtle.* "Gee, come to think of it, I believe I've heard that name before. Something about the Model Railroad Club."

"Oh goodness. Tracee talks about that club all the time. You would think they invented the locomotive."

"Does her husband belong to the club?"

"Tracee's single, although she was dating someone last year who was in the club."

"*Was* dating?"

"It was one of those short-lived things. Not uncommon in these communities. Face it, men at a certain age are only after two things: a nurse or a purse."

Yeesh. "I've never heard it put quite like that. Guess Tracee was smart to walk away."

"I'm not sure if she walked or he walked, but someone did. Anyway, she seems much happier now than she did last fall. Next time you stop by, if she's working, I'll introduce you. She's a lovely lady. Even if all she does is yammer on and on about the Model Railroad Club now that she's an official member and not a visitor."

Yep. One step ahead of you there.

Just then, two ladies walked into the shop, followed by three or four more.

"We've only got fifteen minutes before our Jazzercise class starts across the street," one of them announced. "Where are the towels?"

"So sorry," the brunette said, "looks like I'm needed. Nice chatting with you. Leave your name and number on the counter and we'll call if we get tap shoes."

I was tempted to leave a business card but thought otherwise. I found a small piece of scrap paper in my bag and gave her my cell number. Next to it, I wrote "Sophie" and bolted out the door.

"I may be on to something!" I announced as soon as I got back to the office.

Augusta looked up from her computer and Nate, who had just pulled a drawer open in the file cabinet, turned his head.

The enthusiasm I felt was hard to contain. "Tracee Pearl! She's the lady you interviewed, Nate. The one who said she'd take any action that came her way. *That* Tracee Pearl. I'm positive it's the same woman."

Nate closed the file cabinet drawer and stepped toward me. "You spoke with Tracee? She works at the Resale Shop?"

"No and yes. I spoke with a buxom brunette who told

me Tracee volunteers there and pretty much handles the shoes. The woman told me Tracee was working in the fall, when Roxanne dropped off those tap shoes. Maybe Tracee took her relationship with Wilbur more seriously than she led on with you. Maybe *she* was the other woman. The one he was going to leave Roxanne for. And maybe those tap shoes never saw a sales shelf. Maybe Tracee snuck them out of there intending to kill Wilbur and frame Roxanne."

"Lot of maybes, if you ask me," Augusta said.

Nate crinkled his nose and grimaced. "It's a theory all right. I'll give you that much, but it's a far cry from the solid evidence we're going to need in order to prove Bowman and Ranston wrong. I will, however, dig into Tracee's whereabouts the morning of the murder."

I turned to Augusta and gave her a thumbs-up.

"Still a lot of maybes," she muttered.

"Marshall in his office?" I asked.

Nate went back to the file cabinet and opened the drawer again. "Nope. He's in Laveen, south of Phoenix, and from there to Avondale. At least it's a straight shot."

"New cases?"

"New leads. He tracked down two names from those reprimand letters and set up meetings with those folks."

"Suspects," I said. "They could be suspects."

"Right now, they're 'folks.' Remember, those infractions they were cited for don't merit a full-blown reaction like murder."

I brushed a strand of hair from my brow and took a breath. "Thomas Tartantian's did. That was intellectual theft. Piracy."

"True enough, but that wasn't one of the names."

"Then who? Who?"

"You're sounding like an owl, Phee." Augusta looked up from her computer screen.

Nate laughed. "Might as well give her the names, Augusta. You wrote them down. Otherwise she'll be pestering us all afternoon."

Augusta tapped on her keyboard and moved the mouse. "Gerald Albus, continued tardiness, and Francine Elitsky, excessive absenteeism without a valid reason."

Nate pulled a file folder from the cabinet and closed the drawer. "We're not holding out any great hope that those former employees from Sherrington are suspects, but they may have some insight as to who might have carried a long grudge."

It turned out Marshall had gotten a late start on those meetings and wouldn't be back in time to see me before my seven o'clock engagement at Bagels 'N More. I'd lost so much work time between speaking with Roxanne at the Fourth Avenue Jail and my impromptu stop at the Resale Shop, I decided to stay at the office and work until it was time to drive to Sun City West. I figured I could always grab a bite to eat at the restaurant. After all, that was what they were in business for, not rumormongering.

At six thirty I locked up the place and drove straight to Bagels 'N More. Oddly, the traffic was light and I was the first person to arrive. Or so I thought. What appeared to be a dazzling burst of color in the back of the restaurant turned out to be my aunt Ina's backside. She stood to reposition her blazing crimson ruana wrap on the chair, and at first I didn't realize it was her.

It was only when she turned and called out my name that I rushed over and took a seat next to her.

"Guess we're the first ones to arrive, huh?" I said.

"Good thing, too. I got us this table in the back. Look around. The one to our left is reserved, and the last thing we need is to be in the center of the room should things go south."

"Go south?"

"A debacle, a screaming match, hair pulling, insults. Do you want me to continue?"

"Um, no. I get the idea. But don't you think these women will be civilized?"

My aunt grabbed me by the wrist and shook it. "Tsk-tsk. You haven't been privy to the kinds of things I have. There's nothing worse than two women fighting over the same man. And in this case, there will be three of them. Of course, the man in question is six feet under, but still, it becomes more a matter of possession than sentiment."

I reached for a water glass and took a sip. "How long have you been here? The waitress filled up all the water glasses."

My aunt took a sip of her water as well. "About twenty minutes. Like I said, I didn't want us to wind up in the middle of the room. And I wanted a seat that would afford me full view of the restaurant."

Wow. Broadway dinner theater without the pricey tickets.

At that moment my mother came through the doorway and made a beeline for our table. "Ina! You look like one of those Peruvian women in *National Geographic*. The only thing you're missing is the llama. Why are you dressed like that?"

It was true. My aunt had always been a bit extreme when it came to fashion. Oh, who was I kidding? She was the epitome of hyperbole. And those long braids of hers, which either hung down like a princess from one of those

Wagnerian operas or wrapped around her head like a rope, didn't help matters. Today's ensemble consisted of a banded skirt and an elaborate peasant blouse. Thank goodness the ruana wrap was slung over the chair.

"Nice to see you, too, Harriet," my aunt replied. "I'm getting used to traditional Peruvian attire because Louis and I will be in Lima next month. He's part of an international symposium on indigenous cultural music."

My mother took a seat and rolled her eyes. "Indigenous cultural music? He plays the saxophone, for crying out loud."

My aunt took another sip of water. "Louis is one of those Renaissance men, with many talents and a penchant for learning. He's well-known in the music world. He has connections everywhere."

I imagined my uncle made those connections during his years playing the sax on cruise ships. He also made a boatload of money due to his extraordinary gambling skills.

"No sense wasting time," my mother said. "We'd better move those two tables for four next to us so we'll be able to seat everyone. Give me a hand."

With that, my mother stood and gave the first table a shove so it butted up against ours on the right side. Then she did the same with the other one. "There. Now we've got room for everyone. Oh look! There's Cecilia now. My God. It looks like she's wearing a burial shroud."

"It's not a burial shroud." *Good grief. How would I know what a burial shroud looks like?* "It's a cream-colored pashmina. Although I've never seen one draped quite like that."

"The black shirt and black hose don't help the outfit,"

my aunt muttered. "And why on earth is she wearing a yarmulke?"

I had all I could do to keep my mouth shut for fear of bursting into hysterical laughter.

"It's not a yarmulke," my mother whispered. "It's some sort of hideous cloche with a fake velvet flower on it. Cecilia told me she was going to wear it so the women would be able to spot her in the restaurant."

"And you couldn't talk her out of it?" my aunt asked.

The irony wasn't lost on me, but now wasn't the time to discuss fashion.

"Over here!" My mother waved and Cecilia quickly took a seat facing the entrance. Seconds later Myrna, Louise, and Lucinda walked in and sat down.

"Where's Shirley?" my mother asked.

"Parking the car," they answered in unison.

Then Lucinda added, "She saw a good spot. Someone was leaving as she let us out."

I was smack-dab in the middle of what appeared to be Bagels 'N More's version of the Last Supper. "Um, I hate to say this, but this looks like a tribunal. No one's going to approach this table. Even if they came to claim the Hope Diamond." Then I turned to Cecilia, who was seated at my left. "There's a table for four off to the side. I think that's where you should sit. Much less intimidating for those three women who'll be making an appearance any time now."

"Phee's right," Myrna said. "Besides, we're close enough to hear the conversation. Hurry up, Cecilia, plant yourself at that table before someone else does."

Cecilia stood and edged her way behind our table and over to the adjacent one.

"Hurry," Louise said. "And act nonchalant."

"I'm not sure how to handle this." Cecilia pulled a chair from the table for four and took a seat. "I've never been very good at handling conflict." She clasped her hands together and placed them on the table. "Maybe there won't be any conflict. I'll say a brief prayer for peace in our time."

"Forget the prayer. Forget the peace," my mother said. "Look who's coming our way. Of all people!"

While my mother shushed Cecilia, my gaze locked with the one belonging to a short, gray-haired lady. She waved and gave me a smile. I wanted to smile back, but instead I froze. It was as if I couldn't get any of the muscles on my face to move as Grace Svoboda headed toward us.

CHAPTER 29

My mother, who was seated on the other side of Aunt Ina, leaned over, grabbed my wrist, and shook it. "Do you see who that is? Do you see who that is? Heavens. Wilbur must have gone after anyone in a skirt."

"Shh, Mom. She'll be over here any second."

A chorus of "Who, who, who is that?" followed, but before my mother or I could respond, Grace Svoboda cruised past our table, gave my mother and me a wave, and proceeded to a long, rectangular table on the opposite side of the room. That table had a large Reserved sign on it that read, "RESERVED SUN CITIES ECUMENICAL COUNCIL."

I looked at the ladies and shrugged. "That was Grace Svoboda. My mother and I met her at the G-scale meeting of the Model Railroad Club. Seems like a lovely woman. She and another woman, Evelyn Watross, make sure the club room is tidy and dusted. Someone has to vacuum the dust from those mini villages around the railroad tracks. Those two ladies monitor the volunteers, or something like that."

"I think that's the general idea," my mother said, "but forget about dusting the Railroad Club room, catch that snazzy-looking woman who just walked in. Looks like she might have had bunion surgery, with that large boot on her foot. Still, she might be one of them."

Cecilia, whose head was turned so she could face our table, spun around in time to find herself face-to-face with the waitress.

"It's been crazy tonight." The thirty-something waitress handed Cecilia a menu and then took a step toward our table. "Be with you in a minute, ladies. I'll make sure your water glasses stay filled. I know you're all familiar with our usual fare. The daily specials are on the large chalkboard in front." Then she was back beside Cecilia. "Are you expecting more people in your party?"

"At least one more," came the voice that was the answer to my mother's "catch that snazzy-looking woman."

"Fine," the waitress said. "I'll give you a second to read the menu."

The conversation at our table came to an abrupt halt as everyone turned their attention to Cecilia's table.

"Try not to look too obvious," I whispered.

Just then the waitress asked for our orders. Normally, it took my mother's book club an inordinate amount of time to determine such things as ranch dressing vs. blue cheese or sourdough bread vs. white. This time the orders flew at the waitress in breakneck speed, and she scurried away before anyone had a chance to change their minds.

"We need to make this quick," the woman said to Cecilia. "I told my husband I was running in here for a dozen bagels. He's waiting in the car."

Louise motioned for us to bend forward. Then she spoke in barely a whisper. "Does anyone know who that woman is? I don't think she's a Choo-Choo Chick. I would have noticed her at the Railroad Club meeting we went to. Phooey. We should have invited Herb. If anyone would know, he would."

"I think it's Candace Kane," I said. "I kind of caught a glimpse of her on a cell phone the other night. Long story."

Meanwhile, Cecilia and the woman I believed to be Candace appeared to be having a conversation that was inaudible to the rest of us.

Aunt Ina nudged my mother. "Do something, Harriet. Get Cecilia to speak up."

"What am I supposed to do, Ina? Jab her with a pin?"

"This is terrible," Myrna said. "Cecilia's back is to us. We can't even prompt her if she gets all tongue-tied."

Without bothering to explain, I stood and walked over to Cecilia. "Excuse me. Would you mind terribly if you moved to the seat next to you? Our table is kind of cramped and we need more legroom. I'll shove your chair closer to the table if you can change seats."

I'd heard the expression, "Like a deer in the head-lights," but up until that second I'd never seen anyone who epitomized it better.

Cecilia sat steadfast, as if someone had glued her to the chair and duct-taped her lips.

I tried again. "Please? It would really help our table if you could scooch over to the next chair."

Short of lifting her and dumping her into the other seat, I wasn't sure quite what to do. However, in that brief moment it didn't matter. Another woman approached the table and plunked herself into the chair that faced our table. If Cecilia reminded me of a nun, this woman was Mother Superior, and I'd seen her before.

"I'm Olga Loomis," she said, "and I believe you have something that belongs to me."

Olga Loomis. From the Railroad Club. The one who reminded me of Whistler's mother.

"It better not be what I came here for," the snazzier of the two women said. "Hand it over and I'll be on my way. Trust me, honey, you don't want my husband to barge in."

Wonderful. An unhinged husband to add to the mix.

I pulled out the vacant chair that was sideways to our table and motioned for Cecilia to take it. She stood without saying a word and moved over to the new spot. That meant the third person to arrive would have their back to our table, but it was better than having Cecilia turned completely away from us.

"Thank you." Then, without warning, I watched as the people around us shuffled their chairs to make room for the man who thundered his way to our table. I recognized him immediately and wondered how long it would take for Candace Kane's husband to tip the scale from "upset" to "out-of-control."

His voice was so loud it raised the decibel level in the restaurant. Not to mention a few eyebrows. "How long do you expect me to wait in the car? I thought you were buying bagels, not chitchatting with the locals."

"Barry, sweetie," Candace began, but Olga Loomis stood and pointed her long, bony finger in the man's face.

"Until you learn to approach a table in a civilized manner, I insist you leave immediately. Bad enough we were subjected to your crassness at our Railroad Club meeting, but this is a public establishment and I will summon the management if I have to."

Barry Kane didn't budge an inch. Instead he turned to his wife. "Buy your damn bagels so we can get the hell out of here. I'll wait for you in the car, but if you're not back in ten minutes, you can find another way home." With that, he exited Bagels 'N More in such a huff it reminded me of those *Peanuts* cartoons where Pig-Pen left a trail of dust behind him.

"Someone grab Phee's arm and tell her to sit down," my mother said to the women at her table. "I'm too far away to reach her."

"I can hear you," I whispered. "Everyone can." I moved away from Cecilia's table and plopped myself back in my chair as inconspicuously as possible.

Meanwhile, Candace Kane and Olga Loomis were no closer to collecting the gold charm than the man in the moon.

Cecilia clasped her hands in front of her and all she could do was mutter, "Oh dear, oh dear."

"Listen," Candace said, "you heard my husband. I need to get the hell out of here before he gets upset."

Myrna plopped an elbow on the table and eyed all of us. "Before he gets upset? What the heck was *that*?"

Then Olga Loomis spoke. Loud and clear. "I thought he was doing us a favor and leaving if you're not back in ten minutes."

Candace shook her head. "Nope. That was an idle threat. But trust me, his repeat performance will be worse."

"Not any worse than what's coming through the doorway," Louise said. "Isn't that Herb with his pinochle cronies?"

Sure enough, Herb came marching in, along with his usual entourage: Kevin, Kenny, Bill, and Wayne. Without wasting a second, he motioned for the men to grab a table and then made a beeline for ours.

"If I thought you ladies were having a party, we would have joined you. Why are you at two different tables?" Then he turned his attention to Candace Kane. "Have we met before?"

Holy cannoli! If Barry Kane walks back in here, Herb will be minced meat. "Cecilia's taking care of church business. Church business." I shouted loud enough to be heard across the room.

"Geez," Herb said, "what's she doing? Giving away Vatican secrets?" Then he looked at Candace again. "Herb Garrett. And who do I have the pleasure of—"

Before anyone could answer, our waitresses returned and set up the stand that would hold the tray containing our orders. "I need to get in here," she said to Herb.

The tension building in my neck released slightly as Herb mumbled something to Candace and sulked over to his table. Talk about a close call.

"Hurry up," Candace said to Cecilia. "Give me the gold charm and I'll be out of everyone's hair."

Olga steepled her fingers and took a breath. "The gold charm is mine. I always carry it in my purse. Unfortunately, when I was in the social hall a few weeks ago for bingo, I reached in my purse for a tissue and must have pulled out the little pouch. Undoubtedly it fell, and I didn't realize it until I needed to use that purse again. Imagine my elation when I read that lost-and-found announcement from the Rec Center."

"Nice story, lady," Candace replied, "but that little

doodad belongs to me. It was a gift from someone very close to my heart."

"What on earth are you talking about? It's a commemorative charm for all my diligent work at the Model Railroad Club."

By now, I was at the opposite side of the table, but I could hear every word at Cecilia's. I leaned over and spoke softly. "Will someone close to Cecilia stretch out a leg and give her a kick? Tell her to ask them what the engraving said. But bend down and keep your voice low."

Who was I kidding? No one at my mother's table could keep their voice low.

Myrna gave me a nod, but instead of kicking Cecilia she tried a different tactic. All of a sudden she used what best could be described as an outdoor voice. "That's right, ladies. My salad bowl was engraved. Gee, engravings can tell us so much about a gift."

Cecilia must have gotten the hint because next thing I knew she found her voice and asked Olga and Candace to tell her what their charm engravings said.

"'To Olga Loomis, Choo-Choo Chick Extraordinaire, from the SCW Model RR Club.'"

"I'm so sorry," Cecilia said, "that's not what's engraved on the back of the charm I found. Here, see for yourself."

She pulled out the tiny pouch and showed Olga the inscription. Olga's face turned beet red. So red, her blush was visible from where I was seated. "Harrumph. I earned my pin the respectable way." Then she glared at Candace and, without saying another word, stood and left.

"I'm sorry to have wasted your time," Cecilia said, but at that point Olga was halfway across the room.

Candace motioned for Cecilia to hand over the pouch. "Now will you give me the damn charm so I can get out of here before my husband gives us a repeat performance?"

Next thing I knew the waitress was placing our orders in front of us. Salads, bagels, soups, and cheese spreads. Not the case for Cecilia's table. With the exception of the plain toast Cecilia had ordered, only glasses of water were on her table. And one of them wasn't about to remain upright for long.

Out of nowhere a third woman appeared. Petite, with a pixie-cut hairdo that reminded me of all those fairies in the Disney movies. Only their pixie cuts weren't dyed orange and blue at the tips. And they weren't wearing pink-hued, wire-rimmed glasses. She picked up the nearest water glass and threw the contents in Candace's face. "I should have known you'd make an appearance to claim what isn't yours. Why, you tap-dancing hussy. You make me nauseous. You're nothing more than a man-kissing trollop. You stole my boyfriend right out from under me. At least I can reclaim the token of our short-lived romance."

"'Man-kissing trollop'? At least I wasn't a home-wrecker. I heard about you. You set that ship in motion long before I ever arrived on the scene. Who the hell are you?"

"Wouldn't *you* like to know."

Then Myrna started in again. "Did I ever show you ladies my engraved candlesticks? Beautiful inscription. Nothing like owning an engraved item. They were a gift from my late aunt Velma." If she had said the word "engraved" one more time or any louder, the entire population in Baltimore would have heard her.

"I think Cecilia gets it," I whispered to Myrna. "She's not that spacey. I'm sure she'll ask if those women know what the inscription says. Meanwhile, let's pretend we're eating."

The pixie-cut-hairdo woman sat and crossed her arms while Cecilia handed Candace all the napkins within reach.

Then Cecilia continued. "Let's start by having one of you tell me what the inscription says."

I winked at Myrna and took a breath. Finally, we were on track. Or so I thought. The minute Cecilia asked her question, the women spoke at once. Unfortunately, that was the last civilized thing to occur at Cecilia's table.

CHAPTER 30

Candace's voice was the louder of the two. "You chug and tug in all the right places."

The last time a comment set off a series of actions that would go down in history, it was William Prescott at the Battle of Bunker Hill when he said, "Don't fire until you see the whites of their eyes."

The chug-and-tug comment also took a spot in history—the gossip circles in Sun City West. It also resulted in a response from the Surprise Police Department, who had jurisdiction on that side of Grand Avenue. No sooner had Candace recited the inscription from the back of the gold charm when the pixie-haircut lady threw her body across the table and reached for Candace's neck with her hands.

I knew, in that instant, that if something wasn't done immediately to stop her, the situation would escalate beyond control. It didn't take a psychic to read the tension at that table. And apparently, I wasn't the only one to notice.

My aunt Ina leaped from her seat. "Don't worry. I'll handle this." Then she screamed at the top of her lungs, setting off a much worse series of events. "EEEK! It's a mouse. A large, brown mouse, and it's running under the tables."

Unfortunately, the word "mouse" must have been inaudible. In seconds, people were shrieking.

"A rat! There's a huge rat in here!"

"Brown scorpion. Brown scorpion! Watch out!"

"Did someone say roaches? Where?"

"Bark scorpions! A bite can kill you."

"Rats everywhere! Run! Run!"

In seconds the sound of chairs being moved and people racing to the door permeated the room. Glasses and plates fell from tables as people shoved and pushed their way out of there. Cecilia's table was no exception.

The pixie-hairdo gal pushed herself back from the table and Candace Kane made the fastest getaway on record. Large, black boot on her foot and all. In a blink she managed to crisscross the adjacent tables and join the stampede at the door. I lost sight of her in a matter of seconds.

"I'll be back for my charm!" the pixie-haired woman shouted, but not before toppling over two chairs and dodging everyone in sight.

Screams, shrieks, and squeals competed with the thunder of footsteps. The once-cozy little bagel bistro was now a full-fledged Armageddon. The only good thing for Bagels 'N More was that this wasn't the Instagram, Twitter, or Facebook crowd. There would be no videos popping up to scare future customers away. Or so I thought.

With the exception of Herb, Kevin, Kenny, Wayne, and Bill, who were laughing their heads off at a nearby table, only the women from the Booked 4 Murder Book Club and I remained. Even the Sun Cities Ecumenical Council left their table. I imagined Olga Loomis led the charge.

"Look what you've done, Ina!" my mother exclaimed. "You nearly caused a riot."

I stood to survey the scene and my jaw dropped. "Nearly? Nearly? Um, look around. Aunt Ina *did* cause a riot. And if I'm not mistaken, I hear police sirens. Listen. Yep. Police sirens and they're getting louder."

My aunt puffed out her chest and squared her shoulders. "I prevented a catfight. It was only a matter of seconds. The woman who looked like a punk version of Tinker Bell was about to strangle Candace."

While the turmoil moved to the parking lot, the wait-staff, along with staff from the kitchen, hurried into the room with brooms, dust pans, and large trash containers.

Our waitress motioned to us. "I'll be right there."

"Now what do we do?" Louise asked.

"We pay our bill, leave a generous tip—and by generous I mean more than fifteen percent—and hightail it out of here," my mother answered.

Cecilia hadn't budged from her table. She just sat there shaking her head and muttering, "This is all my fault."

To make matters worse, if that was at all possible, Herb and his crew joined Cecilia and the book club ladies. They grabbed the nearest chairs and plopped themselves down.

"I haven't laughed so hard since that pet parade Harriet's dog was in," Wayne said.

"It's not funny," Cecilia sobbed. She wadded up a wet napkin from the table and proceeded to wipe her face.

"Here, take a clean one," Herb offered.

As Cecilia started to dab her face, our waitress came over. "I don't know what happened. One minute I was in the kitchen putting in an order and the next thing I knew it sounded like the scene from one of those monster movies. And look outside. There are two Surprise Police cars pulling in."

"I'm so sorry," Cecilia said to the waitress. "It's all—"

"A terrible, terrible thing," I blurted out. "Mass hysteria or something. The geriatric crowd can be unpredictable."

At that point my mother shot me a look and I shrugged.

"I suppose," the waitress said. "It'll get chalked up to insurance losses. Lots of broken plates and stuff, but no real physical damage. Most of the people who left are regulars, so we're hoping they'll square up their bills when they return."

Kevin and Kenny glanced at each other and shook their heads. Thankfully, the waitress didn't notice.

"Is there anything else I can get any of you?" she asked.

Yeah. A strong antacid.

"We're all set," a few of the women replied.

The waitress proceeded to hand out the individual bills, and I did a mental eye roll, knowing the next twenty minutes would be spent doing fourth-grade math. When she headed back to the kitchen, I turned to Cecilia. "On a positive note, at least the charm has been narrowed down to two women and not three."

"And one of them is Candace," she said. "You know what that means, don't you? She'll be at all of our Rhythm

Tapper rehearsals plaguing the daylights out of me for that thing. I might as well give it to her and be done with it."

I widened my eyes. "Tell her that if she takes it, it'll be like an admission of guilt regarding Wilbur's death. A piece of jewelry with that kind of an inscription all but shouts 'other woman.' And tell her revenge is the oldest motive for murder. Let's see how fast she distances herself from that charm."

"And if she doesn't?" Cecilia asked.

I bit my lower lip. "Then she's not our killer."

"What if the other woman contacts me? The punk-looking one. She has my name from the Rec Center."

My mother took a deep breath and looked directly at Cecilia. "Tell her the same thing. That the inscribed charm is an admission of guilt. We've got to speed this investigation along somehow. Roxanne is rotting in jail and those sheriff's deputies are more concerned about getting their paperwork done."

As the women haggled over their bills, two police officers conversed with the hostess.

"Better get a move on before we get stuck here," I said.

Surprisingly, no one objected and our entire crew, complete with Herb's cronies, vacated the place in record time. The parking-lot crowd was down to less than a dozen people and none of us wasted any time getting into our cars.

"Call me tomorrow," my mother shouted, "and next time you come up with a plan, Phee, run it by me."

"Hi, hon," Marshall said when I came in the doorway. "You're just in time for the news at nine. Something about a riot at one of the local restaurants. One of the customers caught the whole thing on his cell phone and forwarded it to all four TV stations. Honestly, some of these people are totally out of control. Carrying on like crazies if someone messes up their order."

"Um, yeah, about that . . . it was Bagels 'N More and Aunt Ina sort of caused the riot when she tried to prevent a catfight."

Marshall lowered the sound on the TV and sat up. "Are you all right? What on earth happened?"

I glanced at the TV and sat next to him. "Watch their version first. I'll fill in the rest."

By the time Marshall finished watching the TV and listening to my commentary, he looked as if he'd fought a battle. "Good grief. It just goes from bad to worse. Listen, before things really get out of hand, maybe you should back off a bit and let Nate and me pursue the other leads. You were lucky you didn't get hurt."

"Oh, I wasn't in any real danger. I'm not loony enough to throw myself into a crowd."

"True, but it sounds as if some of the players are more than slightly unpredictable."

"The pixie-haircut lady?" I asked.

"For starters. Did anyone get her name?"

I shook my head. "It might be Tracee Pearl. She was the one who admitted to Nate she had some sort of dalliance with Wilbur. Darn. I should have asked him what she looks like. Don't worry. If she wants that charm badly enough, she'll call Cecilia. Say, how did your meetings go today with Gerald Albus and Francine Elitsky? Any luck?"

"I'm not sure. I wanted to tell you the minute you got home, but then the news came on. Neither of those people had any strong motivation to murder Wilbur, but both of them were really annoyed with what they referred to as 'Wilbur's excessive nitpicking and tattling.' Francine said he was worse than a schoolyard kid, always reporting infractions to Human Resources."

"But how did he wind up with copies of those reprimand letters? Did Francine say?"

"Wilbur was in management and was cc'd on those letters. But why he kept them for years is beyond me. I still need to slog through them. Hopefully I can locate Thomas Tartantian. If anyone had a motive, he did. Wilbur cost him his job and possibly ruined his career."

A few days went by with Nate and Marshall juggling their cases and tracking down leads. Meanwhile, I couldn't seem to track down anything until it was too late. I was convinced the pixie-hairdo woman was Tracee Pearl, but when Nate told me she wore her brown hair in a bun and had readers around her neck on a chain, I knew I had been mistaken. As it turned out, Tracee also had a bona fide alibi for the morning of Wilbur's murder. Nate was able to ascertain she was at Talking Stick Resort in Scottsdale for a concert and stayed overnight. So much for my revenge theory.

As far as the pixie-cut woman went, Cecilia hadn't heard from her. Or Candace Kane, for that matter. According to my mother, Cecilia stashed the gold charm in her fire safe, along with some rosary beads, and decided to wait it out.

"Right now Cecilia has enough on her plate with that tap show," my mother told me when we last spoke. "The

Spring Fling Thing is coming up fast and she's practically a nervous wreck. You *do* plan on attending, don't you? I'll get tickets for you and Marshall. What performance do you want? They have Friday night, Saturday night, and Sunday matinee."

I told her I'd let her know and secretly prayed for an earthquake.

CHAPTER 31

The Spring Fling Thing came up faster than indigestion after a heavy meal, and Marshall and I found ourselves on the way to the opening night performance. A week and a half had gone by with no progress whatsoever on the Wilbur Maines case. Well, no progress as far as our office was concerned. It was an entirely different matter for Deputies Bowman and Ranston. A trial date had been set for Roxanne, and that meant their end of the investigation was completed. To say I was frustrated would be an understatement. I was stymied, baffled, and confounded.

"We need to take a step away from this case," Marshall said.

I grabbed my purse and tossed a lightweight sweater over my shoulder. "You're not going to drop it, are you?"

"Actually, it has been dropped as far as the Maricopa

County Sheriff's Office is concerned, but we live in the same state as your mother, so dropping that investigation would be paramount to putting our heads on a chopping block. No, all I need—*we* need—is to take a breather and let it marinate."

"Marinate? We're not broiling a steak."

"Sometimes when we get too mired under with a case, we tend to overlook the little things that can make a difference. Stepping away for a few days gives us breathing room. No different from taking a break from cleaning or any other chores. Meanwhile, our minds are still at work, and somehow the subconscious thoughts surface and surprise us."

"You've been hanging around Rolo Barnes too long."

Rolo was the cybersleuth our office used whenever we were stuck with encryptions or needed someone to hack into offshore banking accounts in order to track down seasoned thieves or killers. Rolo used to work for the Mankato Police Department and drove me crazy in the process. He had an aversion to certain numbers, so I had to be careful when issuing him a check. When he went into business for himself, he preferred to be paid with kitchen gadgetry in order to keep up with the latest fad diet. If it wasn't for Rolo's purchases, IKEA would have gone out of business long ago.

Marshall laughed. "Where do you think I came up with it? Only Rolo uses food terminology to describe an investigative process."

"My mother and the book club ladies purchased tickets in the front two rows," I said as he started the car. "I'll insist we sit on the end in case you need to make a quick escape."

"Nice thought, hon, but I think we'll be stuck for the

entire performance. None of our cases are about to call me away. Lucky Nate; he's in Sierra Vista for a few days checking on his aunt. And the worst thing about it is, he has to drive with Mr. Fluffypants in the car so she can visit with him."

"Argh. That parrot drives Nate nuts. At least Streetman can't talk."

When we pulled into the parking lot it was packed. Marshall had to circle around the building until he nabbed a spot in the back, near the arts and crafts rooms. A few minutes later we got seated in the second row, with my mother right next to us. Aunt Ina and Uncle Louis were in the front row and, thankfully, she wasn't wearing any of those outrageous hats she owned. Instead, she'd braided her hair with red and mauve ribbons that formed weird-looking tassels at the end.

Shirley and Lucinda were backstage because they had signed up to do costumes as part of Operation Agatha. Louise was in the front row with two of Herb's cronies. Myrna was in our row, and next to her were Herb and the rest of his crew.

"Don't you men make any wisecracks about the ladies' legs, or any of their body parts for that matter," Myrna said to Herb.

"And take the fun out of all this?" he replied.

"I mean it," she said. "This isn't a burlesque show."

Just then, something bumped against my leg. I looked down and saw a huge Vera Bradley tote bag that appeared to be swaying. "I can't believe it," I whispered to my mother. "You've got Streetman in there, don't you?"

"Shh! It'll be fine. I'll put the bag on my lap once they turn out the lights. I didn't want to leave him alone at night."

"Since when?"

"Since I read an article about nocturnal anxieties for dogs."

I shuddered. "Speaking of anxieties, how's Cecilia holding up?"

My mother bent down and repositioned the bag. "What can I tell you? She's a nervous wreck. I'm afraid the slightest little thing might set her off."

"Does she know the dance numbers?"

"Of course. If she were to give a performance in the privacy of her house, it would be spectacular. It's the audience that's an issue. Anyway, I think she'll manage."

"Too bad she wasn't able to hone in on more scuttlebutt regarding any of the dancers who might have had a motive for killing Wilbur. Of course she did find that gold charm, but we already knew about Candace and we have no idea who the woman with the pixie hairdo is."

Louise turned around and put a finger to her lips. "They're blinking the lights. Show's about to start."

The opening number was dazzling. A full cast ensemble with everyone decked out in Arabian costumes and the backdrop that featured minarets and lush gardens. I spotted Cecilia with a group of dancers off to the left, and their timing was impeccable.

Maybe she'll pull this off after all.

The next scene was a marketplace whose dancing vendors and castle guards moved around the stalls with style and precision. I knew Cecilia had a few solos, but I had no idea when. The show continued with Aladdin—played by a fifth grader, according to my mother—making his grand entrance.

By the fourth number I began to relax. The Vera Bradley tote was no longer at my feet, and I figured the dog would be safely contained on my mother's lap. Marshall glanced at his phone for a second, then put it back in his pocket. "Just checking the minicam at the Railroad Club," he said under his breath. "All's well."

Cecilia was in the next number, along with five other tap dancers. She was part of a harem and the only one wearing a bodysuit with a painted belly button. The other women had no problems showing off their midriffs.

Then the women tapped their way offstage and Cecilia moved to the center. The lighting changed from gold and red hues to soft blue and the tempo of the music picked up. It was syncopated and sharp. And the tune was somewhat familiar.

My mother jabbed my elbow and whispered, "It's a pizzicato dance," and that was when all hell broke loose.

Marshall's cell phone alert vibrated and he immediately checked the screen. "Gotta check this out. Someone's near that blasted showcase and it's not the painters. I should know. I've watched them in action a few times as a result of alerts. Evelyn was right. They take their time. Gotta run." He was out of his seat and up the aisle before I could blink. No sooner had that happened when Streetman waggled his way out of the tote and made a beeline for the stage.

"The pizzicato music!" My mother gasped. "Streetman dances to an old tape I have that's called *Pizzicato Moonbeams*. Do something, Phee. You're close enough to grab him."

"Not anymore. Look! He's on the stage already. That little stinker just raced up the side stairs and he's right behind Cecilia. She has no idea he's there."

Wails of laughter filled the audience, and poor Cecilia looked at her belly button before continuing her dance.

Then the dog began to dance. He stood on his hind legs and circled around, first to the left of Cecilia and then to the right. The poor woman was totally oblivious to the fact Streetman had upstaged her.

The music got faster, but that didn't deter either of them. Cecilia kept dancing and Streetman kept twirling.

"For God's sake, Phee," my mother said, "I can't run in heels. Get up there and grab the dog. Hurry before he ruins the performance."

"He's already ruined the performance. The audience thinks it's a comedy."

"Way to go, Harriet!" Herb announced. "Now all of us will be subjected to endless letters from the Rec Center about pets in public buildings."

"Hells bells," Myrna exclaimed. "I've never seen anything like this."

I took a breath and dashed down the center aisle and up the stairs to the stage, but instead of walking on, I backed up into the side curtains and tried to call the dog over. I was positive he heard me, because at one point he turned and looked in my direction, but that was about it. Streetman continued with his little doggy dance, and Cecilia continued with her solo. Had it been a circus performance, I would have given it an A-plus.

One of the male tap dancers, dressed as a sultan, whispered in my ear, "Maybe we can dance him off the stage when this number is over. I'll get the kid who's playing Aladdin to give me a hand. Does the dog like children?"

"I don't know what he likes." *But I've got a long list of what he doesn't.* "He's my mother's dog."

"Okay, no problem. The music's ending and the dancer is exiting stage left. Wow. Catch that applause. Can you believe it? The dog's still dancing."

Then I heard the man call out, "Run the tape of 'Somebody's Got Your Back.'"

A minute or so later the recording came on and the Aladdin kid and the sultan tapped their way onto the stage, each one on either side of the dog. Slowly, they tried to coax the dog offstage, but Streetman wasn't having any part of it.

"Don't try to pick him up!" I shouted. "He snaps!"

Then the unexpected happened. Streetman noticed the oversize shoes the sultan was wearing. Long, pointy things that bowed upward and covered the man's taps. The dog stopped twirling around and sank his teeth into the tip of one of the shoes and refused to let go. He tugged, pulled, and chomped on the fabric, all to the tune of "Somebody's Got Your Back."

The old adage "no good deed goes unpunished" immediately sprang to mind as the dancer tried to shake Streetman off his foot. The audience was beside itself. Gales of laughter everywhere.

The kid who was playing Aladdin announced, "I'm outta here!" and exited stage left, leaving the sultan to contend with my mother's neurotic Chiweenie.

Then, in a flash of genius, I thought of something. No dog was more food-oriented than Streetman. The only problem was, there was no food to bribe him with. Then I remembered the greenroom from the last time I was backstage. That was the place where all the actors hung out when they weren't onstage or in the dressing rooms.

Without wasting a second, I edged my way past emirs, sultans, harem dancers, and genies. Out the rear door on my right and across the corridor to the greenroom.

"Food emergency!" I announced the second I opened the door. "Is there any cheese?"

"I'm not sure that's what you give someone for low sugar," a lady replied.

"It's a dog. We can't get him off the stage."

The dancer sitting next to her opened the small refrigerator door. "Cheddar, Muenster, or Swiss?"

"Everything!!!"

With my hands full of cheese, I retraced my steps until I was once again stage right, a few yards from the dog. "Yummies!" I shouted. "Cheesy yums-yums for Streetman!"

The dog all but knocked me over in an attempt to sink his teeth into the cheese.

"Close the curtain," someone shouted. It was followed by "Play the interlude again!"

The sultan looked shell-shocked as he exited the stage, but not half as stricken as Cecilia.

"How long was the dog on the stage?" she asked after I had scooped Streetman into my arms.

"Oh, not that long really. By the way, you were wonderful."

"Really? The whole time I thought people were laughing at my costume. I didn't know Streetman was on the stage until my number was over. Maybe he'd like to dance the other three and I can sneak out of here."

"Back in five!" It was the stage manager, according to Cecilia. "We're on again. Whatever you do, don't let go of that dog."

Instead of walking back down the stage stairs and into the audience, I took the long way around until I reached the lobby. Marshall was leaning against a wall, his eyes fixed on the screen on his phone. I cleared my throat and he looked up.

"Don't tell me you had to take the dog out for your mother?"

I widened my eyes. "You didn't see what happened?"

"Sorry, hon, I've been glued to this screen ever since that alert came on from the minicam in the model railroad room."

"Pilfering?"

"Nope. Polishing."

"Huh?"

"On a Friday night, no less. Talk about not having a life. If I'm not mistaken, that's Grace Svoboda, and she's polishing that Golden Spike with a cloth. Here, see for yourself."

I grasped the dog with one hand and took the phone with the other. "Yep, she's cleaning all right."

Marshall took back the phone and gave Streetman a pat on the head. "I'll stay here and catch the rest of this. It shouldn't be too much longer. I mean, there's not much stuff in that showcase."

"Okay, see you back inside. And if my mother asks, tell her Streetman outdid himself."

CHAPTER 32

Thankfully the lights were out when I returned to my seat. My mother wasted no time plopping Streetman back in the tote and securing the clasps so he couldn't escape again. Then she proceeded to kiss him on the head. All the while, the Rhythm Tappers continued with their show.

Herb leaned forward and chuckled. "Hey, Phee, got any cheesy yum-yums for the rest of us?"

"Shh!" Myrna said. "It's enough she has to contend with that dog."

"I heard that," my mother replied.

A few minutes later Marshall sat and gave my hand a squeeze. Then he leaned into my ear. "I think the Golden Spike is safe for now, but that Grace Svoboda must have a screw loose. Remind me to tell you about it during intermission."

When the first act ended it was practically bedlam in the theater.

"Regular rush for the restrooms," Herb announced. "That's why I curtail my liquid intake when I go out."

"I'll keep that in mind," Myrna replied. "Meanwhile, step aside. The line probably stretches to Idaho already."

My mother clasped the tote bag close to her chest. "I don't dare make another move with Streetman tucked in here or he might get out. Goodness knows what he'll think of next. He's become quite the entertainer."

Entertainer? Try nuisance, ankle-biter, snapping turtle . . .

Then she proceeded to tell anyone and everyone who was seated in her proximity all about the dog.

"While she's busy yammering," I said to Marshall, "tell me what you observed at the Railroad Club room."

"It was strange to say the least, but then again, I've heard that as we age, our idiosyncrasies tend to grow. It appears as if Grace is compulsive about cleaning. I watched her dust and polish everything in the showcase. That wasn't surprising. But when she repositioned the old newspaper clippings of club events, I was flabbergasted."

"Why? People reposition knickknacks all the time. Framed news articles wouldn't be all that different."

Marshall groaned. "She used a ruler to measure the distance between the frames that housed the photos. Then she remeasured. All of this on a Friday night. Most people have some sort of social life. Bingo, cards, movies . . ."

"At least you didn't have to rush over there for a break-in."

Marshall glanced toward my mother, who was still extolling the virtues of Streetman to a captive audience. "It would've been preferable to this."

I kicked his ankle. Seconds later the house lights blinked and the curtain rose. Cecilia had three solo numbers in this act, and they remained solo numbers. Her dancing partner wasn't about to escape from the Vera Bradley tote this time.

As soon as the performance ended and the Rhythm Tappers took their bows, my mother announced, "I'd better skedaddle out of here before one of those nitpicking women complains to the theater management about the dog. Between you and me, some of those women have absolutely nothing to do but complain about every minuscule thing."

"The dog disrupted a performance," I said. "That's not minuscule."

Herb stood and laughed. "If you ask me, he improved it."

"Shh!" Louise leaned on an elbow and looked at us. "We need to tell Cecilia what a marvelous job she did. What do you say we all go backstage?"

"Better yet," my mother replied, "I'll dig something out of the freezer and make coffee at my place for all of us. One of you just has to let Cecilia know. And don't forget Shirley and Lucinda."

The mere mention of my mother's freezer sent chills down my spine. I'd bet money there were tidbits from the Ice Age taking up space at the bottom of it. Aunt Ina must have had the same reaction because the next thing I knew, she offered to make a run to the Homey Hut with Louis and pick up a few pies. No one objected. Not even my mother.

An hour later we were seated in her living room/kitchen/patio area with hot cups of coffee and assorted fruit pies. Cecilia arrived shortly after everyone else, looking as if she'd seen the ghosts of Christmases Past, Present, and Future.

"Good heavens, Cecilia," Lucinda blurted out. "You look ashen."

"Are you in shock from that disaster with Harriet's dog?" Myrna asked.

Shirley rushed over and escorted Cecilia to one of the floral chairs, then handed her a cup of coffee.

Cecilia's hands were shaking as she moved the cup to her lips. "It was awful. Simply awful."

Herb, who was a few feet away, moved behind Cecilia and tapped her on the shoulder. "Hey, it wasn't all that bad. You could've fallen or something."

"I'm not talking about my tap dancing," she said. "It's what happened after all of you left."

"You got canned from the show?" Herb pulled one of the side chairs closer to Cecilia.

At that point Shirley gave him a not-so-subtle slap on his shoulder, to which he responded, "Hey, all I'm doing is trying to find out what happened."

"Then use some diplomacy," Louise said from across the room. "Can't you see the poor woman is beside herself?" Then she looked at Cecilia. "It can't be all that bad. What on earth is so upsetting? Did someone criticize the show?"

Cecilia wadded up a napkin and rubbed her nose. "No, nothing like that. But when I went backstage to change out of my costume, I overheard two women talking behind a rack of clothes. I don't think they knew I was there."

"So? Did you hear any juicy gossip?" Louise asked.

"I heard one of them say, 'She may act all prim and

proper, but if you ask me, she did the deed and framed Roxanne.'"

"Who?" Louise asked. "Who did the deed? Who did they name?"

Cecilia's voice cracked and the wadded-up napkin she'd used to dab her nose was now in tiny pieces on the floor. "Who do you think? They meant me. Me! They think I killed Wilbur and framed Roxanne so I could get her solos."

"That's ridiculous," Louise said. "What about Candace? She had those solos originally."

By now Cecilia was practically in tears. "It gets worse. Much worse. One of the women thought it was my shoe bag Candace tripped over when she sprained her ankle. And then the other one said, 'Payback's a . . . a . . .' Well, it rhymes with witch. You know what *that* means, don't you? They're going to do something so I trip and fall. Or—oh no. What if they try to kill me?"

"Whoa," Marshall said. "You're putting two and two together and coming up with five. Yeah, it's unsettling all right, but you don't know who they are, so the best you can do is be extra vigilant. Maybe we can find out who was in the dressing room at the end of the show. Try the process of elimination. Who did you see when you left the dressing room? Which dancers were out in the corridor or still onstage?"

"It was all a blur. First that disaster with the dog and then that horrible accusation." Cecilia placed her coffee cup on a small table next to her and wrung her hands. "I hate to disappoint all of you, but I don't think I'm cut out for Operation Agatha. I'll finish up my performances, but that's it. Please tell Roxanne I'm sorry. I'll bake her a cake or something once she gets settled into the Perryville Prison."

"Forget the cake," Lucinda exclaimed. "And since when do you bake? You can't back out of Operation Agatha. Not when we're so close."

Cecilia continued to wring her hands. "Close? We're not close."

Then Louise spoke. "What about that gold charm you found? If you hadn't joined the Rhythm Tappers, you wouldn't have been in the social hall and you wouldn't have discovered that pouch with the charm."

"And I wouldn't have caused that turmoil at Bagels 'N More. My God! I'm terrified to turn on channel five for fear of what they'll show next. Besides, it didn't get us anywhere. All it proves is Wilbur was a cad."

Just then, Marshall's phone alert went off, and he excused himself and walked to the patio door.

"Is it a dead body?" Shirley asked. "Lordy, don't tell me there's another dead body floating around here."

"Those are merely surveillance alerts he gets from places Williams Investigations are monitoring," I said. "No cause for alarm." *Yet.*

Marshall's head was bent down, and it appeared as if he was glued to his iPhone. Meanwhile, my mother busied herself offering everyone additional slices of pie or coffee. Only Herb and my uncle Louis took her up on the offer.

"About that gold charm," my aunt said to Cecilia. "If neither woman comes forth again, it's probably because they've both figured out that claiming the charm points a finger at them. It would mean they were having an affair and could very well be the jilted ex-lover who bludgeoned the man to death."

I winced. "I wouldn't exactly call it 'bludgeoned.' He was hit over the head. A blunt-force thing. Not a bludgeoning." *Like I would know.*

"We need to get back to Operation Agatha," my mother said. "If we waste too much time, they'll be on jury selection and Roxanne might as well find makeup that goes well with orange."

"What did you have in mind?" Shirley asked.

I held my breath and waited until I thought I'd turn blue. "Yes. What did you have in mind? And please don't tell us it involves breaking and entering or something even worse."

"Two things," my mother said. "We have to find out who the pixie-hairdo woman is. Surely someone must have noticed the blue and orange tips. It's not as if we're living in some artsy-fartsy community. And don't give me that look, Ina. You know what I mean."

"I most certainly do, Harriet. We're living in a wasteland of bland makeup, neutral eye shadow, and, above all else, a never-ending sea of gray. Unless, of course, we're talking your hair, in which case none of us have seen its original color since you were in ninth grade."

"Enough with the hair colors," I said. "What's the other thing?"

My mother caught a quick breath. "We find out who said those nasty things about Cecilia before they decide to make good on their threat. Cecilia can't live in fear someone is going to throw her under the bus, so to speak. Operation Agatha will continue its two-pronged format. Of course we'll still infiltrate the Model Railroad Club and the Rhythm Tappers, but now, we'll specialize. Myrna, Louise, Ina, and I will work on tracking down that little pixie-hairdo trollop. Shirley, Lucinda, and Cecilia will find out who was in the dressing room. We'll begin to-morrow."

I heaved a sigh of relief she hadn't mentioned my name. But I should have known better.

Twenty seconds later my mother looked at me. "Is to-morrow one of your Saturdays off?"

Not anymore.

At that instant Marshall returned from the patio. "Everything's fine. Nate and I have alerts on our phones for surveillance monitoring. False alarm."

"Does anyone want any more coffee?" That was my mother's monitoring system, which meant, *It's late and everyone needs to go home.*

I immediately started the ball moving. "Thanks, Mom. Marshall and I have work tomorrow, so we'll be on our way."

Seconds later everyone else made excuses to hightail it out of there.

"Don't forget," my mother said, "Operation Agatha part two begins tomorrow."

Marshall looked pain-stricken and I whispered, "I'll tell you in the car."

CHAPTER 33

"What was the second alert?" I asked when we were back in the car.

"Nothing but nothing. Grace forgot something and went back inside to get it. Cleaning solution. That's what she forgot. She tucked it under her arm and looked both ways, as if she had absconded with someone's bank deposit bag. I zoomed in to be sure that's what she took with her."

"A bottle of cleaning solution? I wonder why she didn't leave it at the club."

By now Marshall had pulled onto R H Johnson Boulevard and turned right on Grand Avenue. "Who knows? Maybe it was her own personal cleaning stuff. People are funny that way."

"Geez, it's not as if you can't buy Lysol or Mr. Clean everywhere."

"It was antibacterial cleanser. Big pink bottle labeled as such. Guess Grace is somewhat of a germaphobe."

"Lately, nothing surprises me anymore."

Sure enough, part two of the never-ending Operation Agatha began the next day. And while I made sure to busy myself at the office in the morning and run errands in the afternoon, I was privy to all the details via endless phone messages from my mother on the landline. Apparently she had given up on cell-phone voice mail.

"Phee? Are you there? Never mind. I thought you picked up. I guess not. Anyway, I wanted you to know Myrna, Louise, and your aunt spent most of the morning contacting the local beauty parlors and salons. None of them have done pixie hair with outrageous colors. Ina suggested we branch out, so I took the Peoria and Litchfield salons. Louise took Glendale because there are more of those beauty shops there. Ina, naturally, had to take Scottsdale, Paradise Valley, and Fountain Hills. And you know what? No pixie dos with orange and blue tips. Call me when you get in."

I deleted the call and moved to the next one. Still my mother.

"You must still be at work. It's after three. We've got the entire city of Phoenix to check and we're doing it alphabetically. Do you have any idea how many salons there are? Myrna pulled off the names from the internet. It would be a big help if you shared M through Q with her; that's the longest list. Call me."

A spasm jerked in my back when I heard the words "it would be a big help." The third message wasn't much better.

"We called Lucinda. She's helping Myrna out with some of the phone calls, but only for an hour or so. She's got to get to the theater for tonight's performance. I told her to email you the names of those places she didn't get a chance to call so you could do it. Thanks goodness Shirley and Lucinda are helping out with the costumes and props. Cecilia said if they weren't going to be in the building, she wouldn't show up to dance. I suppose those nasty comments really rattled her. Call me, Phee."

I was terrified to check my email, envisioning a mile-long list of every salon from North Phoenix to South Mountain. Meanwhile, when I left work, Marshall had been glued to the office, pursuing his own list from those reprimand letters we found in Wilbur's file cabinet. And while he lucked out with two of them, he kept hitting dead ends with the others. When I spoke to him earlier in the day, he was about to call Rolo Barnes to see if he could locate Thomas Tartantian via the guy's bank accounts. That would free Marshall up to work on the other names. Unfortunately, it wouldn't do a darn thing to help me with my list.

Lucinda emailed me twenty-eight beauty salon names. Twenty-eight! I was half tempted to call Lyndy to see if she was willing to take fourteen of them, but I decided otherwise. There was such a thing as pushing a friendship too far. Instead, I prepared pork chops for the oven, made a quick and easy risotto, and got to business with the list. It was four thirty and I didn't expect Marshall for another hour.

Like my mother and the other ladies, I didn't get any-where. At least not right away. Then I had a conversation with someone named Maybelle from Hairs to You.

"Honey," she said, "we haven't done those hairdos since

the seventies. Fine for nightclubbing and gambling casinos, but not so great if you're stuck in one of those professions where you need to look more conservative. Lots of women buy those home dye kits, but the results are unpredictable at best. And with some hair colors, you have to bleach the hair first."

"Wow."

"I know. That's why we're in business. It's hard to get the right color if you're going for blues and oranges. You know, a federal court judge whose hair I style loves to look a bit on the wild side when she goes on vacation. So she bought herself a wig. Flashy one with gold tips and silver streaks. If you want my advice, do the same."

It was as if all of us were walking around in a fog and not thinking of the obvious. A wig! Heck, Roxanne and I went incognito when we searched those storage units. Who wasn't to say the pixie-hairdo woman hadn't done the same when she met with Cecilia. Especially if she had more to hide than her hair.

I thanked Maybelle and told her if I was ever in South Phoenix, I'd check out her salon. Then I returned my mother's calls.

"That would explain it," she said. "This is all Cecilia's fault. She should have looked closer when the woman sat next to her."

"Cecilia was a nervous wreck. She wouldn't have noticed if the woman had fangs."

"So now what? We can't go tracking down every retail and wholesale store that sells wigs."

"True, but maybe Cecilia can remember some other detail about the woman. Like dimples or a beauty mark. Forget eye color. Contacts can change that."

"I don't dare ask her anything until she's done with the final performance of that tap-dance-into-spring thing."

"Good idea. No need to make her any more nervous than she already is."

"I'd better call my sister and the ladies to let them know about the wig. It makes sense, doesn't it?"

"Yeah. I wish everything else did."

"I'll get a report from Shirley and Lucinda about any scuttlebutt they uncover while they're backstage fussing with the costumes. Actually, Shirley's really doing the costumes, if you must know. They've got Lucinda working on props. Apparently, she wasn't too fastidious buttoning up the outfits. Anyway, if someone's talking behind Cecilia's back, hopefully we'll find out who and put a stop to it."

"Sounds good, Mom. Listen, I've got to go. Marshall will be home any minute and we want to have a nice, relaxing dinner."

"If you find out anything, call me. I'm broiling a steak for Streetman and me."

Broiling a steak for her and the dog. Unbelievable. "Um, sure. Talk to you later."

"The dog is getting a steak," I said to Marshall as soon as he stepped inside the house. "You're getting seasoned pork chops and risotto. Don't ask."

He chuckled. "I won't. Listen, I've got good news. Rolo's on the hunt for Thomas Tartantian, but I managed to track down Gloria Rouzoni from Wilbur's letter pile. Let me refresh your memory: petty theft."

"The paper-clip woman?"

"Assorted colored binder clips. Believe it or not, I actually spoke with her. She made no bones about it. She's been harboring a grudge against Wilbur for years. That letter cost her a promotion. And as for those binder clips? She said they were attached to reports she took home, but apparently she returned them without the binder clips, only regular paper clips. Good grief! She finally left Sherrington and took another job for a company outside Davenport before retiring to Lake Worth, Florida. Her response echoed Francine Elitsky's. Said Wilbur all but wore a path to Human Resources with his petty complaints. Still, she was shocked he was murdered."

"I take it you don't think she had any part in it."

"Not if airline manifests prove anything. It took some doing. That's why I never left the office today. Nah, Gloria Rouzoni's not our culprit, but I was hoping she might have some information about her colleague, Thomas Tartantian."

"And?"

"Thomas Tartantian was the brainchild behind Mavis Gear. If it wasn't for him, according to Gloria, Sherrington's stocks never would have climbed to such heights. It was Mavis Gear that literally put them on the map."

"But what about the pirating? Did she know anything about that?"

"When a competitor came up with a similar gear that was less expensive to manufacture, Thomas was accused of giving them the specs."

"Why? Engineers come up with similar ideas and patents all the time."

"Let's just say these were a bit *too* specific."

"Hmm. Still, it would be hard to prove."

"I'm not sure if definitive proof was needed, but it was enough for the company—or Wilbur in this case, because he was the manager—to question Thomas's involvement in the development of that competitor's product. Remember, Thomas wasn't arrested. He wasn't put on trial. He was terminated. Unlike the public sector, private companies don't need to validate their decisions."

"Did Gloria know what happened to Thomas? Where he went?"

"She said he packed up his personal belongings and was escorted out of the building by security. That was the last anyone saw of him or his family. Only a wife, as far as she knew. No kids. Gloria did mention the employees sending him some sort of letter expressing their sorrow for what happened, but it was returned 'Address Unknown.'"

"She wouldn't happen to still have that address, would she?"

"She did, and I'm one step ahead of you. Gloria had an old phone book with her coworkers' names and addresses dating back years. Got Rolo on it. Maybe he'll have better luck than the post office. Come on, let's eat before the pork chops dry out. And while you've got a full mouth, I'll tell you about my day on the phone."

"It can't possibly beat mine. I got suckered into calling beauty parlors, trying to track down that pixie-hairdo woman. What a waste of time. She was probably wearing a wig. We're not giving up, though. She may turn out to be the jilted ex-lover who stole the tap shoe and showed up at the railroad exhibit to make sure Wilbur took his last ride. Once the Rhythm Tappers' performances are done and Cecilia calms down, my mother intends to ask her what else she might remember about the woman other than the hairdo."

"From what you've told me, Roxanne said she brought those tap shoes to the Resale Shop. If so, how did one of them get back in her closet?"

"Oh my gosh. I totally forgot about that. I was going to track down Tracee Pearl, who volunteers at that shop, to ask her. Honestly, I feel as if my mind is a cafeteria tray and the more I load it up, the more food falls off. And don't tell me it's an aging process or I'll scream."

"Relax. I think that's how great minds work."

CHAPTER 34

Sunday came and went like a windstorm, and other than a phone message my mother left regarding Shirley tracking down the "two harpies who bad-mouthed Cecilia" and giving them a "good tongue-lashing," Marshall and I were back at the office on Monday before my eyelids fully opened. He had to meet with a few clients and Nate wasn't expected to return from Sierra Vista until later in the day.

"I have no choice," I said to Augusta when we took a break. "H/O scale meets this Thursday and I've got to attend."

Augusta bit into her donut and motioned for me to keep talking.

"I know. It'll be dreadful, but I've got to find a way to speak with Tracee Pearl about Roxanne's tap shoes."

"Sure you're not developing a liking for model railroads?"

"I've got to admit I like the cute little villages and towns they build around the tracks, but as far as all the work that goes into it, I'd be exhausted. And keeping it dust free—forget it. No, I need to find out what she knows about those tap shoes Roxanne brought into the Resale Shop last fall. I have a hunch they were never sold."

"You mean you have a hunch Tracee took them."

"Uh-huh. And used them to frame Roxanne. After all, she was pretty upfront with Nate about her relationship with Wilbur."

"Locking lips is one thing. Killing the guy is another. And what about stashing the evidence? I've got news for you. She's not going to offer up a confession, if that's what you're hoping."

"I'm not going to come right out and ask her about the tap shoes. I'll wheedle it out of her slowly and watch for her reaction."

"Sure you don't want to rent a polygraph machine?"

"Very funny."

Later that morning Marshall informed me jury selection was taking place for Roxanne's trial. Apparently, Deputy Bowman couldn't wait to shoot off a text message.

"How long does jury selection take?" I asked Marshall.

"It can take two or three days or even over a week. Remember, they have to select jurors the prosecution and defense agree to. That's not always easy."

"For Roxanne's sake, I hope it takes so long they reschedule the trial date."

"Not likely, but I have great faith in Rolo's ability to get us some answers."

"I'll be working on some answers, too. Thursday. At the H/O scale work session."

"Another fun night with your mother and the book club ladies?"

"Lord no! She doesn't know I'm going and I intend to keep it that way. Look, I realize Nate ruled out Tracee Pearl as a suspect, but I'm not so sure. Think he'll mind if I chitchat with her about tap shoes she might have sold last fall at the Resale Shop?"

"If it makes you feel better, I'm sure he won't mind. Nate's not territorial like Bowman and Ranston. Thank goodness. And it won't surprise him if you pick up on something he didn't. People have been known to give different impressions depending on who they're talking to and the circumstances."

"Of course there's still the matter of how one of those shoes wound up back in Roxanne's closet, unless Wilbur and Tracee did some lip-locking at his house while Roxanne was out."

"Good luck finding that out."

"O ye of little faith."

"I'm not so sure that's what that Bible verse was intended for, but I give you credit for perseverance."

As things turned out, I needed all the perseverance I could get. We all did. The next three days didn't bring Williams Investigations any closer to tracking down the real culprit, but on Thursday morning the office received a cryptic email from Rolo that read, "No stone goes uncovered. On the chase at last."

"Is that supposed to be something like, 'The crow flies at midnight'?" I asked. "Because if it is, I'm lost."

Nate and Marshall broke up laughing. "It means he's getting closer to locating Thomas Tartantian."

"We're not the CIA," Augusta said. "He could just say that."

Nate rubbed the nape of his neck and retrieved his coffee cup from the Keurig. "It would take all the fun out of it."

Just then the phone rang, and Augusta picked it up. "For Mr. Williams or Mr. Gregory. It's Deputy Bowman, and he wasn't all that specific."

"I'll do the honors," Marshall said to Nate. "No sense letting your coffee get cold."

The four of us watched for any reaction from Marshall as he listened to Deputy Bowman. The call didn't last but a minute before Marshall thanked him and hung up.

"What?" I asked. "What was he calling about? Did the real killer confess?"

"No. The forensic report came back on the substance found on those rocks at the crime scene."

"Nail polish! I knew it. Augusta was right. It was clear nail polish. But it couldn't have been Roxanne's because she uses shades of coral and red. And Candace Kane seems to wear greenish-blue polish, so—"

"It wasn't nail polish, Phee," Marshall said. "Or glue. It was the residue from the liquid smoke they use to make those trains look like real steam engines when they go around the track. Anyway, Bowman and Ranston aren't all that concerned about it. They figure the residue could have been there a while from old train runs. After all, it was near the junction box, where Wilbur was working before that blow to his head."

"Won't they even consider the possibility someone from the club was with him? Maybe that person had the jar of liquid smoke. My mom and I saw cartons of it in Wilbur's storage unit. Those jars are small. Only two ounces."

"The only possibility they've considered is Roxanne," Nate said. "The call was an investigation formality, that's all. Try not to look so grief-stricken, Phee. This isn't over yet. We haven't exhausted all our leads."

"Me neither. Starting with Tracee Pearl tonight."

Well, Nate was right about one thing. No way was Tracee Pearl the petite woman with the pixie hairdo. Wig or no wig. Tracee was built like an Amazon. The last time I'd seen muscles like that, they belonged to Arnold Schwarzenegger. Next to her, Myrna was the epitome of frailty and charm.

Tracee was wearing a sleeveless, navy tank top and jeans. Her hair hung shoulder-length against the tank top, unlike the tight bun Nate had observed when he spoke with her. If it wasn't for the readers hanging on a long, gold chain around her neck, I would have mistaken her for one of those Hollywood police officers on *Blue Bloods*, *FBI*, or *NCIS: Los Angeles*. It seemed tank tops, tight jeans, and a badge on the waist was the new uniform for female officers. Tracee certainly fit the bill.

It was only when Big Scuttie addressed her at the front table that I realized who she was. Her chest hung inches from the table's surface, and I was afraid she'd fall over. "Honestly," she said, "here's the receipt. I had to go to Hobby Bench this week anyway. Couldn't the G-scalers purchase their own Mega-Steam Smoke Fluid?"

"Come on, Tracee. It's no big deal. I knew you were headed over there, so I told Grace you'd pick up a bottle of the cinnamon-roll scent. You know how they are about scented smoke. Especially Grace. You'd think they were setting up for a church social, not a train run."

"Never mind. The club owes me ten dollars and ninety cents. That includes the tax. And what was her big hurry? The Midnight Run's not for another week."

"Do I have to spell it out for you? You know how anal retentive that woman is. Everything has to be just so."

Suddenly I remembered what Marshall had observed when the alert went off on the minicam by the showcase. He was convinced Grace brought her own bottle of antibacterial cleanser rather than use anything the club had purchased.

"I'm sorry," I said. "I couldn't help but overhear your conversation. Cinnamon-roll-scented smoke fluid? I knew there were scents, but not any that resembled a pastry shop."

"Phee, right?" Big Scuttie asked. "You were here last week. With your mother. Does this mean you're interested in joining our club?"

Tracee stepped aside so BS and I were face-to-face. "I'm still trying to learn more."

"That makes sense. This is Tracee Pearl, by the way. She's been a member of our club since—"

"I'll cut you off there," Tracee said. "Before you tell her it was before George Washington was born."

I laughed and shook her hand.

She moved the sign-in sheet closer to me. "About those liquid smoke scents, they now come in all sorts of aromas. Used to be only hickory, pine, cedar, and original smoke—they came up with peppermint, vanilla, bayberry, gingerbread, and even hot chocolate now. Running trains is a big deal during the Christmas holidays, so I suppose the companies that produce the smoke fluid wanted to capitalize on it."

"I take it Grace has a liking for cinnamon-roll flavor."

Big Scuttie leaned his head against a propped-up elbow and chuckled. "Let's just say she has a dislike for anything that smells like the real deal. Oil, grease, smoke . . . you name it. She practically sanitizes this place once the meetings are over. I've got a buddy in G-scale who told me all about it. Good thing she didn't join our H/O group. Usually members stick to one group or another. Except for Evelyn. You might have met her if you were at the G-scale meeting last week. She was the woman howling about the Golden Spike being moved. Got the full story from my buddy."

"Yes, I was there and I remember."

"Evelyn belongs to both groups. Too bad she couldn't pick a team and stay on it."

Tracee shot Big Scuttie a look. "That's not a nice thing to say."

"All I said was—"

"Forget it. I'm sure Phee doesn't want to hear it." Then she turned to me. "Come on, I'll walk with you into the workroom. I'm designing a new layout that should be up and running by next fall. You can see what I'm up to. I've taken over the entire left-hand corner of the room, but no one seems to mind."

Sure enough, there was a large table on the left and what looked like the beginnings of a track being assembled. Tracee pulled out a folded chair from the alcove and motioned for me to do the same. As I looked around, I noticed various club members painting landscape pieces or assembling train tracks. I recognized a few of them, including Vickie Owen, with her perfectly styled platinum hair and cute little figure. At least Herb wasn't here to annoy her. I glanced around to see if I could spot Evelyn, but no such luck.

"You'll have to forgive Big Scuttie," Tracee said. "He's not the most diplomatic club member we have, but he's a decent guy. Which is more than I can say for the late Wilbur Maines. I'm surprised it took this long for his wife to do him in."

CHAPTER 35

I couldn't believe what I'd heard. Without even trying, I had the opening I needed to pry into Roxanne's tap shoes. I just hoped I'd be more tactful than Walker Scutt. "Yeah, about that I'm not so sure. True, the news said a tap shoe with large cleats was the murder weapon, but I heard Roxanne donated those shoes to charity. To the Resale Shop in Sun City West."

"Where did you hear that?"

"Um, the news, I think."

I tried to gauge her reaction, but it was hard to tell. No faint blush. No eye twitch. Nothing. I prayed the brunette in the Resale Shop hadn't mentioned my visit to the store. I hadn't given her my full name or my nickname, but I couldn't take anything for granted and had to watch what I said to Tracee.

"Oh well," I said. "You know how these stories get around."

She gave me a nod and tapped her teeth. "Hmm. I volunteer at the Resale Shop, and come to think of it, I remember one of the gals talking about selling a pair of tap shoes last fall. Around October. She thought the woman who bought them did so as part of a Halloween costume."

"What made her think that?" I asked.

"Because the woman resembled Aunt Bee from *Mayberry R.F.D.*, only older. She didn't appear to be the dancing type. And it was around the time when the Rec Center held its annual costume party."

I bit my lower lip slightly and tried not to sound too anxious. "Maybe she bought them for someone else."

Tracee shook her head. "Nope. The volunteer told me the woman tried them on and mentioned something about a bunion."

Argh. I might as well join Nate and Marshall in the dead-end club.

There was the off chance the woman made it appear as if she was buying those shoes for a costume when she really had other, more nefarious plans. Then again, I was tracking down a possible suspect, not writing a mystery novel.

"Anyway," Tracee went on, "if it wasn't the tap shoe, it would have been something else. Wilbur had a horrible habit of leading women on. At least I didn't take him seriously, but, between you and me, he was a damn good kisser."

"So, you, uh, er, um . . ."

"Relax. We swapped saliva, that's all. I'm not proud of it, but it wasn't the end of the world either. And I had no reason to do him in. Unlike his wife. I suppose she reached her limit with his affairs. Can't say I blame her. Did you know he was even seeing two women from this club at once? And that was long after we were done with our brief whatever you'd call it."

"Two more women?" I asked.

"Don't look so shocked. This is a senior community, not a monastery. About a month before Wilbur was found dead he was seen making out in the workroom after an H/O scale meeting. To top it off, he was with another Choo-Choo Chick in the parking lot after the meeting ended. They couldn't get into his car fast enough. Can you imagine?"

Not only can I imagine, I can probably recite their names. Or at least provide a decent description.

My mouth felt as if someone had stuffed it with cotton. "Um, that's terrible. Then again, those kisses probably didn't mean much. It's not as if he gave those women diamonds or anything."

"Not diamonds, but I heard from Evelyn that at least one of them was seen wearing a gold train charm around her neck, and I seriously doubt she bought it for herself. Boy, does that get me riled. Damn cheapskate never bought me anything. Not even a pack of gum. Still, he did get my heart rate up, and I suppose that's good for the health."

"So, you never found out who that woman was? The one with the gold chain?"

"Evelyn, who happens to be as prissy as they come, refused to tell me because she didn't want anything to 'compromise our lovely work relations in the club.' Oh brother. Needless to say, I kept eyeballing the women around here, but I've never seen anyone wearing that charm. Not that it matters. Still, I'm curious."

Fat chance I'd be able to get Evelyn to spill the beans. Cecilia is on her own for now.

"Hey, Tracee!" someone shouted. "Got any extra sheets of extruded foam? I left mine in the truck and don't feel like walking back."

"There are some in the closet. Just replace it, okay?"

"Thanks."

"Maybe Evelyn was right," Tracee said. "We do need decent working relationships around here."

I pulled my chair closer to the layout table and watched as Tracee placed small pieces of track in a loop formation. "Too bad the setup at Beardsley has to remain fixed. I'd love to design a new layout for the G-scale. Between you and me, it's not very imaginative."

"I really didn't take a good look at it. I was there when Wilbur's body was discovered."

"Oh. How awful. Are you an early morning walker?"

"No. I'm an early morning sleeper if I can help it. My mother's friend is the walker who came upon the body and then called us." *More or less.* "From what I saw, it looked as if Wilbur was repairing something in a circuit board."

"Wilbur was always repairing, tweaking, or fiddling with that circuit board. It wouldn't have surprised me in the least if someone deliberately messed with it so they could get Wilbur out of the house at an ungodly hour to fix it."

"As in premeditated murder?"

"Murder?" Tracee dropped the small pliers from her hand and looked ashen. "Oh no. That's not what I meant at all. I figured someone messed with the guy. That's it. Wilbur could be such a pain in the butt at times. No, I think Roxanne killed him. True, Big Scuttie and Montrose were ticked about the restraining orders, but not to the point of murder. My money is on something much more personal. Anyway, I told all this to one of the detectives on the case."

"Uh-huh. I heard the Sheriff's Office and their consulting detectives were interviewing all the club members." *I wonder how long I can pull this off before she finds out I work for one of those consulting detectives.*

"I'll say. I had the pleasure of two such interviews. Although the second one was short. The detective inquired about my whereabouts that morning. Lucky for me, I spent the night at Talking Stick Casino. Ever go there?"

"It's on my list."

"Hey, speaking of lists, put the Midnight Run on yours. It's a week from tomorrow at dusk. Real neat community event, and it only happens twice a year at Beardsley Rec Center. We run the trains, and unlike their regular runs, we use smoke fluid to make them appear like real locomotives. Of course this time the air won't be permeated with an authentic scent like oil or wood. Thanks to Grace, who's in charge of this spring's event, our trains are going to smell like the corner bakery."

"Uh, yeah. I kind of overheard you and Walker Scutt when I came in."

"Then you know the aroma of cinnamon rolls will fill the air and everyone will be asking where they can buy them. Grace should have thought of that. We could have made good money."

I laughed. "Maybe she'll consider it next year."

"I doubt it. You don't know Grace. Anyway, we rent a popcorn machine and also sell hot dogs and soft drinks. And this year we'll even have kettle corn. It's a great fundraiser for us. We set up a big grill right next door to the train track by the horseshoe pits and wait for all those Sun City West grandkids to show up."

"Don't tell her the rest of it, Tracee," a guy called out from the table behind us. "You'll scare her away."

Tracee turned her head. "Thanks a heap." Then she looked at me and groaned. "Every year, heaven knows why, Grace or Evelyn delivers a boring, mind-numbing talk about the completion of the Transcontinental Railroad. I'm hoping this year will be different and they say a few words about Wilbur. It's the closest to a memorial he'll get, seeing as his wife is awaiting trial."

"I'll make sure to put it on my calendar. Bakery scents and boring speeches notwithstanding."

I left the Model Railroad Club work session having made very little progress regarding the tap shoe that wound up in Roxanne's closet after it was donated to the resale charity shop. I did, however, glean more information than needed regarding liquid smoke scents, Golden Spike lectures, and Tracee's admission of guilt regarding kissing Wilbur. Big deal. Who hadn't the guy kissed? As for that tap shoe, it had now become more valuable than the Hope Diamond as far as I was concerned.

"We need to put the Midnight Run on our calendar for next Friday," I said to Marshall as soon as I got in the house. "It'll draw a big crowd and maybe we'll stumble on a decent clue. How do you stand this? Every little snippet of information I get has tentacles on it. I feel as if we're overlooking something, but I don't know what."

"Whoa. Slow down and kick off your shoes. I picked up Italian sandwiches from the deli. You must be starved by now. And as for the investigation, you'll be pleased to know Rolo discovered something 'gadgetry worthy.'"

"'Gadgetry worthy'?"

"Yep. Those were his words. Means it's going to cost us. Too bad it's another dead end."

"What? What did he discover? What dead end?"

"Thomas Tartantian is alive and well in Hong Kong. In fact, he's the CEO of Nan Tian Industries. Nan Tian. Not an anagram, but close enough. According to Rolo, Nan Tian is the number-one producer of minigears for ATM machines. Rolo tracked him down by following the money trail dating back to when Thomas was fired. Investments, purchases, loans . . . Thomas was able to parlay his wealth, so to speak, like a seasoned gambler. His expertise in mechanics obviously helped with his start-up company. This was right under our noses all the time. I guess you know what this means, don't you?"

I groaned. "That he wasn't harboring a lifelong grudge against Wilbur?"

"Hardly. In fact, if it wasn't for Wilbur getting him canned, he never would have taken that giant leap to start his own business on the other side of the globe."

"My mother was right. Roxanne is going to rot in jail. Railroaded for a murder she didn't commit."

"Look, even if a jury does find her guilty and evidence to the contrary surfaces after the fact, she'll be exonerated. I would also expect her lawyer to appeal a guilty decision."

"Still not very hopeful," I mumbled.

"I think Nate would disagree. Thomas Tartantian isn't the only suspect on that reprimand letter list. Sure, the infractions were minor, but that doesn't mean the reactions from the letter holders were. This morning he picked up where I left off and gave Gloria Rouzoni another call."

"The paper-clip lady?" I laughed.

"Uh-huh. Nate wondered what she could tell him about the other names on the list."

"And?"

"The two winners of the insubordination letters, Jenko and Norton, were cited for wearing jeans to work, which went against company policy. Didn't matter they were designer jeans, according to Gloria. Wilbur blew those women into HR like a windstorm."

"Yikes. I'm surprised the guy wasn't drawn and quartered by half the employees. Seems strange he was murdered years later. And in Sun City West of all places."

"Which brings me to my next train of thought. Maybe the motive was more recent."

"Guess we're back to Choo-Choo Chicks and Rhythm Tappers, huh?"

"It would seem so. That Midnight Run you mentioned may put all the players in the right place for one of them to break down and confess."

"And how's that going to happen?" I asked.

"I haven't gotten there yet. Give me time. Meanwhile, let's get into those Italian subs before they get too soggy from the oil."

"I'm famished. I don't care how soggy they get."

CHAPTER 36

It seemed as if we were ruling out suspects faster than identifying them. The scorned-lover idea evaporated into thin air because, as Tracee pointed out, no one took Wilbur seriously. And that included Candace. The only things she took seriously were her possessions, and Wilbur had been one of them. And while the jealousy angle between Candace and the mystery pixie-haired woman might have played out in a verbal assault at Bagels 'N More, I seriously doubted Candace was our killer.

With no viable suspect on the horizon for the Midnight Run, I wasn't quite sure what to expect. What I didn't expect, however, was a new plan to emerge from my mother's imagination.

It was Sunday afternoon when the "brainchild" hit her, and naturally she called me. "Operation Agatha will increase its intensity at that midnight train run."

I was stunned. "'Increase its intensity'? What on earth do you mean?"

"We only took care of half the issues. Cecilia doesn't have to worry about being bad-mouthed in this community thanks to Shirley's intervention, but we have no idea who the woman with the spiked orange and blue hair is."

"I wouldn't call it 'spiked,' but—oh never mind."

"Never mind is right. We have a better plan. And all of the book club ladies will be taking part."

Heaven help us.

"I don't know about you, Phee, but I happen to listen to those detectives on TV."

"You mean those actors?"

"Let me finish. All of them say the same thing—go back to the scene of the crime. Well, that's exactly what's going to happen on Friday at dusk. Of course the crime took place at dawn, but we can't have everything."

"Oh dear God, no. Do *not* tell me you plan to reenact the murder?"

"Of course not. We simply plan to mill around and spread the word the killer is in the crowd. That's the other part of what they say on TV. The murderer always returns to the scene of the crime."

"You'll start a panic. Haven't the book club ladies done enough? First Aunt Ina at the restaurant—and for your information, Bagels 'N More had to undergo a surprise health inspection. It was on the news. Then, Streetman's impromptu performance during the Rhythm Tappers' show. I'm sure the man who played the part of the sultan won't go near a pair of tap shoes again."

"You're being overly dramatic."

"I don't think so. Nate and Marshall intend to be at the

Midnight Run. If anyone knows how to question people inconspicuously, they do. Like all of us, they believe Roxanne is innocent, and they're working behind the scenes to prove it."

"Then tell them to move to the front of the stage, because this is the last chance we have."

"Now who's being dramatic?"

It pained me to admit it, but my mother did have a point. If none of those people from Sherrington Manufacturing in Iowa had anything to do with Wilbur's death, it meant someone from a closer circle probably did. I knew all the Model Railroad Club members and friends would most likely be there, but I wasn't so sure about Roxanne's friends from the Rhythm Tappers. That was why I decided to intervene.

As soon as I got off the phone with my mother, I called Cecilia and asked her to call a few of the Rhythm Tappers to tell them it would be the least they could do for Roxanne. As I explained to Cecilia, "The Midnight Run is the closest thing to a memorial for Wilbur, and Roxanne is behind bars, so their attendance would be appreciated."

Three hours later she called me back to say, "I called everyone on the list and believe it or not, they agreed to go. I even spoke with Candace, who told me to forget about the gold charm. You were right, Phee. She doesn't want to be implicated."

Then I made one more phone call to my friend Lyndy, who informed me she wouldn't miss the Midnight Run for the world because her aunt had told her it was really a sting operation to catch the killer.

"You don't actually believe that, do you?" I asked.

"Of course not. But face it, it'll be better than any comedy show we've seen in a while."

* * *

On Friday morning Nate drove to the Fourth Avenue Jail to have a chat with Roxanne about the timeline. Even though he and Marshall had been through it before, both of them felt as if something was missing.

"It can seem like the most inconsequential of details, but sometimes people fail to disclose things they observed because they think those recollections don't matter or won't have any bearing on the case," Nate said as he got ready to head out of the office for downtown Phoenix.

I had just put some files away and was standing near the door. "Are you hoping Roxanne will remember something?"

"It's a Hail Mary, but yes. She was the one who drove her husband to the model railroad exhibit that morning. Maybe revisiting that ride will refresh her memory."

"I hope so. Because all we're left with is a possible derailment tonight if those book club ladies go through with part two of Operation Agatha."

"Bite your tongue."

It was a little before eight when the sun started to set. Coral, turquoise, and pink tones filled the skies, and with evening temps expected to remain in the low seventies, it was a perfect time for the Midnight Run. Nate had told us he'd be there as well but wasn't sure when.

Marshall and I had grabbed sandwiches at Arby's before pulling into the Beardsley parking lot. Somehow the thought of elbowing through a crowd of grandkids in order to buy grilled hot dogs wasn't all that appealing.

"Check out the lineup of Buicks," Marshall announced. "Your mother and her friends must be here already."

"Better yet, check out the line in front of that popcorn machine. If I'm not mistaken, that's my aunt Ina in some sort of a bonnet. Yeesh. And look, there's Shirley and Lucinda right behind her."

"It's a full house all right. The crowd stretches from the railroad exhibit all the way to the horseshoe pits."

"Look! That's Vickie Owen by the soft drink table. I recognize the platinum hair. She should have worn a hat like my aunt."

"Why?" Marshall asked.

"Because Herb will be circling around her like a vulture. He nearly scared her away at the H/O scale meeting we attended, but that won't stop him."

Marshall laughed. "At least your mother left the dog at home."

"How do you know?"

"Because that's her heading this way and she's not carrying one of those floral tote bags."

I thanked the gods under my breath.

"Phee! Marshall! It's about time you got here." My mother's voice reached across the lawn to the edge of the parking lot, where we stood. "Hurry up, the crowd's gathering by the train tracks. Oh, and not a word about Wilbur's dead body. There are lots of children here."

And now they all know about the dead body, thanks to you.

My mother was right about the children. They seemed to be everywhere. Running, shrieking, throwing popcorn at each other, and climbing over the berms that separated the railroad tracks from the horseshoe pits. A few of the people I recognized from the Model Railroad Club were guarding the main G-scale track as if it was about to be attacked by vandals. They weren't far off.

In addition to the garden scale railroad that encompassed the Beardsley Park exhibit, I noticed a few tables had been set up with smaller train layouts. Apparently, the H/O scalers wanted their share of the action, too. Big Scuttie was standing in front of one of those tables with at least a dozen or so kids surrounding him. I figured the guy must be in his glory.

"Boy does this bring back memories," Marshall said. "I had a Lionel train as a kid. It went to my cousin Bruce when he turned ten."

"Why did you give it up?"

He squeezed my shoulder. "I discovered girls."

I didn't think it possible, but my mother's voice got louder. "We can all revisit memory lane later. The program is about to start. You'll want to get a good spot so you can hear what's going on. This is a huge crowd. Cecilia told me she called the Rhythm Tappers and all of them should be here."

By now we were halfway across the lawn area and only a few yards from the railroad track. I thought back to that morning when I climbed over the trains to check out what I had hoped to be a long palm frond or wooden pole. Then I thought about Nate's comment regarding details that could have been missed, but I was positive I was in the clear.

I elbowed my mother and pointed. "Say, isn't that Montrose over there? Looks like he's chatting it up with Evelyn. Hold on a second, Olga is about to join them."

"Probably boring Railroad Club business," my mother

replied. "Hurry up, we want to be near the tracks. And keep your ears open for any mention of Roxanne or the murder."

I must have done at least three mental eye rolls as we nudged through the crowd. I kept my eyes on Montrose, Evelyn, and Olga, but I wasn't exactly sure why. None of them were on my radar as the killer.

Seconds later Montrose and Evelyn walked to a small podium that had been placed in front of the garden track. It was equipped with a microphone, and I imagined the same electrical source used for the outdoor lighting was what powered the mic.

Montrose took the microphone and cleared his throat. "Welcome, everyone, to the Sun City West Model Railroad Club's Midnight Run. I see the kettle corn is a big hit, and so is the Thomas the Tank Engine for the little ones. Our Model Railroad Club is open to all Sun City West residents, and we hope you'll consider joining. We have G-scale and H/O scale, so dig out those old trains you have packed away and come to one of our meetings."

Then he handed the mic to Evelyn. She motioned with her hand, and all of a sudden Grace was at her side. "I'm Evelyn Watross, and this is Grace Svoboda. We're in charge of the housekeeping at our club room. Also, the archives and our museum area. As some of you know, we preface the Midnight Run with a delightful look back at history. Specifically, the completion of the Transcontinental Railroad."

Just then, someone shouted, "Your speech last year took longer to finish than the Transcontinental Railroad!"

Evelyn seemed to ignore the comment. "As much as Grace and I would like to regale you with stories about our nation's history, specifically the Golden Spike and its relevance, we'll instead offer a tribute to our late president, Wilbur Maines, who died on these very train tracks."

One of the kids immediately piped up, "Can we see the dead body?" He was quickly shushed by an adult.

Evelyn continued. "Wilbur Maines was, by all accounts a—"

"Lying, cheating womanizer who got what he deserved." It was a woman's voice that could be heard above the crowd. I couldn't tell who it was, but the speaker made everyone in the vicinity gasp. Except perhaps for those folks who were familiar with rumors of Wilbur's dalliances.

Then Montrose took the mic from Evelyn and demanded the crowd refrain from making derogatory remarks. "There are young children in the audience. Keep that in mind." He clicked off the microphone and turned to Evelyn. Unfortunately, Grace picked up the mic and turned it back on. She was about to speak when Montrose's voice could be heard all over the park. "Wrap it up, Evelyn. We want to get the damn train running."

Guffaws and chuckles came from everywhere, but there was one I recognized immediately—Nate's. He stood a few yards to the left of the podium and waved at Marshall and me.

"Think he had any luck with Roxanne today?" I whispered to Marshall.

A second later his phone vibrated. "Hmm. A text from Nate. To answer your question, I'd say yes. Nate's just waiting for Rolo to finish up his end of the investigation. Not easy tracking down all those players from Sherrington."

At that moment Grace spoke the most welcome words of the night, "Let the Wilbur Maines Memorial Train Run begin."

With that, the ladies walked away from the podium, as Montrose had done minutes before. Next thing I knew, a train horn sounded and everyone jockeyed past me to get to the tracks. Everyone except Vickie Owen. She was headed in the opposite direction, with Cecilia at her heels.

CHAPTER 37

I grabbed Marshall's arm and motioned to the parking lot. "Cecilia's chasing after Vickie Owen and I don't think it has anything to do with the Rhythm Tappers. Vickie's a Choo-Choo Chick. Something's up for sure."

Without waiting for Marshall to respond, I took off after Cecilia. Thankfully, my mother didn't notice because she had already elbowed her way to the train tracks for Wilbur's memorial run.

Mountaintop hikes and walks with Lyndy paid off because I managed to be a few yards behind Cecilia in a matter of minutes. Those tap dance rehearsals must have done wonders for Cecilia's stamina because she kept running without pausing to catch a breath. As I got closer, I could hear her yell, "Killer! Killer! I know who you are. You won't get away with it."

I wasn't sure what Cecilia knew or how she knew it, but I was certain of one thing: Cecilia had just accused Vickie of murder. I was stunned. So stunned I momentarily slowed down, and that was when Cecilia tore off her black cardigan and threw it over Vickie's head, as if she was capturing a hawk or a falcon.

Vickie stumbled to the ground and the sweater got caught up in her hair. By that time I was only a few feet away.

"What's going on?" I shouted.

"This crazy woman attacked me for no reason." Vickie got to her knees and tossed the sweater off to her side, where Cecilia promptly picked it up.

"Everything all right?" Marshall was a few yards away and moving quickly toward us.

"No!" we all replied in unison. After that it was anyone's guess at what was said. Cecilia kept shouting what sounded like "murderess," while Vickie returned the favor with a few retorts of her own. Those retorts might or might not have consisted of four-letter words, but I couldn't be sure.

"It's over," Cecilia said to Vickie. "I know who you are. You're the woman who met me at Bagels 'N More to claim the gold charm. When I stood next to you a few minutes ago I noticed that birthmark by the side of your eye. It looked familiar, and then I remembered where I'd seen it. Nice touch with the wig and tinted glasses. You were having an affair with Wilbur and it went south, didn't it? So you wanted revenge and set up Roxanne to take the blame. Murderess! Heathen murderess!"

"You're wrong. Completely wrong and a bit unbalanced, I might add. That's why I ran when you accused me. I didn't murder Wilbur Maines. I was trying to find out who did. That's why I showed up in disguise at the restaurant. Darn it. I should have used concealer on that beauty mark."

Marshall and I exchanged glances while Vickie continued to speak directly to Cecilia.

"Wilbur's death wreaked havoc on our club. Overnight the club members became suspicious of one another. The G-scalers thought someone in H/O scale did it and vice versa. When I saw the posting about the gold train charm I was positive it belonged to his killer. You see, I'd heard rumors about him having an affair and doling out tokens of affection to his lover. I figured he jilted her and she got even. Same theory you had, but obviously with a different suspect."

Cecilia shook out her sweater and put it on. "So, that was all an act at the restaurant?"

Vickie nodded. "Not my proudest moment, but yes. I tried to get a reaction from that blond tap dancer, but no go."

"Excuse me," I said to Vickie. "If it was all an act, how come you knew the inscription on the charm?"

Vickie took a deep breath. "It was a darned good guess. Wilbur made a play for me, and at the time he used that expression. It stuck with me. Once I got the first words out, I knew I was in the clear. What an awful waste of time, not to mention the aftermath. I only wanted our club to go back to the way it was. Friendly. Inviting. Enjoyable."

"I'm sorry about throwing my sweater over your head," Cecilia said to Vickie. "And calling you a heathen murderess."

"I suppose that was understandable, given the circumstances. I guess my performance at Bagels 'N More was pretty convincing. Maybe I should join the theater group."

Oh yeah. You can ask my mother. Ghost sightings, a body on the catwalk . . . I bit my lower lip and grimaced. "Um, only if you're looking for more drama. And no pun intended."

"Okay, ladies," Marshall said. "Now that we've got all that settled we'd better get back to the train run before it's over." Then he looked directly at Vickie. "Next time you decide to track down a murderer, please don't. No sense putting yourself in danger."

"I'll second that," came a familiar voice from a yard or so away. It was Nate, and he strode toward us, rubbing his chin. "Thought there might be some trouble here, but I was mistaken."

With that, the five of us speed walked back to the train tracks in time to hear another announcement. "Hooray for the Midnight Run!"

Cecilia wormed her way to where my mother, my aunt, and the book club ladies were standing, while Marshall, Nate, and I opted to plant ourselves a few yards away with a direct view of the large garden track. Miraculously, no one stood in our way. The Thomas the Tank Engine, as well as the other smaller exhibits, was still bursting at the seams with kids. Of course there were scads of them where we stood as well.

Another train horn sounded and the Midnight Run kept going. The engineer's cabin moved past us, followed by passenger cars, dining cars, freight cars, and tank cars. It was endless, with no caboose in sight. A sweet, smoky smell permeated the air as the faux locomotive steam drifted from the train. Mega-Steam Smoke Fluid. I remembered Tracee's conversation with Big Scuttie about her purchase at Hobby Bench. Suddenly, my mind reverted back to the morning when I discovered Wilbur's body.

I was positive I'd detected the aroma of cinnamon rolls that morning, but I'd attributed it to being hungry. Now I smelled it again. Stronger this time, but the same cloyingly sweet smell. Then my stomach tightened, and I recalled something else Tracee had said. Something about the woman who'd purchased the tap shoes from the Resale Shop. The volunteer who sold the shoes said the woman resembled Aunt Bee from *Mayberry R.F.D.*

Only one Choo-Choo Chick fit that description, and in an instant I was certain I knew who murdered Wilbur. And it wasn't with Roxanne's old tap shoe. My stomach was now churning and my hands began to sweat. It was as if bits and pieces of unrelated information somehow gelled in my mind, forcing me into a conclusion that made absolutely no sense. Still, in my mind it was irrefutable. Even if I was unsure of the motive.

By now the caboose had made its appearance as the train continued on for its second run. The delicious scent of vanilla and cinnamon wafted by, and one by one I studied the faces in the crowd until I spotted the killer. I figured if Cecilia could make a blatant accusation, so could I.

In retrospect, I should have said something to Marshall or Nate, but my adrenaline kicked in and next thing I knew, I skirted to the front of the podium where Evelyn, Grace, and Montrose were standing. I had to do something before I lost my nerve.

"It was the Golden Spike," I shouted over the train's horn. "That's what killed Wilbur. Not his wife's tap shoe, although that was a pretty good touch. Hmm, as I recall, weren't two of you in Wilbur's house last fall on club business? Yes, that was a side conversation at the club meeting I attended. Real easy to use the guest bathroom and then sneak into the master bedroom to plant the shoe in Roxanne's closet."

"What on earth are you babbling about?" Montrose asked.

"Yes. What?" Grace added.

"I think you know. In fact, I'm positive of it. Ever hear of something called Touch DNA? It's the process forensic teams use to extract the teeniest, tiniest bits of human cells from objects that come in contact with them."

Evelyn let out a strong huff of air and crinkled her nose. "We most certainly do not know."

"Let me extrapolate for you." I took a quick breath and looked around. No one was paying any attention to us. "Regular cleaning solutions don't remove DNA evidence. They water it down, making it harder for a determination, but it's still there. People think antibacterial cleansers can do the trick, but they're mistaken. Truth is, only anti-DNA cleaning products like those erase-and-replace sprays that are touted on the internet can really get the job done."

Then I looked directly at Grace. "Is that why you waited until the painting and shelving crew had completed their work in the model railroad museum room to clean the Golden Spike at such an ungodly hour? Well, it doesn't matter, because right now the Golden Spike is on its way to the Maricopa Crime Lab."

Boy, when I lie, I really lie.

Without saying a word, Grace took off as if someone had set her clothing on fire. She thundered through the crowd and into the parking lot.

"What just happened?" Montrose asked.

"Other than having one of our esteemed club members accused of murder?" Evelyn snapped.

I didn't wait to continue the conversation. I made a beeline for the parking lot.

"Phee!" Marshall shouted from behind me. "What's going on?"

"Call Bowman and Ranston," I screeched. "Grace is the killer. She's on her way over to the Model Railroad Club. Hurry!"

"Got it!"

In that instant I knew beyond all doubt I had made the right choice in my decision to marry Marshall Gregory. He trusted my judgment, and that was all there was to it. Grace got into a light-beige Hyundai and steamed across the parking lot. Only by now, the ground resembled an obstacle course. Popcorn was strewn everywhere. And not little bits of it. Handfuls. Fistfuls. Like tiny pellets of hail after a storm. Only this storm was entitled "The Grandkids."

Grace's car skidded across the lot as she headed to the Beardsley Road exit, but she didn't make the turn. Instead, her car swerved to the left and bounced over one of those long, concrete parking-lot barriers for handicapped vehicles. The tires were still spinning when Marshall and I got there, and I immediately noticed the pink license plate holder in the shape of a pig that read, "Iowa Born and Raised."

Nate stood off to the side, cell phone in hand. From the look of things, he was texting someone, and I figured it had to be Bowman or Ranston.

Lucky for Grace the airbag didn't deploy or she might have been injured from the impact. Marshall pulled the door open and asked if she was all right, but before he finished, I leaned in and announced, "It's over. Don't make it worse." *Yep, the catch-all phrase used by every crime-drama cop known to TV viewers.*

"Tell her to stay put!" Nate shouted.

Marshall and I stepped back as he rushed over to the car. Leaning his elbow against the top frame of the driver's side door, he spoke slowly, enunciating every word. "Right now there's enough circumstantial evidence to have you arrested for the murder of Wilbur Maines. In less than an hour it will be concrete evidence. You can choose to cooperate with the sheriff's deputies when they arrive on the scene or not. Your choice. But rest assured, they have a solid case."

Then he gave me a nudge. "Nice work, kiddo, but we had this, you know."

CHAPTER 38

Grace rested her head on the steering wheel and sobbed. I reached into my pocket, pulled out a crumpled Kleenex, and handed it to her. She dabbed her eyes, blew into the tissue, and all but choked on her words. "Wilbur Maines was the most despicable human being to set foot on this earth. Fussy, petty, and relentless. He made mountains out of molehills, and by doing so, destroyed careers and households."

Iowa Born and Raised. My gosh! The Sherrington reprimand letters? Was that the motive?

"I thought I'd never cross paths with that worm once I retired and moved to Arizona, but I was wrong. When I joined the Model Railroad Club, I recognized him immediately."

"And that's when you devised an ingenious plot to murder him?" I asked.

"I wouldn't exactly call it murder. It was more of a plan to knock him out of commission for a while. And get his wife to take the blame. It was serendipitous really. I happened to go into the Resale Shop last fall to mill around for bargains. That's when I saw those tap shoes for sale. I knew immediately whose they were because the initials were stitched into the tongue of the shoe. I also knew I had a business meeting with Montrose and Wilbur a few days later at Wilbur's house."

My pulse quickened. I was right! I was right with my hunch. "So you planted a shoe in Roxanne's closet and held on to the other one."

"Uh-huh. It was only a matter of time. And that time came in late March. It was a Friday night, and I arrived early for bingo at the social hall. Roxanne was still there, following a dance practice. She was in such a hurry to get out, she left her little screwdriver sitting on one of the chairs. Call it my ah-ha moment, but in that second I knew I had everything in place to get even with her wretched husband."

A siren hit my eardrums. "I think the deputies will be pulling in here any second. Maybe you should wait and give them your statement."

Grace balled up the tissue and leaned back. "My statement is that I didn't murder Wilbur Maines. He kind of died on his own. After I clocked him over the head."

"Psst!" Nate said to me. "I need a word with you and Marshall. Ms. Svoboda isn't going anywhere."

I stepped away from the car, as did Marshall.

"We had Grace dead to rights," Nate said. "When I met with Roxanne this morning we went over the timeline. She didn't see anyone or anything out of the ordinary when she dropped her husband off at the train exhibit. But she did recall the tail end of the conversation that woke him up in the first place. According to her, Wilbur said something like, 'Yeah, yeah, damn circuit board. By the way, got your special wood polish for the showcase. You and Evelyn can thank me later.' Special wood polish. It had to be Grace who made the call."

Out of the blue Evelyn whizzed past the three of us and charged over to the car where Grace was still seated. Evelyn's arms flailed and she seemed almost out of breath. "The Golden Spike? You used our precious Golden Spike to kill Wilbur Maines? You desecrated our pride and joy? Why, that's unconscionable. Absolutely unconscionable. What were you thinking? That replica should never have been tampered with." Then she took a step away while still muttering, "The Golden Spike. Our precious Golden Spike."

Then Nate started to walk back to the car, when all of a sudden Evelyn brushed past him and was now face-to-face with Grace. "Why couldn't you have used a crowbar? Or one of those tire things from the trunk of your car?"

Before Grace could answer, Evelyn grabbed the sleeve of Nate's shirt. "I'm pressing charges for the destruction of property. Or unlawful use of property, whatever works. Write that down. I'm pressing charges."

"We're not law enforcement, ma'am. You'll need to take that up with the Maricopa County Sheriff's Office, but frankly, Ms. Svoboda will be facing other, more salient charges."

The siren sound was all but on top of us, and I spun my head to look down Beardsley Road. Sure enough, a vehicle with red and blue flashers was headed our way.

Marshall approached Evelyn and motioned for her to calm down. "You'll have plenty of time to file a complaint. Right now I strongly suggest you head back to the train track and let the deputies do their job. I'm sure you don't want to get caught up in any of this."

"I suppose you're right. But it's not over." Then, she tromped over to Grace's car again. "I hope you realize this will put poor Olga over the edge. And she trusted you, too. Took all that time to show you how to wire a train's circuit board. And how did you repay her? By violating the sanctity of our Golden Spike replica."

With that, Evelyn brushed some loose hairs from her brow and marched across the parking lot as if she was going into battle.

"That doesn't look good," I said to Nate and Marshall. "She could get the crowd into an uproar. Right now they have no idea what's going on here. For all they know, Grace has a flat tire or something."

"Good point," Marshall said. "How about if you go back there and get that rumor started? We'll do our best to speed things up with Bowman and Ranston."

"Tell Bowman my mother has Streetman with her. Point to the crowd and tell him you think that's her and it looks like she's on her way over here. They'll read Grace her Miranda rights and scurry her off in their car in a hurry. Bank on it."

Unlike Evelyn, who tromped all over the scattered popcorn in the parking lot, I walked with caution but took long strides. Once back in the crowd, I found my mother. "Hmm, I think Grace got a flat tire or something. But don't worry. Nate and Marshall are helping her."

"How much help does she need?" my mother asked. "Looks like they called the posse."

"Yeah, well, maybe Grace will need to have the car towed. Newer models don't have spare tires, or even those donut things."

My two-second conversation with my mother worked. She immediately began to spread the rumor of a flat tire to anyone and everyone within a three-foot radius. That was, until Montrose Lamont had a side conversation with my uncle Louis. And while I prayed they were talking about music or gigs or whatever musicians talked about, I had a sinking feeling they weren't.

My worst nightmare was confirmed when Montrose pointed to the parking lot and my uncle Louis announced, "Think they're going to arrest her?"

My aunt Ina, who was only a few feet away from her husband, responded with a resonating, "Who? Who? I must have missed something."

"You didn't miss anything." Then I looked at the crowd.

Thankfully, most of the people were still focused on the large, garden-scale train making its run around the tracks. The kids were getting restless, as evidenced by whining, moaning, and tossing more popcorn. This time at one another. I wondered how long it would take before the crowd focused its attention on the parking lot and not the Midnight Run.

Next thing I knew, Montrose answered my uncle's question. "Oh, they'll arrest her all right. I heard it straight from the horse's mouth."

Wonderful. I've now become the horse's mouth.

I wasn't sure quite what to do or say at that moment, but it didn't matter. Everyone in a four-foot radius heard him loud and clear. And they all had something to say.

"Who's getting arrested?"

"Wilbur's killer!"

"Who is it?"

"Don't know. It's not on my Facebook feed."

The voices in the crowd got louder, and if I thought the kids were antsy, their grandparents were worse. I decided to try a new tactic. One I'd learned from my mother and my aunt. Say something loud enough and people will believe you. I took a deep breath and did my own pointing at the parking lot. "Who wants to help Grace with her flat tire? I'm sure those deputies have other things to do."

Suddenly, the crowd turned back to the train track and the pounding in my chest subsided. The train horn sounded again, followed by another announcement. This time by Big Scuttie. "Thank you, folks, for remembering Wilbur Maines and giving him the send-off he deserved. We'll have one more run around the tracks before calling it a night. Get your popcorn while you can, and don't forget those hot dogs."

Then someone shouted, "Where are the cinnamon rolls? I smell cinnamon rolls."

When I looked at the parking lot again the sheriff's car was gone. A few minutes later Nate and Marshall found me in the crowd.

Marshall gave me a peck on the cheek and whispered, "Grace is on her way to the posse station. A tow truck is coming for her car. It's really wedged in."

"Good. People will think it's the flat tire."

"For the time being. I guarantee someone will pick up the chatter on Bowman and Ranston's scanner and KPHO or another local station will have it on the ten o'clock news."

"Your fiancé is right." Nate looked around. "Much as I hate to say this, we really should let your mother know what's going on. She'll find out soon enough. We might as well be upfront."

I locked my fingers together and pressed so tight I was afraid my knuckles would turn white. "You do realize she'll blab it to all the book club ladies. Heck, that will take thirty seconds. They're all here. And Herb. He's here, too, somewhere. I spotted him earlier with some of his pinochle guys."

Then something came to me out of the blue. "I have an idea. I'll tell her Marshall and I are going to stop by her house when this is over so we can chat about our wedding ceremony. Believe me, she'll want to talk. We can tell her then."

Nate laughed. "I'll head over to the posse station and call you folks in a bit."

Sure enough, my mother was ecstatic when I mentioned going back to her house. "We should ask your aunt and uncle to join us, too. I'll put on a fresh pot of coffee."

A fresh pot of coffee. Aunt Ina and Uncle Louis don't know how lucky they are.

"Oh," she added, "before I forget, the book ladies decided to meet for brunch tomorrow at ten. Join us if you don't have to work."

I mumbled something about invoices, billing, and spreadsheets.

"Okay, see you at the house."

I was positive Evelyn wouldn't be able to keep her mouth shut, but it didn't matter. Once Marshall and I, along with Aunt Ina and Uncle Louis, finished our coffee and our discussion about the wedding, my mother turned on the nightly news. As Nate predicted, the "Breaking News" banner flashed across the screen and one of the anchors announced, "This just in. An arrest has been made in the Wilbur Maines murder that took place in Sun City West. That's all the news we have at this point. For details, visit our website, and be sure to tune into our station tomorrow morning for the early bird segment."

"Actually," Marshall said, "that's the real reason we came back here. We wanted you to know firsthand who committed the crime. It was Grace Svoboda, from the Railroad Club."

My mother gasped. "So, it wasn't a flat tire after all. What was it? Did she attempt to knock off someone else at the Midnight Run?"

My uncle Louis added another teaspoon of sugar to his coffee and stirred. "Montrose told me she was going to be arrested, but I figured it was hearsay."

"Not this time," I said. "But what I don't understand is her motive. She certainly wasn't having an affair with him."

Marshall took out his phone and glanced at us. "Only one way to find out. Nate was on to something back at the park, but we didn't have a chance to talk. I'll catch him at the posse station. Give me a minute."

He stood and walked to the counter while my aunt and my mother offered up enough motives to keep most hard-boiled detective authors in business for quite a while. And when they weren't offering motives, they were offering bits of cookies to Streetman.

"Rolo's perseverance paid off," Marshall said.

"That's the cybersleuth our office uses," I quickly added. It was easier than saying, "The international hacker who has thus far managed to elude Interpol, the CIA, and the FBI."

My mother grabbed a cookie, broke it in half, and handed a piece to the dog. "Well, don't just sit there, tell us why she did it."

CHAPTER 39

"Revenge," Marshall said. "One of the oldest motives in the book."

"Revenge? For what?" I was still stymied.

"Remember those reprimand letters you found at Wilbur's storage unit?"

"Uh-huh. But Grace's name wasn't on them."

He smiled. "I know. That's because she never worked for Sherrington. But she did live in Des Moines, where Catapult Construction Equipment is located. And Catapult is where Wilbur enjoyed another stint as a manager."

"I don't get it."

"You will. Seems Wilbur's penchant for pettiness when it came to workplace rules didn't disappear when he took his new job. Too bad he didn't keep copies of *those* reprimand letters in his storage unit."

My uncle Louis moaned and leaned into the table. "I'm not getting any younger. Get to the point."

Marshall nodded. "Grace's brother worked for Catapult. Over twenty-five years and no problems until Wilbur cited him for piracy. Same deal as Thomas Tartantian, only Grace's brother didn't become CEO of a major company. He lost his job, his wife divorced him, and he died a few years later, broke and living in a halfway house. And get this: after all was said and done, it was determined the man never pirated anything. But by then it was too late. Wilbur retired with a decent pension before the company could fire him for misconstruing information."

The room got so quiet the only noise was the dog chewing on one of his toys. I steepled my fingers and took a breath. "How on earth did Rolo find all of that out?"

"The guy's a shark. Only instead of hunting prey, he hunts information. He hacked into a multitude of business and industry databases, not to mention the usual government ones, and made connections. That's how he narrowed down the killer to Grace."

"You mean to tell me all we had to do was sit back and wait?"

"Heck no. Honestly, hon, you put us all to shame by solving the case with old-fashioned sleuthing."

"Yeah, but without the motive. Glad we've got Rolo on speed dial. Might as well add IKEA, too." Then I looked at my aunt. "Rolo likes to be paid with kitchen gadgetry."

"Forget about Rolo for a minute and think about Roxanne. They should release her right now," my mother exclaimed.

Marshall groaned. "It's the weekend. And that involves paperwork. It's not like TV or the movies. If she's lucky, she'll be out on Monday."

Sure enough, Marshall was right. Jane Ellis-Engle, Roxanne's criminal defense áttorney, had all charges against her client dismissed. She picked Roxanne up on Monday afternoon and drove her back to Sun City West.

In the days that followed, the news of Grace's arrest traveled through my mother's community like a swarm of bees, only faster. And while I certainly didn't condone what Grace had done, I understood what drove her to the moment when she picked up the Golden Spike and clobbered Wilbur with it.

According to the news anchors, who ran the story all week long, Grace admitted to donning one of those food handler gloves and using Roxanne's screwdriver to open the circuit box, making it look as if someone had pried it open and disconnected some wires. She then left the screwdriver in plain sight. When Wilbur arrived to fix the box Grace showed up under the guise that she wanted him to smell the cinnamon smoke fluid and inadvertently dripped some on the rocks. When Wilbur was engaged with the circuit box she used that moment to remove the Spike from under her coat and hit him over the head.

Roxanne returned to the Rhythm Tappers in plenty of time to prepare for the Fall Follies. Unfortunately, the same couldn't be said for Cecilia, who vowed never to dance in public again. She did, however, keep her tap shoes, according to my mother.

"You never know," my mother said when I stopped by her house a week later, "the Rhythm Tappers may do a show that calls for ankle-length clothing. Or maybe even a dancing dog. Which reminds me, you never gave me an answer about Streetman taking part in your wedding ceremony."

The little Chiweenie looked up from his spot near the coffee table when he heard his name. His ears picked up and his eyes got wide.

Call it a moment of weakness. Or maybe even delirium, but I reached down and patted him on the head. "A short dance. A very short dance. Stick him in your tote and I'll bring my iPod."

After all, weddings were supposed to be memorable, weren't they?

STREETMAN'S WALKING MAP

A Neighborhood Walking Guide to Sun City West

A – Watch out for crazy screaming lady! She goes nuts if Streetman so much as sniffs at her lawn.

B, I, Q, R, U, Z – Danger! Sago Palms. Keep him away from those houses.

C – Go to big red rock on edge of property. Streetman likes to pee on it.

D – Nice jacaranda tree on corner of the lot. Let him sniff there awhile.

E – Go to fence in rear. It's okay. He likes to visit with the two Pomeranians.

F, G, H– Golf ball alert! These houses are on the golf course. Who knows when one of those balls makes it to the street? Keep a wide berth.

I – Hissing cat in the front window. Only a concern when the window's open.

J – Toad sanctuary. They have a water feature that attracts Sonoran Desert Toads. Keep Streetman away.

K – Three nice boxwood beauties that Streetman likes to pee on. It's a rental and so far no one has complained.

L – Steer Clear! They use rat poison around the house. I know because I watched their exterminator one morning.

M, N, O – These are his favorite locations for business. Take more than one bag.

P – Don't go past this house. Streetman doesn't like to walk much farther. Unless you want to carry him.

S – Very nice lady from Myrna's bunco group lives here. She gives Streetman treats.

T – Steer clear. They had a beehive in this area last year.

V – Just like letter P. Streetman doesn't like to walk much farther than this house.

W – Watch out for speeders on this corner. Tighten leash.

X, Y – Streetman will sometimes do his business here. Or maybe even a second time after M, N, or O.

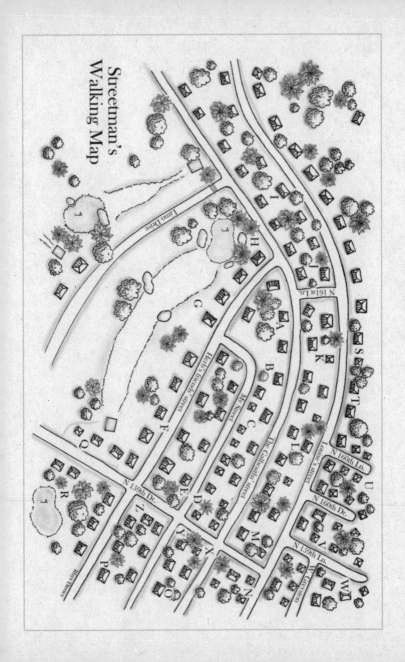

Keep reading for a special excerpt of *Broadcast 4 Murder* by J. C. Eaton!

BROADCAST 4 MURDER
J. C. EATON

All of Arizona's Sun City West heard Sophie "Phee" Kimball's mom scream bloody murder, but it's up to the reluctant sleuth to find the killer . . .

Phee's mother, Harriet, is going to be a star! At least, that's how the Sun City West retiree describes her chance to host a live radio program of her book club's "Booked 4 Murder Mystery Hour" on Arizona's KSCW. But instead of chatting about charming cozies, Harriet ends up screaming bloody murder over the airwaves after discovering the body of Howard Buell, the station's programming director, in a closet—with a pair of sewing shears shoved into his chest.

The number-one suspect is Howard's ex-girlfriend Sylvia Strattlemeyer, who believed she was going to host a *sewing* talk show before Harriet was offered the spot. But not only do the fingerprints found on the scissors not match Sylvia's, they belong to a woman who passed away twenty years ago at the age of ninety-seven. Now, with the whole town on pins and needles, it's up to Phee to stitch together enough clues from the past to uncover the identity of a killer in the present . . .

Look for* Broadcast 4 Murder, *on sale now.

CHAPTER 1

Harriet Plunkett's House,
Sun City West, Arizona

Myrna Mittleson, all five-foot-nine of her, charged out of my mother's house and nearly bumped into me on the walkway. "Oops! Sorry, Phee! I'm in a rush to get to the beauty parlor. God bless the state of Iowa!"

It was a Saturday morning in late January, and I was returning a large salad bowl I had borrowed for a neighborhood dish-to-pass party. Before I could utter a word, Myrna blew past me and raced to her car, a nondescript beige sedan. *God bless the state of Iowa?* I knew my mother's Booked 4 Murder book club friends leaned toward the eccentric side, but for the life of me, I had no idea what Myrna was talking about.

The door to the house was still ajar and my mother stepped outside.

"Did you hear that?" I asked. "Iowa? I thought she was from Brooklyn."

My mother ushered me inside. "She is. But right now we're enamored with the state of Iowa."

"Huh? Why? I don't get it."

"Quick! Come in. Close the door behind you before Streetman runs out. I think I heard a bird chirping and he's likely to run after it."

I looked around the room and spied the little Chiweenie sitting on the couch, trying to tear off what looked like a Christmas tree plastered to his back.

"Um, I don't think so. And what's he wearing? Is that supposed to be a Christmas tree with a hoop skirt under it?"

"It's one of Shirley's designs. We're getting an early start for the Christmas in July program."

"Good grief! The holiday event was only a few weeks ago."

"You have to plan early in these retirement communities."

"Your dog is planning early. Look! He pulled off one of those dangling ornaments."

My mother groaned, walked over to Streetman, and removed the costume. "We'll try later," she said to the dog.

I shuddered. "Anyway, here's your salad bowl, and for heaven's sake, please tell me what's this business with Iowa. Not another retirement community you're looking into, I hope."

"Good grief no! I'm not leaving Arizona. I love Sun City West. Best thing I did was get out of those Minnesota winters. Same deal with Myrna, only she's from New York."

I tried not to roll my eyes and nodded as my mother continued.

"Last night Myrna and I got the most wonderful news about Vernadeen Stibbens. Sit down and I'll tell you all about it. I was going to call you, but I knew you'd be stopping by on your way to work."

I was totally lost but used to the way my mother's conversations circumvented the main idea until boomeranging back to the point. I plopped myself down on a floral chair so as not to disturb the dog's position on the couch. God forbid I upset that neurotic little ball of fur.

My mother put the salad bowl on the coffee table, grabbed the chair next to mine, and leaned toward me. "Vernadeen Stibbens was asked to be one of the judges for the sewing contest for the Iowa State Fair, and she'll be on the homemaking committee as well. She still has her condo in Davenport, so technically she's a resident there. She was one of the judges for that contest back in 1995. Can you imagine? She'll be reprising her role once again."

"And you and Myrna are doing cartwheels because someone you know is going to be on a committee? Or worse yet, judging someone's stitching? I don't get it."

"If you'd let me finish, Phee, I'd explain. Vernadeen Stibbens has her own live radio show on KSCW, the voice of Sun City West, every Tuesday morning. *Sewing Chats with Vernadeen*. Of course, they tape it and run it over and over again during the week."

"I'm still—"

"Shh! I'm not done. Anyway, Vernadeen will be gone most of the spring and summer because of her role at the state fair. That means *Sewing Chats* will no longer be on the local airwaves."

"And that's a cause for celebration?"

My mother shuffled in her chair and the dog immediately jumped down from the couch. "Isn't that adorable?

He thinks Mommy is going to give him a treat. I can't disappoint him. Hold on a second."

My mother walked to the kitchen and returned with a dog biscuit. The dog immediately devoured it.

"Now," she said. "Where was I? Oh yes, Vernadeen's show. It was deadly. Topics like nuances of double stitching and harmonious hemming with cross-stitches. Herb Garrett from across the street said he recorded it for nights when he had insomnia. When he found out she had been one of the state fair judges, he asked how many people she put to sleep with her commentary."

"I'm still not sure why you and Myrna are so over-joyed."

My mother patted the dog's head as she grinned from ear to ear. "Myrna and I are rejoicing because we've been asked to take over Vernadeen's slot on the radio with our own show."

My jaw dropped and I had to remind myself to breathe. *Heaven help us.* "Ah-ha! And now the real reason! But what show? What are you and Myrna going to talk about? You don't sew and Myrna wouldn't know a cross-stitch from a straight stitch. Now, if you said Shirley Johnson, I could understand. She's a talented milliner and teddy bear maker, but you and Myrna? Seriously?"

"Oh for goodness' sake, Phee. We're not going to have a sewing program. We're going to have our own murder mystery show! No one knows more about mysteries than our Booked 4 Murder book club. Cozies, forensic, hard-boiled . . . You name it, we'll talk about it. Myrna even has her own little segment planned for elements of sus-pense."

"The only element of suspense I can think of is when Aunt Ina finds out."

"Oy! Don't remind me. I'd better give my sister a call before she hears about it from the grapevine. You know how people around here can gossip."

Intimately. I know this intimately. "Um, when do you and Myrna get started?"

"Tuesday morning we're going over to the radio station to meet with the station manager to find out what's involved. It can't be all that hard. If I have any questions, I can always ask Herb."

"Herb Garrett?"

"Of course Herb Garrett. How many Herbs do I know? He and his pinochle buddies have their own show on Thursday nights: *Pinochle Pointers*. Once our show gets underway, Myrna and I will have guest speakers from our club. Cecilia and Shirley are already chomping at the bit to do a program about household poisonings as they relate to murder mysteries."

"Gee, I'm surprised Louise Munson doesn't have one planned about parrots that kill. Especially given the one she owns."

"Don't give her any ideas. Those things bite. I suppose Ina will want her own segment, too. I can just see it now. She'll be rattling off about obscure authors from countries none of us have heard of."

"Er, um, yeah. I suppose. Look, Mom, I've got to get going. I'm working from ten to noon this morning and it's already nine twenty. I'll talk to you later. Thanks for the salad bowl."

I made a beeline for the door before she insisted I pet Streetman or, worse yet, give him some "kissies." Besides, he seemed perfectly content back on the couch.

"I'll call you later. On your real phone. I hate when

that cell phone of yours goes to voice mail. It always cuts me off."

"Okay, fine. Later. Love you!"

I was out the door and buckled up in my car just as Cecilia Flanagan pulled up. Her old, black Buick was unmistakable. Yep, word did travel fast, especially with my mother at the other end of the phone line. I imagined Cecilia had stopped by to get all the juicy gossip about Sun City West's latest radio show. I beeped the horn and waved as I pulled away from the curb and headed to Williams Investigations in Glendale, where I'm employed. I have my own office and appropriate door sign that reads, "Sophie Kimball, Bookkeeper/Accountant," even though everyone calls me "Phee."

Nate Williams, the owner of the detective agency, was a longtime friend of mine, and like me, had worked for the Mankato Police Department in Minnesota. When he retired as an investigator, he moved out west and convinced me to take a leave of absence from my job in accounts receivable to do his accounting. It was an offer I couldn't refuse, and one that got better the following year, when another detective from the Mankato Police Department, Marshall Gregory, also retired and joined the business.

I'd had a crush on Marshall for years and, unbeknownst to me, he felt the same way. Maybe Nate figured that out all along and pulled the right strings. Now, almost two years later, Marshall and I were sharing a house together and slowly broaching the subject of marriage. *Slowly*, because I was still in shock, following my Aunt Ina's nearly catastrophic wedding ceremony to three-time divorcé Louis Melinsky. Besides, as my friend Lyndy put it, "You're both in your forties and consenting adults. What else do you need?" Even my daughter, Kalese, a teacher in St. Cloud, agreed when I called to tell her about my living arrangements. I figured it was because she wanted me to be as relaxed about her living arrangements if and when the time came for her to drop a bombshell like that.

I chuckled as I watched Cecilia exit her car. Still the same black skirt and white blouse. *Uh-huh. I know a former nun when I see one. Even if my mother says it isn't so.* I figured that by five this evening, the Greater Phoenix community would know that my mother and her book club would be hosting *Murder Mysteries to Die For*, or whatever title they decided to give the show. As long as she didn't invite me to be a guest, I would be in the clear.

Augusta, our secretary, was at her desk, coffee cup in one hand and fingers furiously hitting her computer keyboard with the other, when I breezed into the office.

"I don't know how you can type with one hand," I said.

"Hey, good morning to you, too, Phee. I learned how to do that when I had carpal tunnel surgery a few years ago. I take it Marshall's still on that case in Florence, huh?"

"Oh yeah. He left at an ungodly hour. He got a new lead on the whereabouts of that not-so-deadbeat dad. Can you imagine? The guy absconded with their four-year-old in the middle of the night. The wife thinks they may be with friends of his somewhere near Apache Junction."

"Why didn't she just go to the sheriff's office and have an Amber alert issued?"

"According to Marshall, the woman's madly in love with the guy and thinks he'll eventually return. She didn't want to sully his name. Can you believe it? Still, she wanted him found. That's why she hired us."

Augusta groaned and took a sip of her coffee. "Nate's downtown, by the way, with the office manager at Home Products Plus. I don't expect him to come up for air any time soon."

"Yeesh. That's a snarly case for sure. The manager's convinced someone's got a rogue operation going since their inventory dwindled without explanation."

Just then the phone rang, and Augusta picked up, but not before adjusting her tightly sprayed bouffant hairdo.

"I'll catch up later." I walked to my office. At least my work was clear-cut and reasonable: invoices to send and a few bills to reconcile. Since Marshall was out on a case, I decided to stick around and grab lunch with Augusta, something I did once in a while because our office usually closed at noon on Saturdays.

When I told her about my mother's latest endeavor as we munched on baked subs from the deli around the corner, Augusta grimaced. "A radio show? A murder mystery radio show? Let's hope it turns out better than her last theatrical performance. Last thing you need is another murder."

I let my fork slip back onto the plate. "Bite your tongue. I'm sure they'll just be talking about murders." Too bad I was wrong.